About the author

Blair Wylie is a retired Canadian oil and gas engineer and manager. He worked thirty-five years in a number of interesting places, including the Arctic, Western Siberia, the North Sea, Newfoundland, and Trinidad and Tobago. In his second career as a writer, he prefers to stay in the plausible world with respect to science, and character studies. His stories place everyday people in awkward if not outright terrifying situations, then have them discover hidden strengths while they rescue themselves. He hopes readers will come away feeling better about themselves, and about the future in general.

COVERT ALLIANCE

Blair Wylie

COVERT ALLIANCE

Vanguard Press

VANGUARD PAPERBACK

© Copyright 2019
Blair Wylie

The right of Blair Wylie to be identified as author of
this work has been asserted by him in accordance with the
Copyright, Designs and Patents Act 1988.

All Rights Reserved

No reproduction, copy or transmission of this publication may
be made without written permission.
No paragraph of this publication may be reproduced, copied
or transmitted save with the written permission of the
publisher, or in accordance with the provisions of the
Copyright Act 1956 (as amended).

Any person who commits any unauthorised act in relation to
this publication may be liable to criminal
prosecution and civil claims for damages.

A CIP catalogue record for this title is
available from the British Library.

ISBN 978 1 784656 68 3

*Vanguard Press is an imprint of
Pegasus Elliot MacKenzie Publishers Ltd.*
www.pegasuspublishers.com

First Published in 2019

**Vanguard Press
Sheraton House Castle Park
Cambridge England**

Printed & Bound in Great Britain

1

When the moderator noted that the university auditorium had filled to capacity, she asked a technician at the back of the hall to slowly dim the lights. As she had hoped, the many loud and excited conversations in the two-hundred-person amphitheatre gradually tapered-off.

After a few minutes, when only the stage at the front and lower end of the hall were illuminated, only a few whispers could be heard. As the moderator slowly made her way down the darkened central aisle, and up the front stairs to the stage, even the whispering came to an end.

The moderator was an attractive, middle-aged woman, with olive-coloured skin, and short, curly hair that she had fashionably dyed a trendy shade of light purple.

When the moderator reached the podium, she took a few moments to look around. She smiled as she tried to survey the audience seated before her within the darkened amphitheatre. Then some people started clapping, and a few people even rose to their feet to clap loudly.

The moderator pointed and waved at a few people that were seated in the front row. She had recognised the Minister of Science and Technology, Doctor Abdul O'Shea. Then she gasped and clapped her hands above her head with a laugh when she also noted the presence of General Jorge Kepler. He was sitting with his arms crossed near Doctor O'Shea.

General Kepler had been an outspoken critic of the evening's topic of discussion, the 'Second Continent Pyramid Project'. No one, including the moderator, had expected to see *anyone* from the security forces at this elite gathering of scientists.

The moderator was pleased that she could not make out any reporters in the audience. She concluded they must either be sitting towards the back of the hall, or they had been unable to finagle a way into the hall. Members of the media had not been formally invited of course, because the government had unfortunately attached a 'Top Secret' classification to the university's research project.

The moderator adjusted the height of the microphone on the podium in front of her. Then she smiled broadly, and said in a strong, clear, soprano voice, "Welcome everyone! For those who may not know me, I am Doctor

Sita Mugabe, Dean of Anthropology at Abubakar University, here in First Town, Prime Continent.

"It is my honour this evening to introduce our featured speaker, and in fact our *only* speaker tonight, the distinguished and always controversial Professor Gunter Rabinowitz!

"Doctor Rabinowitz has recently returned from four months of intensive archaeological research in the vast and dangerous interior wilderness of Second Continent. As everyone knows, Second Continent is far away in the southern hemisphere on the other side of New Earth. A few human settlements on Second Continent have been established around the coast, however the interior region remains a true wilderness area, which is still only accessible by aircraft, or more accurately, by helicopters.

"Many of you might be surprised to hear that there was once a small native, or rather genetically-modified, hominid population on Second Continent! We believe that the infamous and alien 'Masters' of our antiquity had probably established one or two coastal plantations on the continent thousands of years ago. And we know that the Masters used slave labour in their otherwise very advanced agricultural and industrial endeavours.

"About one hundred and twelve years ago, with our assistance, the last remaining Second Continent hominids chose to resettle on Third Continent, that we also call

North Continent. It is an arctic and sub-arctic place, but it is still very rich in wildlife. They moved there together with all of the other members of their noble species, from all over New Earth. Together, they now manage their own affairs. To protect their more primitive culture, our intercourse with them is restricted to rather infrequent, barter-based trade. But our relationship with them has always been peaceful, and we believe mutually beneficial.

"Now, to return to the topic of tonight's lecture and discussion, we expect what you will hear will generate a *lot* of questions. We will be fielding those questions at the *end* of Doctor Rabinowitz's presentation. So *please*, I ask you to let Doctor Rabinowitz speak *without interruption* until he tells us he is finished!

"Then, as your moderator, I will manage the question and answer session. If you raise your hand, I will point at you. Then you will tell us who you are, and then you may ask your question. You may ask only *one* question, as we want to give everyone here tonight a chance to directly engage with Doctor Rabinowitz.

"And now, with the introduction and administrative formalities now completed, please join me in welcoming this evening's *very special* guest speaker, the renowned and greatly esteemed, Professor Gunter Rabinowitz!" The moderator then sat down on a wooden chair that was positioned about ten metres to the right of the podium, and she immediately focused her attention on the audience. During the long introduction, Doctor Rabinowitz had been impatiently pacing around in the left wing of the stage behind a curtain. As he suddenly appeared and quickly made his way over to the podium in the centre of the stage, everyone could see that he was small in stature, but obviously very fit. He looked a lot younger than his sixty-two years. He had a perpetually tanned face, a meticulously trimmed grey beard, and rather longish, very straight, grey hair that he only tied in a ponytail for formal gatherings like this one.

When the professor reached the podium, the audience responded with a mixture of polite clapping, a few cheers, a few boos and even a few obscene catcalls. Most people remained sitting, and most people were embarrassed to hear a few people high up at the back of the hall yelling their obscenities.

Doctor Rabinowitz took a moment to survey the audience just as the moderator had done. He recognised many people sitting close to the stage. He simply smiled back at everyone as the noise in the hall gradually subsided. Then he had a quick glance at his prepared notes that he had placed on the podium in front of him, and began his presentation. His voice was surprisingly deep and gravely for a relatively small man. It instantly commanded attention.

"Welcome, both fans and critics alike!" Doctor Rabinowitz yelled with a laugh, with his fists tightly clenched and his muscular arms stretched straight out from his sides. Some people at the back of the hall yelled back with fresh insults as he then repositioned his notes. Doctor Rabinowitz firmly grasped the sides of the podium in his usual manner when delivering a lecture. Then he boomed, "As you can clearly see, I'm back! And *miraculously*, I'm still in one piece!

"That may surprise some people. And I can sense that my obvious *survival* disappoints a few people here tonight, especially the rather passionate and vocal group of critics that I cannot see at the back of this fine hall.

"My critics seem to be mostly upset with the *cost* of my expedition, viewing it as a complete waste of intellectual talent and scarce resources. Well, perhaps we can check in with them again at the end of my presentation to see if their negative and cynical opinions have changed?

"Some of you will remember that about eight years ago, I published a paper that revealed some *mysterious aspects* surrounding the mammoth stone pyramid that is located in the central jungle area of Second Continent. I wrote that paper just after making my first visit to the site. I used my own funds for that venture, by the way, with only a modest endowment from the university. Tonight, I will start by reviewing some of these mysterious aspects, to help set the context for our more recent and frankly more alarming discoveries.

"We believe that the pyramid is the only ancient megalithic structure on New Earth. In fact, we have found no other prehistoric stone structures *of any kind* on our adopted planet, *anywhere*. But of course, these structures *could* in fact exist. They could be just hidden from our view by say a jungle, or by a covering of glacial detritus, or even by the ocean. And if so, I am sure that in time, we will find *all* of them. After all, we are a species *driven* by our curiosity!

"When I wrote the paper, only the top fifteen metres or so of the one-hundred-and five-metre-tall pyramid could be seen above the thick jungle canopy. We know now that the base of the pyramid is in fact sixteen metres below the present-day forest floor. It is set on stable bedrock, which means the pyramid itself is very stable.

"By examining and analysing the natural organic material that has accumulated around the pyramid, we estimated that it has been there for at least *one hundred and twenty-four thousand* New Earth years!

"The sides of the pyramid are very steep. In fact, they are at a *precise* sixty degree angle to the horizontal. The pyramid is also *precisely* oriented with its four base corners pointing to the cardinal directions relative to the axis of spin of New Earth.

"The pyramid is glossy black in colour, because it is made of a very hard, igneous and basaltic-type rock. Furthermore, the surface of the pyramid has been uniformly vitrified, also with impressive precision, using some sort of intense heat application process. It is as smooth as obsidian or volcanic glass, and the seams between the stone blocks have been fused into near invisibility. Therefore, the pyramid cannot be climbed by human beings without special equipment, such as devices that use suction cups. And to add to the many research challenges, the pyramid is in the middle of a jungle filled with very aggressive, very hungry and very successful predatory animals!

"So, it really should be no great surprise to anyone that we knew very little about this great pyramid at the time I wrote my paper! After all, we have only been on this planet for three hundred and eighty-seven years, and we have had many other *priorities*. I get that! I am a passionate archaeologist, but I understand *priorities*, like *survival*! Really I do!

"But on my first expedition, as my brave, small band of graduate students fended off the slobbering beasts that wanted to eat us, I managed to manoeuvre a drone around the top of the pyramid. Some video clips from these pioneering drone flights will now come up on the screen behind me as I talk further.

"As you can see, there are some peculiar aspects to the rock surface, especially towards the top of the structure. There appear to be dull-coloured sections in a number of places. We managed to land a specialised drone on one of these dull-coloured sections. That allowed us to successfully drill-up a sample of what we thought was a different form of 'vitrified rock'.

"That was no easy feat! Most drones do not like to be tilted. That is how they manage to fly so successfully! But we eventually managed it after a few tries, and we gathered our samples for follow-up lab analyses. Those analyses showed that the powdered material we recovered was in fact a mixture of polymers, monocrystalline silicon and gallium arsenide.

"My friends, that is the stuff used to make efficient photovoltaic cells!

"An obvious scientific push-back is that just because the material we found *could* make a solar cell does not mean that the dull surfaces at the top of the pyramid *are in fact* solar cells. And we have heard that particular cynical challenge many times from our most able and *distinguished* colleagues, as you can well imagine!

"But we saw something else at the top of the pyramid that caught our attention. It also seemed completely out of sorts for something supposedly built by primitive, native and ancient hominids.

"Now, please look carefully at the screen behind me. Wait for it... yes, okay, here it comes... see! There is clearly a capstone on the pyramid, with an obvious seam! The capstone is about one-and-a-half metres high. That gives it a mass of over *forty-three hundred* kilograms, assuming it is made of a basalt-like rock, which we now know that it is.

"Our little drones certainly could not have lifted that stone out of the way to let us peer down inside the pyramid! Only a heavy-lift helicopter or a tall crane could manage that Herculean feat!

"Now, do you think the ancient builders had such sophisticated lifting devices when they installed their capstone? But let us park that rather disturbing question for now.

"Okay, now look carefully at the nature of the seam at the base of the capstone. The gap is about fifty centimetres wide. All of our drones had difficulty just approaching that seam, because there is a rush of gas coming out of it through small recessed channels! These square channels have been precisely cut, and they are all spaced at regular intervals within the gap.

"But thankfully we eventually *did* manage to land and park a drone directly over the seam, using some rather creative modifications. Then we successfully acquired a sample of the gas coming out of the seam for further analysis.

"'Why did we do that?' you probably would ask me, if our highly-disciplined moderator would let you. Why, because we desperately wanted to know what is *inside* this fantastic structure, of course! We thought that anything coming from inside of it, even a gas sample, might give us another clue.

"As it turned out, subsequent analyses of our gas sample just led to more questions. The gas proved to be mostly air, just like the stuff we breathe everywhere on New Earth. It comes out of the pyramid with a temperature of fifteen degrees Celsius and a relative humidity of about ninety percent.

"But incredibly, we determined that our air sample contained two viruses, and *only* two viruses! No other microbes, pathogens, contaminants, pollutants, organic or inorganic compounds were detected in the air sample.

"To be more precise, only two 'Fisher Six Xenonucleotide' viruses were detected in the air sample. These two members of an exotic and unique microbial species had never before been classified. This very peculiar type of virus is known to mutate fairly rapidly. So far, five hundred and seventeen other strains of this virus have been classified. There are undoubtedly *thousands* of additional strains that we just have not found yet, or bothered to classify.

"This family of viruses resembles the parasitic viruses that we unwittingly brought with us from Earth, with a protein-coat, and genetic material contained inside that protective coat. The viruses use the cells in living animals to obtain sustenance, and to propagate.

"However, instead of Earth-like DNA with its four base polymers, the genetic material contained within the Fisher family of viruses is what we call an 'XNA' or Xeno Nucleic Acid. It is a massive, double-helix molecule composed of *six* base polymers, held together by hydrogen bonds.

"I am sure that many of you here tonight are well aware of this XNA virus, and are now asking yourselves, 'So what?'" After all, every living animal on New Earth, both native and imported, including ourselves, seems to be carrying this virus in one of its many mutated forms. We all seem to be unwitting hosts for its survival and propagation. But like every other creature we know about, this XNA virus does not seem to affect us in any appreciable way.

"To take this line of inquiry further into the realm of discomfort, all of us first learned about an aggressive, intelligent alien species, the infamous 'Masters', in our elementary school lessons. We know they have visited New Earth in the past, and as recently as when we first arrived on this planet. But did you know they *also* have six-base XNA for their genetic material?

"I ask you now, is that much more than mere *coincidence*?

"I propose, most emphatically, that as scientists, we *must* ask ourselves why two particular strains of the Fisher virus are coming out of this pyramid! Furthermore, we must ask ourselves what is the *source* of these two viruses!

"More specifically, are they being *synthesized* by some kind of very sophisticated device or machine within the pyramid? And if so, is their presence in the airflow from the pyramid somehow linked to the mysterious and horrible Masters of antiquity?

"I will now share with you one more discovery from our first expedition before we move on. We set up our tent camp in an area of new-growth vegetation beside a lake that is within walking distance of the pyramid. We had to land on this lake with a float helicopter until we had sufficiently cleared the thick vegetation away to make ourselves a proper helipad.

"The lake is remarkable! It is oval in shape, and very deep, with vertically-sheer, solid-rock sides. It did not take much in the way of sophisticated investigative work to confirm that this lake is in fact a *quarry* that has filled up naturally with ground water. Without any doubt, we know that this quarry was the source of the stone that was used to build the pyramid.

"Furthermore, we initially thought our camp site was located in a recent forest fire area. But we found to our horror that it was a relatively recent *blast* site!

"Dead trees that were lying under the thick foliage and accumulated compost were arranged in a precise radial pattern, as one would expect to find around the centre of a ground-based explosion! Furthermore, we detected unusually high background gamma radiation at our camp site, with the highest intensity noted in a shallow central crater. We gathered soil samples in that crater, and subsequent isotopic analyses confirmed a relatively low-yield thermonuclear device must have been detonated there!

"Furthermore, half-life radioactive isotope analysis was used to estimate the probable time of the detonation. We believe the explosion happened when the Masters last visited us, just after we first arrived on New Earth!

"So, incredibly, we believed we had found *yet another* potential link with the Masters! And we used these links, and the many mysteries surrounding the pyramid itself, to lobby for a second, more extensive and yes, for all you critics out there, a more *expensive* and *logistically complicated* investigation of the site.

"What we really wanted to do next was to find out what exactly is *inside* this remarkable pyramid. And we wanted to do our follow-up investigative work in such a way as to not damage the pyramid.

"Since it is obviously unique, it is, after all, of great historical significance and value. And as our military friends pointed out to us, most emphatically, there may be cleverly-placed defensive devices installed within the structure, especially if there could *indeed* be some sort of link with the mysterious, technologically-advanced and aggressive Masters who are now part of our folklore.

"So, we agreed that we did not want to unwittingly set off, for example, a hidden, embedded explosive device of some kind by physically tunnelling into the rock, or by doing any blasting.

"Fortunately, after seven arduous years of lobbying, my close colleagues and I eventually obtained the funding we needed for the next phase of the Pyramid Project through an obscure budgetary line-item included in the federal government's Resource Allocation Plan. The Pyramid Project was classified as 'Top Secret' because no one knew where it might lead us.

"We invited the military to participate *directly* in our operations, but they declined without providing an explanation. Thankfully, the government magnanimously decided to let us proceed anyway.

"As an aside, to this day, our military leaders have been *openly opposed* to the Pyramid Project. When pressed, they always cite its perceived high cost and quote 'low probability for success' unquote. They have been *continually* creating logistical and supply-chain barriers wherever they can.

"But I'm not here tonight to cry over sour grapes! After all, as you will soon see, in the end we successfully managed to manoeuvre our way around the many bureaucratic barriers that were put up to block our quest for knowledge.

"We started by re-designing, manufacturing and mobilizing highly-specialized equipment. We borrowed heavily from the vast experience of oil and gas explorers.

"We are not allowed by law to drill for oil on New Earth, of course, but we *do* drill for natural gas. Liquefied natural gas is used in some transportation applications, and we use the heavier-hydrocarbon, liquid condensate that is sometimes associated with natural gas for making plastics.

"But the technology used for drilling and evaluating oil and gas wells has not changed much since we left Earth, where it was highly developed. And of course, we have access to all pertinent archived technical records.

"We expanded our campsite by the lake to provide space for our vast array of specialized equipment, and for the hundred or so technical people comprising the expanded investigation team. And we roped-off the crater, of course, to keep people safely away from the low-level residual radiation.

"Our first challenging operation was to remove the capstone. We employed expert climbers, and a helicopter with a number of sling-loads, to install a work platform just below the capstone. We used suction cup devices to fix the platform to the hard, slippery surface of the pyramid. Then a heavy-lift helicopter was manoeuvred overhead, and the capstone was successfully plucked straight upwards and out of the way!

"Thankfully, we found that the capstone had not been fixed in place with some kind of mortar or adhesive. Rather, we found out that it must have just been sitting there contentedly under its own weight, for eons.

"Subsequent analysis has confirmed the capstone is entirely *stone*, and nothing else.

"But surprisingly, just beneath the capstone we found a perfectly smooth, vertical conduit with an inside circular bore of about a hundred and five centimetres! It runs straight down into the pyramid. The stream of air we noted earlier coming out from beneath the capstone was still coming up that conduit.

"The conduit is lined with a twelve centimetre thick ceramic casing, fixed in place with a cement or adhesive made from crushed volcanic ash and fired limestone. The conduit has many silver conductive wires embedded in its ceramic matrix. The technology used to make it is therefore very advanced! Electrical power, data and telemetry could *all* be fed through those wires. But please, just store that information away somewhere in your brains for now.

"We then installed a mast with a weight-compensating sheave directly over the conduit opening. Then, as gas-well drillers would say, 'we rigged-up for wireline logging'. Our modular winch and data management control shack were firmly anchored to the ground at the base of the pyramid. The idea was to treat the conduit as a wellbore, and run passive and active probes, or 'sondes', up and down the conduit.

"Our goals were to investigate near wellbore rock and pore fluid properties, and to see if there was anything of interest inside the pyramid near the conduit. Our cased 'well' was filled with air, so direct resistive measurements were not possible. But we used cameras, gamma ray detection tools, electromagnetic induction tools, sonic tools, 'compensated neutron' tools, 'densilog' tools, nuclear magnetic resonance imaging tools, calliper tools and cement bond evaluation tools. You see, gas field 'roughnecks' have *lots* of interesting tools at their disposal, not just wrenches!

"We successfully confirmed that the conduit is completely and securely bonded to nothing but the same, rather boring, dense basaltic rock right to the base of the pyramid, where the conduit terminates. The small bit of porosity in the rock is water-filled, and the entrained water is probably primordial, since the rock has essentially no permeability.

"But we also confirmed that there is a sump at the base of the 'well', with an intersecting pipe about five metres above the bottom of the sump! The entrance to the intersecting, horizontal pipe is screened off, with what appears to be a ceramic baffle. We then confirmed with spinner surveys that the air flow originates from behind the screen or baffle.

"So, frustratingly, our primary questions remained unanswered. We still wanted to know if there is anything of *interest* inside this pyramid that can tell us something about its builders, and why they built it!

"We then switched our efforts to three-dimensional internal mapping, using natural cosmic ray muon tomography, combined with ground-penetrating radar, and an elaborate seismic geophysical data acquisition program.

"Seismic surveys are *another* vestige of the ancient Earth mineral and petroleum exploration era. We used caissons to dig down to the bedrock on the four sides of the pyramid. Then we lowered heavy-weight 'thumper devices' down each caisson. Then we installed geophones and muon sensors with great precision all over the pyramid itself, and around the pyramid.

"Then we started thumping, one thump at a time, so we could listen and monitor carefully, and record all the reverberations at each geophone. We also staged a geophone and muon sensor in our 'well' at regular intervals so we could further improve our three-dimensional imaging. And of course, we took a ground-penetrating radar shot at each of our external geophone locations.

"The dataset we gathered was obviously immense! We now had in our possession a very large, mixed-bag of muon scatter plots, seismic squiggles and fuzzy radar images! We used complicated algorithms, and the *awesome* number-crunching power of the liquid helium cooled, quantum, multi-parallel, supercomputer in this university, first to analyse these data, and then to integrate and refine the resulting images to achieve a reasonably high resolution.

"And you people here tonight, both enthusiastic colleagues and diehard sceptics alike, will now join the very small, extremely privileged group of people fortunate enough to know the *results* of our comprehensive analyses!

"Now, please study the screen behind me carefully as I continue speaking. To help you along, I'll use this laser pointer to highlight a few things as I talk, and as the recording rotates the three-dimensional synthesized images around for us.

"As you can see, the pipe that intersects the bottom of the 'well' inside the pyramid leads to a *cavity*. This cavity is a perfect cube, with sides about eight metres long. Observe that there are four things that look like boxes adjacent to opposite walls in the cavity, two on each side. These boxes are also perfect cubes, and about two metres long per side. But we cannot tell what they are! Two boxes on one side appear to be mostly filled with liquid, possibly water or an aqueous solution, and the other two boxes appear to contain solid objects, and possibly metallic objects.

"The rest of the pyramid is entirely made of stone. Except for… wait for it… wait for it… *a scale model of the New Earth Solar System*! See!

"Imagine that our star Sol is in the centre of the 'well', and the flat base of the pyramid is the orbital plane. Moving away from Sol, along a natural logarithmic scale, here we find the three rocky planets, Shinwari, Fisher, and our adopted home, New Earth!

"And see, here is our moon Addy around New Earth! And here are the seven outer gas-giant planets, Abubakar, Tarantino, Smith, Rasmussen, Langlois, Mercado and Bahazhoni… *complete with all of their many moons*!

"And everything, everywhere, is *exactly to scale,* except for the distances between planets, which we presume had to be displayed logarithmically so everything would fit nicely within the pyramid.

"And everything, everywhere, is *frozen* at a moment in time, as one would expect with a static representation of a *very dynamic* system.

"The position of planets in Sol's system recurs about every three thousand, five hundred and seventy-one New Earth years. The last time the planetary system looked like the static representation in the pyramid was about five hundred and twelve years ago. And if you recall, our analysis of the organic material built up around the pyramid indicated that the massive stone structure must be at least two hundred and forty times *older* than five hundred and twelve years!

"But, when you include the position of all the many *moons* in this analysis, the last time the *entire* Sol-system looked like the pyramid representation was about *one hundred and twenty-nine thousand years ago*!

"People, colleagues, and scientific friends, I *strongly suggest* this analysis is in *very close* and excellent agreement with our independent estimate of the age of the pyramid derived from the depth of the organic material surrounding it!

"But here is where it gets *especially* interesting, if any of you could still somehow be bored! The builders *must* have used a very dense metal, perhaps lead or uranium, to represent the planets and moons in their physical model because they show up so clearly in our suite of non-invasive imaging techniques.

"And I therefore believe that the builders *must* have known, or at least hoped, that we would first try sonic and radar-probing methods to investigate the interior of their pyramid.

"Yes, we could have just dug it all up, and found their impressive solar system map that way, in the manner I suppose that primitive treasure-seekers or pioneer amateur archaeologists on Earth sometimes employed.

"But, our sonic and radar energy *must* have stimulated something within the pyramid to cause this particular moon around this particular gas-giant planet *to vibrate like a transponder*!

"You see, around Tarantino, the fifth planet out from Sol, is this moon, Adatia, the third largest moon around Tarantino. When vibrating, Adatia is much 'brighter' in sonic waveforms than every other planet and moon in the builder's Sol-system map! It is pulsing in our three-dimensional seismic image to highlight the fact that it would only vibrate for a few seconds after every one of our thumps or radar pulses! There *must* be an energy source in the pyramid to trigger, control and induce that vibration! Perhaps the solar cells at the top of the pyramid provide electrical current that runs down the silver wires that are embedded within the ceramic conduit, to some sort of battery?

"And furthermore, perhaps a *virus-producing* machine of some kind is also positioned inside the cavity near the base of the pyramid? And perhaps that device is also powered to some degree by solar cells?

"Surely, colleagues, I have sparked your interest by *now*?

"But before we start taking your *many* questions, please also consider this aspect!

"The builders *must* be trying to draw our attention, in a very sophisticated and rather ostentatious manner, to a very particular, very distant moon.

"Why? Why would they do that?

"And what do we know about this particular moon, that we have named Adatia?

"Well, we have only looked at it from a very long way away using our New Earth telescopes, and with the help of a single, multi-planet, exploratory satellite that quickly flew by it, on its way somewhere else, about ten years back. But we suspect that Adatia resembles the moon Europa that orbits Jupiter, a gas-giant planet in Earth's solar system.

"Adatia is about the same size as Earth's moon. It probably has an iron-nickel core. Its surface is smooth, frozen water, with a deep ocean below the ice layer. It has a very thin, mostly nitrogen and oxygen atmosphere. Tidal flexing is probably heating the underlying ocean to some degree, and moving the surface ice around like tectonic plates. And it *might* be a place where life could originate and evolve, that is, if the ocean is not too salty or toxic. Earth-based explorers unfortunately found that to be the case with Europa.

"Now, there is a lot more I can tell you, but not all of it will be of general interest. So, with Doctor Mugabe's help, I think we should now move to our question... our question and answer..." He stuttered to a stop.

Doctor Rabinowitz and everyone else in the hall now realised with stunned surprise that General Kepler must have quietly risen from his seat and climbed up on to the stage. He was now striding at a brisk pace towards the podium. The moderator leapt to her feet, but the General ignored her. Armed guards were also streaming through the main auditorium door, and the lights suddenly came up everywhere in the amphitheatre.

With an angry, grim expression on his face, General Kepler firmly pushed Doctor Rabinowitz away from behind the podium by pushing on his left shoulder with the back of his massive, hairy right hand.

Then the general leaned towards the microphone and boomed loudly, "This presentation is now *over*, people! There will be no question and answer session, *by military order*! You all signed secrecy and confidentiality agreements to get in here. *Remember that*, or suffer very grave consequences!

"All right, everyone, stand up now, and leave, *immediately*, and in an orderly manner, through the main door at the back of the hall. Upon departure, your face will be recorded on video, to confirm your presence here today."

Then the general placed his large, hairy left hand over the microphone and said quietly, "Except for *you*, Doctor Rabinowitz, and your *co-conspirator* Doctor Mugabe. You two will come with me now, and the minister of science, and an escort of armed guards. You are not under arrest, *yet*. But, we now have many questions of our own for you, as you *bloody well should know*!"

2

After an unexpected and frustrating hour long wait, General Kepler, the Minister of Defence and Security, and Doctor O'Shea, the Minister of Science and Technology, were finally told they could enter Prime Minister Wong's office.

As the ministerial pair were entering the foyer of the large, open-plan suite, Patricia Hernandez, the Minister of Resource Planning, almost bumped into them. She seemed to be eager to leave the office in a great hurry. She was young, ambitious, pretty and red-haired. She was also considered super-intelligent, and a bit nerdy, by everyone who knew her. Minister Hernandez was also struggling to hang on to a large bundle of documents. The blank look on her face suggested her mind was completely focused on something else.

"General Jorge, Doctor Abdul, sorry to keep you guys waiting so long!" Prime Minister Wong said pleasantly as he greeted them with firm handshakes in the middle of the cavernous office. "Please, gentlemen, have a seat… no, no, over here! Let's use the lounge area today where it will be more *comfortable* for everyone. You know, I'm frankly *tired* of sitting behind my humungous and cluttered desk! It constantly reminds me of how much more work I have to do today!"

After the three men had taken their seats, Prime Minister Wong took a moment to study the faces of his two visitors. He noted they both looked a bit stressed, and maybe even a bit fatigued. Phillip Wong felt a bit that way too, but like Minister Hernandez, he had no intention of revealing that to anyone.

Phillip Wong was slim and fit, and looked a lot younger than his forty-one years. His hair was still jet-black, and he exuded youthful confidence at all times. He was inwardly pleased about his many accomplishments without appearing to be vain about them. He was at heart a very good man. He was quick to publicly praise the members of his Cabinet whenever he could, and by extension, the elaborate government apparatus they collectively controlled.

So, Prime Minister Wong always had a large group of loyal followers. He had one more year remaining in his five-year term of office, and he was looking forward to running for another term. His wife was very supportive of him in both their public and private lives. Unfortunately, their eighteen year marriage had not produced any children. Doctors had consistently advised them that they were both, 'probably infertile to a significant degree', which really meant they both were *completely* infertile. However, they chose not to dwell too much on that sad reality. Instead, they devoted themselves to public service, him to government, and her to re-training injured and disabled people who wanted to join the workforce, or to change jobs.

General Jorge Kepler was an imposing, handsome, bear-like man. He was tall and muscular, and had a deep voice. And he had thick black hair everywhere except on his head, which he meticulously shaved for complete and unashamed baldness. Kepler had just turned forty, and he had reached the highest possible rank in the combined-service security organization.

In every rank and in every role, Kepler had always been extremely capable and professional. He was proud of his uniform, and he always wore it whenever he thought he might be caught on camera. He had never married, although a dozen or so women had tried to seduce him, some successfully. A few gay men had also made advances to him, but he was not at all inclined that way. He really was devoted only to his job, and to the security of the four New Earth continents that had been settled to various degrees by human beings.

Doctor Abdul O'Shea was a quiet and introverted man. But he was as intelligent as he looked. When he decided to speak, wise people paid very close attention to what he chose to say. He was freckled and fair-skinned, and his greying hair still had a reddish tint. He wore thick, black-rimmed glasses, and he walked a bit on the slow side, as well as a bit hunched over from spending too many long hours in dark university halls while totally absorbed in study.

But Doctor O'Shea had never worried very much about his posture or his appearance. He was in his mid-fifties, and he was completely devoted to his wife, who was a physics professor, and to their two very bright daughters, who were now both attending university, in 'preliminary, yet to be determined' undergraduate programs.

Prime Minister Wong relaxed into his comfortable leather chair and said quietly, "Right, gentlemen, let's get started then, shall we? This should not take us too long.

"Minister Hernandez and I have both carefully studied the transcripts and the video recording of the contentious Professor Rabinowitz presentation. So, we're fully up to speed with the many issues it raises. No one else will ever be allowed to see that recording, or to read the transcripts, of course.

"Now, have you completed your interviews with Doctor Rabinowitz, and with Doctor Mugabe?"

"Yes, we have," growled General Kepler. Then he barked loudly, "It's been a complete freaking waste of our time! They both have *refused* to answer our questions, even the most basic ones! This looks like a bloody-minded *conspiracy* to me! They just want to undermine our authority, and waste our precious resources for their own selfish, academic *glory-seeking*, or whatever the hell motivates them to act like fools in public…" He trailed off with another growl.

"If I may, I can perhaps offer some insight into their mindset, being a fellow scientist," interjected Doctor O'Shea quietly. He paused for a moment to gather his thoughts. Then he said, "Yes, they are both on the defensive right now, that's for sure. But that is completely understandable! They see nothing wrong with what they have done, that is, from a scientific and professorial point of view.

"Doctor Rabinowitz believes he has made many highly significant discoveries, and the next logical step in his mind is to openly publish and communicate the results of his recent work to his peer community, for rigorous challenge and debate. That is what *true* science is all about, after all.

"But I pointed out to him, and to Doctor Mugabe, that they should have recognized the political and social sensitivities involved with this startling, possibly world-shattering suite of *incredible* discoveries. And I told them they should have remembered and respected the government that funded the extremely expensive archaeological research work on Second Continent.

"And then, to be absolutely clear, I *strongly* suggested they should have presented the Pyramid Project findings to *us* first, that is, to 'we three', in *private*. That way, we could have controlled the public messaging properly, and calmly and rationally coordinated the next logical steps."

"And how did they respond to your obvious words of wisdom, Doctor O'Shea?" asked the prime minister with a grim smile.

"They both got their professorial backs up, and said they would say no more to us without their *freaking lawyers* present!" snarled General Kepler. He was unusually angry and worked-up.

"General, I directed my question to Minister O'Shea, not to you!" admonished Wong sternly. "Let's keep this strictly *professional*, shall we? This is not at all like you, General, and that greatly disturbs me. These clearly are very serious matters. But we are all on the same side, right? So, Abdul?"

"General Kepler is mostly right about what he says," O'Shea replied slowly. Then he sighed and said, "Except, I sensed they both realised they have screwed-up, big time. They both looked *terribly* embarrassed at the end of our discussion. They are professionals too, and self-critical to a very high degree. And we *did* eventually glean from them what they think should happen next."

"I think Minister Hernandez and I have already guessed what they want," said Prime Minister Wong with a shake of his head. "They want us to send a highly-specialized, robotic probe directly to this strange moon, and immediately, if possible. Right?"

"That is exactly right, Prime Minister!" replied O'Shea with surprise and a sudden smile. He was impressed that Wong and Hernandez had picked up on the logical next course of action.

"To waste more money and divert more scarce resources away from where we can do the most good!" exploded General Kepler angrily. "We should lock them both up before they do us *any more* harm!"

Prime Minister Wong suddenly jumped to his feet, stomped over to the window, and stared at the outside world for a long moment. It was a sunny, pleasant, late summer day, but unfortunately, he did not have any time to fully appreciate it.

Instead, he turned around, and stared hard at General Kepler. The general initially stared back, but after a few moments he seemed to melt a bit as self-doubt appeared. Finally, Wong said quietly, "You are missing the obvious security angle here, General, and that *greatly* disappoints me.

"I want you to study the video recording and presentation transcript again, with *deeper, unbiased* focus this time. And then I want you to come back to us with a rigorous, *unbiased* appraisal. Furthermore, I want you to seek out some trustworthy, outside, *objective* help with your analysis, because I frankly think you could use it. Of course, your advisors will need to obtain the very highest security clearances before you can involve them. That means *I* will have to formally agree to their involvement. But we can work that through the formal channels, as always.

"I *want* all of this, General, because I may have a different perspective than you of the 'big picture'. It is apparent to me that an ancient, intelligent, advanced alien race put *immense* effort into building a physically impressive structure, possibly for the sole purpose of directing the attention of intelligent creatures *like ourselves* to a particular, distant moon in our Sol-system. And for some reason, they may also have wanted to continually generate two exotic virus strains far out into the future. Of course, this virus production operation may be a complete red herring, or something that is occurring either naturally or accidentally through currently unknown processes.

"The bottom line though, General, is I want your recommendations on what this proposed 'deep Sol-system' probe should be capable of doing, *from a security aspect*. There are now almost eighty million human beings on this planet, spread out over four of the five continents. Should we now be worried about the continuation of our peaceful civilisation? And if so, is this an *urgent* matter, one we should deal with *proactively*? Furthermore, should we upgrade our military capability in some manner, to potentially neutralize a new threat to our very *survival*?

"I think it is obvious that we currently do not have enough information to answer such difficult questions. So, we will just have to gather *more* information, that's all! And I believe we have to do that immediately, *starting with this probe*!

"To close, I have instructed Minister Hernandez to start looking at how to include a relatively long-distance space probe mission into our Resource Allocation Plan."

General Kepler sat quietly for a few moments. Then he took a deep breath, stood up to attention, saluted smartly and said crisply, "Yes, sir! Will that be all, sir?"

Prime Minister Wong also came to attention, and saluted awkwardly in return. By law, he was also *de facto* Commander-in-Chief, but it was a role he was very uncomfortable with.

Then Wong relaxed, and said with a smile, "No, General, Jorge, please take it easy and sit down again for a few minutes. Thanks! Because there is also of course the immediate *pressing* matter of what to do with Doctor Mugabe and Doctor Rabinowitz. Any ideas, both of you?"

There was an awkward silence for a few moments. General Kepler was still stinging a bit from the prime minister's rebuke. Minister O'Shea looked at Kepler with sympathy, then cleared his throat and said quietly, "I don't believe the two professors are rabid revolutionaries, or anything like that. And I don't think they have done anything that actually approaches *treason*.

"But then again, they have struggled over their lives, both of them, to accept over-rule when it comes to their academic pursuits. They have enjoyed a *lot* of freedom in the university environment, and they are both well-respected leaders in their chosen fields. And they have *a lot* of like-minded friends! So, I think they could do more mischief if we just turned them loose again after, say, just a 'hand-slap reprimand'."

"Keep your friends close, and your enemies closer," General Kepler offered bluntly. Then he explained, "Gentlemen, the word 'enemy' can describe people that do *mischief* against the state, not just invaders bent on conquest, or hardened criminals bent on thievery, or worse. Anyway, following that particular creed has worked very well for me over the years."

"Yes, I think the general is absolutely right about that," said Minister O'Shea in support. Then he smiled at the general, and the general smiled back at him.

"Right, I agree too," said Wong emphatically. Then he added, "Yes, we *will* involve them immediately in the Probe Project. We'll start by asking them what they think the probe should be able to do *exactly*. And we'll give them well-defined roles within the Project where we can monitor them closely, and if necessary, restrict their activities and control who they talk to. But for now, until this Project is officially sanctioned, please keep them under very close observation, General."

Prime Minister Wong paused to stretch his back, and then he said, "Okay, let's meet again in, say, a month's time. Minister Hernandez will join us next time. There are *huge* practical considerations to consider as well, like carving-out sufficient funds, and providing proper resourcing!

"Please do your very best to have your detailed recommendations ready for us to review and consider in our next meeting, General.

"No, on second thought, we will want your recommendations *too*, Doctor O'Shea, of course, sorry! And I encourage both of you to consult with each other, *continuously*, so we can all align sooner rather than later on mission objectives. But I suppose it could still take a couple of iterations over a couple of months to get to the final solution. We have to be realistic about these things, of course.

"Okay? Two *emphatic* nods, in unison! That is always *great* to see! Then, I'll bid you both adieu. Have a great day, gentlemen! Enjoy the sunshine outside if you can! I truly wish that *I* could…" He trailed off with a sad look etched on his tired face.

3

The morning was dragging on, and Doctor Gunter Rabinowitz had still not made his promised appearance for a scheduled clandestine meeting with Doctor Sita Mugabe.

Their meeting had been quickly arranged in the 'white noise' security of a busy university hallway. The two tenured professors had agreed in whispers that Sita should leave her home two days later for an early morning 'recreational nature walk'. She was to depart her home at precisely half-an-hour before Sol-rise.

It was late autumn, and unfortunately, it turned out that the meeting would be occurring on an overcast, windy, drizzly and cold day. With this witch's brew of obscuring climatic conditions, actual Sol-rise would not be an observable event, rather just a trivial note in the morning weather forecast.

Sita was becoming increasingly worried. Still, she kept walking to the east along the forest trail that ran beside the northern shoreline of Long Lake. She stopped periodically, making it look like she was specifically observing something natural or wild in her surroundings. In actuality, she was paying very close attention to *everything* surrounding her. As such, she was fairly certain she was not being followed.

The trail had started near the centre of First Town, where Sita lived by herself in a lower-level flat. Long Lake had once been the southern boundary of the first human settlement on New Earth. That settlement, of course, had started out as little more than a crude wooden fort. In fact, it had once been called 'Hill Fort'.

The surrounding forest was a very creepy place in the dim light. There were many strange rustling sounds, presumably from small wild animals. There were also eerie creaking noises as the gusty wind rubbed bare, gnarly branches together.

Suddenly, Sita heard a very strange high-pitched squeal of sorts over to her left. She stopped and listened for a few moments, and then she heard it again. She could see no path into the forest in the murky light. But she decided she must try to investigate the source of the sound anyway. So, she bravely forced her way through wet shrubbery and undergrowth, and entered into the thick, dark, mostly evergreen forest.

After about a hundred stumbling paces, she froze in panic when a strong hand suddenly shot out of a bush at her side and firmly grabbed on to her right triceps.

"Take it easy, Sita," she heard in a sharp whisper in her right ear. "It's me, Gunter. Come over this way a bit. It will be safe enough. Come on, let's move. Quickly!"

Gunter released his grip, and Sita followed his shadowy, dripping-wet form through the underbrush. The bushes were prickly and unyielding. Leafless branches scratched and whipped across their faces. After five or so minutes of awkward, strenuous struggle, they emerged into a very small clearing. Sita noted that the space was *just* large enough for a small portable table, and two collapsible canvas stools, that had obviously been set up for their use by Gunter.

"Let's sit down here, Sita," suggested Gunter in a quiet voice. Then he said, "I don't think we'll have to actually whisper any more, but we should probably keep it down as much as we can. There is *no telling* where the security force put their spy microphones these days. But enough with the conspiracy theories! Would you like some hot coffee? I brought along a thermos jug full of the stuff."

Sita sat down cautiously opposite Gunter. The stools were a bit wobbly on the soft, mucky ground. Then she carefully looked around at their cramped, dark and dripping surroundings. Then she smiled weakly and said quietly, "Sure, let's have some coffee, Gunter."

Gunter kept his leather gloves on while he filled two tin-plated metal cups with steaming coffee. He gingerly handed a cup to Sita, who was not wearing gloves, and said, "Careful, Sita, use the handle! The thermos jug has kept it *really* hot, obviously!" Then he took a small sip from his own cup, smiled broadly with satisfaction, sighed with genuine pleasure, and added, "Yes, that *is* a good brew, even if I say so myself!"

After they had both enjoyed a couple of rejuvenating sips of their coffee, Sita asked quietly, "So, what's been happening, Gunter? I really did not want to abandon the space probe advisory council, like the press has made out that I did. But frankly, the early discussions were *way* over my head. And I can contribute far more to the university in so many other ways."

"Trust me, no one in the know blames you for pulling out, Sita," replied Gunter as he stifled a sneeze. He pulled a handkerchief from his coat pocket, and blew his nose as quietly as he could. Then he sniffed and said, "Sorry, I hope that's just an allergy from being outside, you know, from mould or dust."

After another sniffle, Gunter said, "A week ago, I would have said that all you missed was a lot of freaking *frustration*. It's been pretty clear that the probe mission was not going to have much of a science focus. Our ideas were just being politely noted without comment or feedback of any kind.

"And clearly, they still don't trust anyone outside of the military. By '*they*' I mean the members of the

Cabinet. It's not just you and I that have been under their covert observation, unfortunately. But the military, at least, may have lost interest in day-to-day surveillance of us to a degree. Let's hope so, anyway.

"You see, three days ago, high-level members of the military told us that they have made a final decision. They said the government has agreed to all of *their* proposed mission parameters, and full funding of course. They told us the prime minister is going to make a public statement in a few days. And I thought you should hear what the statement will likely be, in advance. *I* think you've earned that courtesy, even if *they* don't."

Gunter took three quick sips from his coffee cup before continuing. Then he smacked his lips and said, "One thing they eventually *did* appreciate from us was the suggestion that the key to a successful mission was a comprehensive investigation below the ice sheet on the moon we call Adatia. If there is any life there, it will *almost certainly* be in the ocean below the ice. That is, if the ocean there is anything like we think it is.

"The real problem is that we don't have any idea how thick that ice is! It could be kilometres thick!

"One would need much more than a 'typical' lander from a space probe to drill a hole through that ice, or I suppose melt a way through it. And the no doubt intense natural radiation on the moon's surface precludes expanding the Project into a far more elaborate and costly manned mission.

"One *fool* of a Colonel actually proposed using a *nuclear bomb* to blast and melt a hole through the ice so we could then deploy a remote-operated mini-submarine! General Kepler, to his credit, pointed out that intelligent life on the moon, if it's there, would not be very impressed with us as a species if the first thing we did was set off a nuclear weapon right over their heads!

"So, what they seemed to have finally arrived at is a rather *pathetic* compromise, but one that could at least tell intelligent lifeforms that we have the ability to send a probe to their moon, and that we are moderately intelligent ourselves, in spite of our political foibles.

"The compromise solution is a two-and-a-half tonne spacecraft with two parts, an orbiter and a lander. The orbiter will have a dual-frequency ice-penetrating radar instrument to see if a thin spot in the ice exists, or maybe a fissure of some kind. If so, we will then have a place to target to see if we can penetrate or bypass the ice sheet to reach the underlying ocean.

"Thankfully, from a science perspective, other passive sensors on the probe will include a thermal-emission imaging system, a mapping-imaging spectrometer, a mass spectrometer, a visible light and ultraviolet radiation imaging system, and a magnetometer.

And also, thankfully, the military-types saw the logic, or humanity I guess, in not using *active* sensors, like proton or neutron beams, because they could potentially harm native lifeforms, even simple lifeforms.

"Even if a thin spot or crack in the ice cannot be found, the lander will *still* descend to the surface. It will actually be a very advanced rover, with artificial intelligence. It will be able to plunge into water, and even swim down a hundred metres or so. It will have a few instruments that might help us to detect simple carbon-based lifeforms.

"But mostly the lander will just send out sonic, radio and microwave messages of greeting in many Earth languages. The idea is to attract curious lifeforms, and hopefully *intelligent* lifeforms, close enough to the lander to be captured visually with an elaborate array of multi-frequency cameras.

"There was absurd talk about installing a *telephone* of sorts on the lander so an intelligent being could talk with us back on New Earth *directly*! Aside from the obvious language incompatibility issues, there is the *huge* time lag issue of course. The place is about one-billion three hundred and fifty million kilometres away! So, just one-way electromagnetic communication will take *seventy-six minutes*!

"So, instead, we will have the ability to speak our welcoming gibberish in a number of different ways, then listen with microphones and antennas, and carefully observe with cameras what happens in response. We will be able to do all of that with the lander, on the surface ice in the very thin atmosphere, or underwater if it manages to find a way to get into the underlying ocean.

"As I sort of mentioned before, there is an *intense* magnetosphere around the gas-giant planet of Tarantino. On the plus side, the radiation should effectively sterilize any New Earth microbes that manage somehow to cling to the surface of our lander, and survive the long journey through space. After all, we would not want to kill any native lifeforms on Adatia with a nasty little assortment of free-loading New Earth microbes!

"Titanium shielding will help protect the electronics that will be located towards the centre of both the orbiter and the lander. The orbiter and the lander will both be powered by radioisotope thermoelectric generators, fuelled with plutonium two-thirty-nine. Plutonium is, of course, highly radioactive, and highly toxic. But hopefully, any lifeforms that we might find on Adatia will not try to eat, breathe or even touch our fuel!

"Everyone is hopeful that a huge, three-stage chemical rocket will start the probe on its journey from New Earth to Adatia in about two years' time, assuming no significant funding, engineering or construction problems arise.

"To gather sufficient momentum, the probe will have to do close fly-bys of planet Fisher, and our planet New Earth, and the planet Abubakar. So, the probe will take almost seven years just to get there! And then, it will probably require a few months to conduct elliptical and transverse orbital surveys of the Adatia moon to adequately map its surface, and help us to select a prime landing spot for the lander-rover.

"So unfortunately, Sita, we may be nine long years away from learning anything useful from the mission!"

"My goodness, that long?" gasped Sita in response. Then she said, "But maybe an experienced engineer or space-scientist would not have been surprised by that physical reality? Yet more proof, I guess, that I should never have been involved with the planning of this mission."

"Well, another reason I wanted to talk with you today is to warn you that the government does not quite see it that way," replied Gunter very quietly. Suddenly there was a high-pitched squawking sound just at the edge of hearing. He stopped and listened carefully for a long moment, and then he shook his head and said hopefully, "Just an Iguanoraptor, I think. They can glide to the ground from treetops. They're harmless, and not very big, thankfully.

"Listen, Sita, they're not going to let you stay on the outside any longer. They're going to tell you tomorrow that you're back on the Project team, fully.

"You see, they have realised that if intelligent life is actually discovered by our probe, they'll want a professional like yourself to help them to understand it, and to communicate effectively with it. They know you're kind of unique in the academic world with your vast knowledge of social, cultural and linguistic anthropology.

"But nine years is indeed a long time! So, you might want to bring someone else into the picture, or at least start considering that. No offense, Sita, but none of us are getting any younger!

"Maybe there is a promising graduate student in your program that you could discreetly start mentoring for the job? If so, when it makes sense to proceed to the indoctrination step, I'll help you make the formal pitch to the government to get your selected protégé's full inclusion on the mission team.

"Frankly, I'm doing the same myself now. I mean, starting to groom my own successor, that is. However, I don't think archaeology will play an important role going forward. But I hope I'm completely wrong about that, of course."

Sita stared straight ahead into the nearby bushes for a long moment, clearly deep in thought. Then she replied quietly, "Yes, I can see the logic in all of that, Gunter. And I do have someone in mind that I've been closely mentoring, for other important projects, obviously.

"So, okay, Gunter, that all sounds good. Now, is there anything else on your mind today? I must admit, you've given me a lot to think about as it is!"

Gunter laughed heartily, and a bit too loudly. He stopped himself abruptly, and looked around sheepishly. Then he said, "No, Sita, that's about it for today, I guess. I hope we can start enjoying a cup of coffee together soon, in somewhat more hospitable and open surroundings. I'm thinking about some place as stuffy and mundane as our faculty lounge. Geez, I haven't been in that little nook for a very long time!

"Oh my, that was quite a shiver, Sita! I can see you're starting to feel the raw cold like I am. So, why don't you start heading back first, and I'll head out right after I have another cup of coffee, using a different path of course? And I think you should take your time going home, you know, make it look like you're actually on a nature appreciation walk. And, hopefully you'll feel a lot warmer when you start moving again."

"No problem, Gunter, thanks!" Sita replied with a chuckle. "And thanks for all of the really interesting news. Sincerely! It was a very brave and considerate thing to do, meeting with me like this.

"And maybe I actually will have a nice, relaxing nature walk on my way back home now!"

4

Everyone in the mission control centre was feeling a degree of frustration with the long wait. But everyone also knew there was nothing anyone could do about it.

They were waiting for a 'check-in confirmation signal' from the orbital part of the probe that they had recently helped guide into orbit around the distant moon they called Adatia. It was possible, but probably unlikely, that the orbiter would also tell them that the lander-rover part of the probe had succeeded in reconnoitring the ocean under the ice sheet that covered the entire surface of Adatia.

Of course, *whatever* the signal told them would be seventy-six minutes in the past. One could never overcome the physical fact that the speed photons travel in a vacuum is very fast but finite, and that speed is *exactly the same* everywhere in the universe.

Some of the scientists and engineers in mission control had pondered the bizarre world of quantum physics. Photons were very funny creatures. They either were completely stationary and invisible, or they travelled at light speed. There was nothing in between for a photon. Furthermore, experiments could *prove* they were particles of matter. And other experiments could *prove* they were electromagnetic wavelets! So, what the heck was a photon, really?

Professor Sita Mugabe knew nothing about photons and quantum mechanics, but she knew a whole lot about how human beings had behaved within many different cultural settings. And she knew with certainty that human beings were a *lot* less predictable than photons.

Her young protégé, Assistant Professor Francis Maldonado, believed that one could accurately predict how very large *groups* of people would react to specific stimuli. The theory might have been first popularised by an ancient Earth science fiction writer. She thought that all one needed were the right equations and algorithms arranged logically in a properly designed computer program.

Sita was sceptical of the theory, and she thought that Francis was a bit naïve to buy into it. But she also did not want to curb her protégés' youthful enthusiasm by openly expressing pessimism and doubt. After all, historically, great discoveries had been made by people who had ignored peer challenge, and endeavoured to persevere.

But Sita and Francis now had to divert their full attention to the Probe Project. They had been allowed, or rather strongly encouraged, to sit at one of the many monitoring stations in the over-crowded control room.

Sita was aging well, but she was glad the youthful and energetic Francis was with her. They had agreed that Francis would be taking the lead should they ever be asked to contribute something *tangible* to the Project.

There was of course no way of knowing where any of this might be leading them.

Sita looked at the young male engineer sitting directly to her right. He was busily working away at a complicated-looking console. After a few moments, the young man realized he was being watched. He turned and smiled at Sita. Sita seized the opportunity, leaned closer to the handsome young man and whispered, "So, how much longer will it be, Sergei?"

Program Engineer Sergei Kharlamov was wearing an ear-muff type of headset, but through context, he thought he could guess what Sita had just asked him. So, he closed his right hand over the little microphone in front of his mouth, and whispered, "How much longer, I think you asked me?" Sita nodded back with a smile, so he answered pleasantly, "About five minutes, ma'am, at least for the preliminary 'alert part' of the signal.

"What it says next depends on how the artificial intelligence parts of the machine on the surface of the moon, and in its companion machine in orbit, interpret sensor information, and jointly figure out what to say to us. It's all a bit complicated, sorry…" He trailed off, and looked embarrassed at not being able to offer a more definitive answer to a layperson.

Sita just nodded politely and whispered, "Thanks, Sergei, that's really all I needed to know."

Then Sergei for the first time had a close look at Francis, who was sitting on the other side of Sita. Then he blushed before quickly turning back to monitor the console in front of him.

Sita figured yet *another* young man had been instantly smitten by the very pretty and fascinating Francis.

Then Sita had a quick look herself at Francis. She was wide-eyed, and clearly excited. Francis seemed to be excited about *everything* to do with the Project. And her excitement had obviously just peaked. This was a totally new experience for both of them.

Francis was twenty-eight years old, but she could have passed for nineteen. She was petite in stature, with short, thick, dark brown hair. She was also a *brilliant* linguist as well as a renowned social and cultural anthropologist.

Francis had many other interests, too. Her favourite hobby was tracing the roots of the many first and last names in use on New Earth. The cultural norm for the last century or so had been for young couples to search through the old Earth historical archives for names that they thought they could identify with in some way. Francis had been glad to help her young friends find *just* the right first name for their babies. One could now also choose to adopt a new last name or family name, however that practice rarely occurred.

The activity at the many consoles in the large room was no doubt purposeful, but totally baffling in its complexity. Sita wondered how everyone could possibly be working cooperatively together.

Sita wished Gunter could have been here on this milestone day. But tragically, he had passed away about a year before after suffering a heart attack.

Sita remembered sadly that the Project leaders had basically phased out Gunter's role. No one could see why an archaeologist would be needed going forward. Frankly, neither could Gunter, but his interest had never waned. And really, how could anyone possibly know for *sure* what would be needed?

Sita now knew she had a bit of time, so she mused to herself about the last nine years. Remarkably, the Project had progressed as originally planned with very few difficulties. The media had accepted and promoted the idea that the probe was considered absolutely necessary 'for the advancement of science'. Coverage had been sporadic, but many updates had been provided on where the departing probe was in relation to New Earth, and to the distant moon Adatia.

But media coverage had *really* intensified over the last few weeks. The orbital mapping phase had yielded a fantastic discovery. Amazingly, right after orbital insertion around the distant moon, a kilometre-long fissure had opened up in the moon's surface ice sheet!

But even stranger, the fissure now seemed to be continuously opening and closing, on a cycle of about one New Earth day. Whenever the fissure opened up, a geyser of condensed water vapour would spew into the near-vacuum surrounding the moon. The vapour would instantly freeze into a cloud of ice crystals, which would dissipate as the ice crystals gradually fell back to the moon's surface.

So, selecting the landing site for the lander-rover had been easier than anyone had anticipated. The lander had descended smoothly, and successfully made 'moon-fall' close to one side of the fissure.

The lander had then turned itself into a rover. Human 'drivers' on New Earth instructed the rover to move back and forth along the side of the fissure to gather data. The rover sent acquired data back to New Earth via the part of the probe that had remained in orbit around Adatia.

Some of these data included optical images. Uploading data to New Earth had to occur in bunches, because line-of-sight contact was required between the transmitter and the receiver. The same constraint applied when relaying new instructions to the rover via the orbital probe.

The lander-rover continuously announced its presence on the surface of the moon by emitting an 'introductory message of greeting' in radio and other electromagnetic frequencies. The message was just a repeating series of beeps corresponding to the prime numbers up to seventeen, those being two, three, five, seven, eleven, thirteen and seventeen. Unfortunately the same message could not be delivered in sonic frequencies because the atmosphere on the moon was essentially non-existent. But a sonic form of the message would be delivered when, or rather if, the rover somehow managed to enter the ocean.

Analysis of the data received on New Earth suggested there was about a thirty-metre drop from the undisturbed part of the ice sheet to the ocean surface exposed by the fissure. When the fissure opened, the widest gap was in the order of two hundred metres. However, the opening and closing of the fissure was creating a rubble zone. But when the fissure was fully opened, the slope down to the water looked to be something the rover *might* be able to traverse.

So, the rover had recently been told to carefully make its way down to the ocean surface, drive itself into the water and then submerge itself deep enough to avoid being crushed when the fissure closed again.

Because of the need to steer around obstructions and select the best path to traverse in *real time*, the rover had to perform everything by itself, using its artificial-intelligence control-module. It was told to collect data continuously when submerged in the water and under the ice. It was also told to use its own judgement about how and when to re-surface in open water, establish line-of-sight contact with the orbiter in space, and upload the data it had collected for further transmission to New Earth.

Sita and Francis were suddenly aware that people had begun talking quietly together in little groups within the mission control centre. After ten minutes or so, some of the group discussions in the room became loud, and even a bit heated or angry. And then everyone, everywhere, was looking very anxious and very worried.

This time Francis whispered to the nearby engineer, "Sergei, what on New Earth is going on around here?"

Sergei took his headset completely off this time. He looked sad and confused. Then he mumbled, "Something has gone *terribly* wrong! We did not receive the normal check-in confirmation signal from the probe when line-of-sight was re-established.

"Instead we received an unusually terse message that the rover had entered the water. Then we received a series of images from orbit showing the fissure closing again. The images all had time-text notes, of course.

"It looks like the fissure completely closed *right after* the rover first entered the water! And it almost certainly did not have sufficient time to submerge itself out of harm's way!"

"You mean, the rover might have been crushed and *destroyed* when the fissure in the ice sheet closed?" asked Francis a bit frantically.

"Yes, that is *exactly* what it means!" replied Sergei while shaking his head. He now looked to be in a state of shock. Then he said quietly, "Look, I better not say any more to you guys. See why? Some guards are coming this way! I suspect you will now be asked to leave the mission control room, and right away.

"I'm sorry, I have *truly* enjoyed your company…" He trailed off with a stifled sob, while lowering his head and covering his face with his hands.

5

Prime Minister Phillip Wong was now in his third term of office. The historical precedent established for competent and politically astute New Earth 'supreme leaders' was only two terms in office. But there was no actual law preventing a third term, and Wong's left-of-centre party had been perceived as performing exceptionally well by the electorate.

But suddenly, Phillip Wong had become very worried about his political future. The dramatic and inexplicable failure of the deep-space probe mission was probably a game-changer. It had consumed a vast amount of resources, and yielded very little in the way of new scientific knowledge. Wong had promised that great discoveries would undoubtedly be made to enhance the all-important Resource Development Plan. And that certainly had not happened.

It was now approaching ten o'clock in the evening, and Prime Minister Wong was alone in his cavernous government office. He was a morning person, so he was feeling rather tired, and a bit out of sorts. But General Kepler had *insisted* on the need for an immediate meeting with him to discuss 'startling new information'. The prime minister had subsequently asked that Science Minister O'Shea and Resource Minister Hernandez sit in on the impromptu meeting as well.

At precisely ten o'clock, the top general in the world, and the two other inner-cabinet ministers, were ushered in to the prime minister's office by Janet Osaka. Janet was the prime minister's personal administrative assistant. She was a morning person too, and she looked visibly angered by having to stay at her post so late into the evening.

Prime Minister Wong decided to completely ignore the presence of Janet Osaka. He found that was the best way to remind her that her role was completely subservient, and that she was very fortunate to have such a job. He rose from his desk and motioned for everyone else to take a seat in the adjoining lounge area. Then he waited beside his desk without further comment until Janet had stomped out of the room, and loudly closed the door behind her. He sighed, and wondered again if it was time to look for a new assistant.

The prime minister walked over and took a seat beside the others. Then he asked pleasantly but bluntly, "So, General Kepler, what's happening?"

General Jorge Kepler looked even more out of sorts than Phillip Wong was feeling. His face was unusually flushed. There was a pitcher of ice water on the low coffee table in front of him. Kepler reached for the pitcher, then clumsily poured himself a glass of water. His hands were shaking! He took a long drink of water, spilling a few drops from a corner of his mouth. Then he wiped his mouth with the back of his left hand, and awkwardly thumped his water glass back down on the table.

Then General Kepler took a deep breath, and said in a wavering voice, "Prime Minister, and fellow Ministers, we have just received a message from space. It reached us about twelve hours ago. It did not come from our Adatia moon orbital probe, or from any of our other satellites. It was a digital signal in a radio frequency. It was actually picked up by a radio telescope.

"The message began with what we have just deciphered as a digital-code translation table. You know, a series of zeroes and ones, that we are now certain correspond to the twenty-six letters in our English alphabet, as well as our ten numerals from zero to nine. The translation table was repeated twice. Then the actual message was delivered, three times in succession."

General Kepler deliberately paused for a few moments to let the others consider the implications of this remarkable information. Then he said a little more steadily, "The message came from *our* moon – Addy! It was clearly in English, and without punctuation. But we think we have managed to properly insert some logical punctuation into it. Now, let me read to you the slightly-edited message."

The general then pulled a single piece of neatly folded paper from an inside pocket of his uniform jacket. He carefully unfolded the piece of paper, and slowly read out loud:

'We need to talk. We want a meeting. Three of our emissaries will meet with three of your emissaries. Meet us on your moon, exactly two of your years from now. Come to where the beacon has just been activated. You have proven yourselves to be technologically advanced. But you are also naive. We will explain our views about you in our meeting. Your probe to the ice-covered moon around the fifth planet has been completely destroyed. Do not attempt to send another probe to that moon. Ever. We are the guardians of the lifeforms that are evolving there. And we are far more technologically advanced than you are.'

No one said anything for a very long moment. The general carefully re-folded the piece of paper he had brought with him and handed it to the prime minister.

The prime minister looked shaken and totally confused. He just held on to the folded piece of paper, and his eyes darted around to glance at the sombre faces of the other people in the room.

Then Minister Abdul O'Shea simply mumbled, "*Wow.*" He was clearly reeling from the news as well.

Minister Patricia Hernandez regained her composure first, and she said quietly, "Okay, *wow* as well, no doubt. Now, is there anything else you can tell us, General?"

"Ah, yes, sorry," Kepler mumbled. He reached into another inside pocket of his uniform jacket, and pulled out another precisely-folded piece of paper. He gently unfolded the sheet of paper and smoothed it out on the table in front of him. The others leaned closer to be able to look at the document.

The letter-sized page was completely filled with a high-resolution image of the near side of New Earth's moon, Addy.

General Kepler pointed at a small red dot on the surface of the moon and said, "The, ah, *beacon*, is right here. Three-dimensional, or I guess four-dimensional, triangulation also places the origin of the radio message we just received in exactly the same place. It is a steep-sided, small circular crater, about sixty metres across. It is probably the collapsed roof of a lava tube. It appears black in visible light, so it must be pretty deep."

"A lava tube?" asked the prime minister slowly. He still seemed a bit dazed. Then he shook his head, and added, "Is that significant, General, somehow?"

"Ah, yes, possibly," replied Minister O'Shea. He looked at General Kepler, and the general nodded back at his friend with a weak smile to suggest he should continue. So O'Shea said, "The discovery of lava tubes on Earth's moon led to the planning and development of cost-effective subsurface bases. The tubes provide natural radiation shielding and protection from meteor strikes. And they can be sealed airtight to make effective shelters for human habitation. They also provide a really effective and secure way to *hide* a moon base, I suppose.

"We think our moon is similar to Earth's moon in many respects, except it is smaller, and it may be richer in valuable metallic elements, like iron and nickel. Addy must have been there a long time, because it is has synchronous rotation through tidal locking, like Earth's moon. That means we always see the same side of Addy from our vantage point on the surface of New Earth."

There was another long pause, then Minister Hernandez asked bluntly, "So, now what, guys?"

"Yes, *now what*, of course," mused Prime Minister Wong out loud. Then he said, "Ah, sorry! Definitely as an aside, and for your ears only, this obviously startling development *may* just have saved my political career. I mean, the great expense of the probe mission has now been *completely justified*!

"But that is not really that important right now, is it, considering the far greater implications and ramifications?

"The answer to Minister Hernandez's *excellent* question is obvious to me. *Now* we must figure out a way to show up on time for our meeting, of course! I don't mean 'us' specifically, but rather the three completely trustworthy, extremely fit and highly competent people that we will send to Addy to represent us."

"I completely agree with you from a security perspective, Prime Minister," said General Kepler immediately. He looked to be more in control of his emotions. Then he added calmly, "We are likely dealing with aliens that possess highly superior technology, and probably by extension, more advanced weaponry. So, we absolutely need to determine right away if they are friends or foes! We frankly have *no way* to know right now what kind of a threat they are to us. So, we *definitely* have to establish the threat level we could be up against, whatever the cost!"

"Yes, well, the *cost* will of course be *astronomical*, General," mumbled Minister Hernandez, who was also the guardian of the overarching Resource Allocation Plan.

"Okay, but is this meet-and-greet mission to Addy something we can actually *do*?" asked the prime minister a bit frantically.

"Yes, thankfully it is, Prime Minister," replied Minister O'Shea with confidence. Then he smiled and said, "You see, we have *proven* designs for moon landers and chemical-rocket boosters in our archives. An uncertain, up-front research and development phase is therefore not required. But two years is still a very short timeframe for building the *right* space craft and a suitable launch vehicle for it. And selecting and training a suitable crew will also be a significant challenge for us."

"So, obviously, we will just have to begin *immediately*, that's clear!" said the prime minister emphatically. Then he added in the same loud voice, "And how do we do that? Do we go public with this, and right away? That would no doubt make our citizenry as frightened and anxious as we are right now, but that also might help get them onside quickly?"

"Okay, that germ of an idea might have some merit, Prime Minister," replied Minister Hernandez slowly. Then she sighed, and said, "But, I think we should put some very careful thought into how exactly we go public! I'm just thinking out loud, but in this case a simple press statement will almost certainly not be good enough. I think we'll have to follow up with well-planned public consultations. This news will stress a *lot* of people out, like it has us."

"That is exactly why we cannot 'go public' with any of this, damn it!" growled Kepler abruptly. When he saw the others recoil in reaction to his stern words, he looked a bit sheepish and explained, "Sorry about that, guys. Look, only a few radio astronomers heard this message in its raw, cryptic form. We know exactly who these astronomers are, and they know that we know. They have all just been ordered into secrecy, and all of their raw data recordings have been confiscated. We can *definitely* keep a completely sealed lid on this!

"So far, only a few security-force code experts have deciphered the message. And those guys all have top-level security clearances, and therefore are sworn to secrecy."

After a long pause to think, Prime Minister Wong said quietly, "Right, if we do not go public with the full truth, then we will need a plausible cover story. Maybe we could release something, without fanfare of course, about a *subtle* message that we think *may* have been detected during the probe mission that seems to suggest we should visit our own moon, Addy?

"Furthermore, we could say we all believe it is high-time we started exploring for the valuable resources we think probably exist on our moon? And, maybe we should add that we plan in time to establish a small human-occupied base on Addy, and make it into something like a highly useful communication satellite?

"Folks, for your benefit only, as I have yet to reveal this publicly, I've got another three years left in this term of office, and I have literally just decided not to run again.

"I think I can withstand the political fallout from the failed probe mission to remain in office if I can somehow positively link it to an exciting new manned mission to Addy. And it will help, no doubt, if I can also stress this is just the start of an exciting manned space program that will have both a strategic and commercial upside.

"Sorry, I have been having a bit of a discussion with myself, out loud! But, the more I think about it, that *last* point may be the one to stress with the citizenry.

"The probe mission got us back into the space business, that's all! We are *finally* ready to take the obvious, next bold step. And there may *indeed* be great riches on Addy!

"So, I'll start working right away with the Parliamentary Press Secretary, and proceed right away with that line of public communication."

Then after a longish pause, Prime Minister Wong said informally and in a friendly manner, "Patricia and Abdul, after this Addy mission is announced publically, I want you both to work with your respective ministries to jointly come up with a detailed plan for this new mission, and how we will resource it. Let me know when you have something ready for me to look at. I think we'll let the general manage the construction and operational phases. This will also require very high security, and that's the general's business, too.

"Now, is there anything else we should talk about before we break up for tonight?"

"Ah, yes, there is something else I believe, Prime Minister," replied Minister O'Shea slowly. Then he explained, "We need to watch the sky around us very carefully, and far more carefully than we have been doing. You see, I don't think the three visiting emissaries are actually on our moon, I mean *right now*.

"Rather, I think they will have to travel there from somewhere else, just like we will have to do. If we detect their spacecraft early enough, we *might* be able to determine its point of origin. I think the obviously intelligent beings that sent us this message, and who admit to destroying our deep-space probe, are probably living somewhere in our Sol-system. But we might have to wait until our meeting with them for verification. That is, if they should decide to tell us where they live."

The prime minister looked confused again, and very tired. Then he said quietly, "Okay, Abdul, and Patricia, include a more comprehensive space-monitoring proposal in your detailed plan as well. But please, avoid saying too much, if anything, about *why* this add-on is suddenly deemed necessary.

"All of this prep-work has to be kept top secret, of course. Now, is there anything else, folks? No? Okay, then let's break it off now, and try to get some rest. That may prove to be futile, I know, tonight anyway.

"But we're about to get a *lot* busier, and we'll all need to find ways to get proper rest between many spurts of high activity if we are going to pull off this moon-mission successfully!"

Prime Minister Wong then abruptly stood up, and the others followed suit. Then he shook everyone's hand, and escorted them to his office door. When they had left, he returned to sit down behind his cluttered desk.

He knew he could not hope to fall asleep after such an intensely disturbing discussion. However, he wondered if a bit more work might distract him enough for a bit of successful meditation before daybreak. But then he suspected he was only fooling himself.

6

Assistant Professor Francis Maldonado arrived early for the mysterious meeting at Government House. She had received a letter from something called the Privy Council telling her exactly where she was to go, and exactly when she was to arrive.

But she had not been told what the meeting would be about, or who else would be in attendance.

Francis had never heard of the Privy Council, so she did a word search to find out about it via the internet. Apparently, it was a rather secretive group of retired ex-Cabinet Ministers who provided advice directly to the prime minister. It was not commonly known who was on the Council at any given time. And the word search did not reveal if the advice was proactively offered, or only provided upon the request of the prime minister.

Francis always arrived early for meetings, and she decided this one would be no different. She strongly believed arriving late for *any* meeting demonstrated either an anti-social lack of consideration for others, or brazen rudeness. And trying to arrive exactly on time, well, that just increased the risk of arriving late through unforeseen circumstances.

As a result, she found herself sitting alone in a richly-furnished meeting room deep within an administrative wing of the federal parliament building. An immaculately uniformed guard had carefully checked her credentials, and then he had escorted her into the meeting room.

The guard was both friendly and grandfatherly. At a side counter in the large room, he had poured her a big mug full of steaming, highly-aromatic coffee. It tasted as rich and fine as it smelled. Francis wondered if this might be one of the many perquisites enjoyed within inner-government circles.

When the guard had left the room, Francis sat down on a plush leather chair near the end of a twelve-seat, highly-polished, wooden table. She used the quiet time to reflect a bit on the previous couple of weeks.

The Dean of Anthropology had insisted that her annual medical check-up had to be *greatly* expanded to include a week-long series of elaborate physical, behavioural and mental-aptitude tests. When asked for an explanation, the Dean had simply shrugged in a cavalier manner and said, 'Francis, apparently it stems from a new government edict that now applies to everyone in positions like ours. We just have to accept these things when they happen.'

The Dean's explanation did not sit well with Francis. No one else seemed to know anything about this 'new edict' with respect to more comprehensive medical check-ups, and psychological profiling.

Francis was startled out of her inner wool-gathering when the elderly guard reappeared. This time he was leading a tall, uniformed man into the meeting room. The military man stopped abruptly just inside the doorway, and looked around carefully. He appeared to be greatly concerned about something. Then he stared long and hard at Francis. He smiled at her briefly, then he asked the guard politely, "Are you *sure* this is the right room, Master Sergeant? I presumed this was going to be a discussion about military matters."

The guard simply smiled back at him and said quietly, "Yes, we are quite sure that this is the right room, Colonel Knudsen. Now, please take a seat, sir. And, would you like some fresh coffee?"

"Ah, yes, please! And I am *Lieutenant* Colonel *Nils* Knudsen," replied the tall young man. He still looked a bit confused, so he asked, "Are you *still* sure I'm in the right place, Master Sergeant?"

The guard just nodded in reply this time, and directed Colonel Knudsen to the plush chair opposite Francis. Then the guard brought the young officer a full mug of steaming coffee, and left the room.

Lieutenant Colonel Knudsen could have played the part of a Norse god in a Wagner opera. He had short blond hair, and was very well-groomed, to the point of perfection. His well-tailored Air Force uniform enhanced his obviously muscular and athletic physique. Francis could not help but admire his good looks, especially his piercing, blue eyes.

And the young Colonel was instantly struck dumb by the stunning beauty of the exotic, brunette, and obviously young lady sitting across the table from him. He was at a complete loss for words as he carefully studied her fascinating face. He was astounded by the discovery that he could find no flaw.

After a few awkward moments, Colonel Knudsen offered his hand across the table to Francis, and said in a deep baritone voice, "Hello there! I don't believe we have met before. You just heard who I am, but that may not help you very much? Would you tell me who *you* are?"

Francis shook his hand firmly, smiled politely, and said, "I am Associate Professor Francis Maldonado, from Abubakar University. I am a cultural, linguistic and social anthropologist."

"From Abubakar University, and an anthropologist," mused the young Lieutenant Colonel out loud. Then he shook his head and said, "Nope, sorry! That doesn't help me much, not at all. You see, I'm a test pilot! Do you have any idea what this meeting is about, Professor Maldonado?"

Francis recoiled with surprise. Then she laughed heartily and said, "Please call me *Francis*, Colonel Knudsen! You have just made me even *more* uncertain about the nature of this meeting! You see, I was just told in writing by the Privy Council to attend a meeting here today. And they offered me no explanation."

"The Privy Council?" exclaimed Colonel Knudsen with unrestrained surprise. Then he added quietly, "They advise the prime minister, don't they? This is *very* curious. You know, I was simply ordered to attend by my commanding officer. She offered no explanation either, and we are really not supposed to ask in the military, you know, just obey."

Just then, the elderly guard reappeared. This time he was leading two more uniformed male officers into the room, and an older man dressed in a well-tailored civilian suit. Francis and Colonel Knudsen both stood up immediately. They both recognized General Jorge Kepler and retired Cabinet Minister Abdul O'Shea. Colonel Knudsen also recognized the other officer, and offered him a slight welcoming nod of his head.

The attending guard then asked, "Would you gentlemen like a cup of coffee as well?" All three of the men he was escorting accepted his offer. General Kepler sat down at the very end of the table, and the other officer sat down next to Colonel Knudsen. Doctor O'Shea sat down next to Francis.

Francis and Colonel Knudsen both realized there were not going to be any immediate introductions or handshakes, so they both just sat down again. The guard left the room after delivering the three mugs of coffee. He quietly closed the door to the meeting room behind him.

"It's no secret that I like punctuality, so I think we are off to a very good start," began General Kepler gruffly. Then he boomed loudly, "Lieutenant Colonel Knudsen, we have met once before, I believe. You quickly showed me around a flight simulator facility last year. Now, I also understand that you may know Major Weismann here?"

"I know Major Weismann very well, sir," replied Colonel Knudsen formally. He smiled at Weismann, and added, "We have worked on a number of really interesting research projects together."

"Right, then that's good," replied General Kepler abruptly. He then opened a thick file folder that he had brought with him, glared hard at Francis and said, "But you probably do not know who this highly intelligent young lady is, and *vice versa*. So, I'll run quickly through some introductions before we start.

"I am General Jorge Kepler. I command the Combined Security Forces. We also have with us today a retired Minister of Science and Technology, Doctor Abdul O'Shea, who is now an esteemed member of the Privy Council.

"I will now have to refer to my notes, unfortunately."

Kepler had aged well. He still shaved all of the hair off of his large, blemish-free head. He was very fit, so it was actually quite difficult to guess his age.

O'Shea had grey, thinning hair, and he was noticeably hunched over from years of neglected posture and the onset of osteoarthritis. But he looked to be alert, and very interested in the proceedings.

General Kepler looked at Francis again, this time with just the hint of a smile, and said pleasantly, "This is Doctor Francis Maldonado, Associate Professor of Anthropology at Abubakar University." Then he glanced at his notes again and added, "Twenty-eight, single, the very best in her academic field. Gymnast, all-collegiate gold medal winner in combined exercises. Passed all the qualifying tests with flying colours. In fact, no one has *ever* scored higher on an aggregate basis. Congratulations, Doctor."

Kepler then glanced quickly at Knudsen, looked back at his notes and growled, "Air Force Lieutenant Colonel Nils Knudsen. Thirty-four, single, highly-decorated for bravery, never in combat, of course. No wars! Been flying since he was sixteen. Only pilot to flat spin an F-12 from twenty thousand metres up and live to tell about it. And he did that *on purpose*, because he is a *test pilot*. The best one we have, actually, but we know he won't ever let high praise like that go to his head. That's because he is also an officer on active duty. *Very* active duty, I might add. Successfully checked-out on every type of helicopter and airplane on New Earth. Over ten thousand hours flying time as Pilot-in-Command."

Kepler then glanced quickly at the other officer. The man had short, curly, black hair and was wearing black-rimmed glasses. He had a clean shaven, plain-looking face, but like O'Shea, he looked as intelligent as he actually was. He was wiry in physique, and obviously very fit. Kepler looked at his notes again and said loudly, "Major Asher Weismann, Air Force reservist. Thirty-six, married, two kids. Right into triathlons, and he's won a few. He is also *Doctor* Weismann, Associate Professor of Astrophysics and Space Engineering at Abubakar University. Knows *all about* spacecraft, the Sol-system, stars, aerodynamics, control systems, the Theory of Relativity, and a mess of other hair-brained stuff I could never come close to understanding. He also has four thousand hours flying time in many types of aircraft, and some helicopters."

General Kepler then snapped his leather file-folder shut, and barked, "So, why are we all here today? No, don't bother to guess! I'll cut right to the chase!

"You are now Team A! There will also be a back-up Team B, but you will never meet those people, and hopefully we will not need to put any of those other folks to actual work.

"What this really means is that you are now all 'Astronauts in Training', and furthermore, you are also now New Earth Ambassadors. You are soon going to make a visit to our moon, *Addy*. If all goes right, you should be leaving New Earth about twenty-three months from now.

"We are working very hard to have a working rocket and spacecraft combination ready for you by then. Actually, we *have* to have it ready for you by then! And you *have* to be fully-fledged astronauts by then! Because you will have the honour and privilege of attending a scheduled meeting with three highly-intelligent alien creatures who want to talk to us, or rather to *you* three people, *very badly* it seems!

"This is not just a load of BS, so start dealing with it, and *right now*, people!

"Now, and quickly, do you have any questions?" He then methodically scanned around the table. He noted that Doctor O'Shea was frowning back at him. The three younger people all looked a bit confused, and a bit anxious. So he laughed, and added, "Or, is there anything *else* we should tell them before they recover their wits enough to ask us questions, Doctor O'Shea?"

"General Kepler, I think they are entitled to hear something about the context before we proceed to fielding their questions," replied Doctor O'Shea, trying hard to avoid sounding too critical. General Kepler was renowned for being concise, but he was also famous for being overly blunt, to the point of appearing to be a bully. O'Shea had long believed Kepler would be more effective if he initially tried harder to respectfully win people over to his views with supporting facts and logic.

"Okay, then see what you can do for them in, ah, ten minutes, tops, Doctor O'Shea," replied the general, while looking at his watch.

Doctor O'Shea then quickly but methodically summarized the events that had led up to the current situation. Then he provided the latest news that even General Kepler had not heard yet.

"The alien spacecraft is en route to our moon, Addy, and we know that for sure now," he said quietly while carefully observing the general's face for a reaction. When he saw Kepler immediately frown back at him, he added, "It really is not difficult to see the approaching vessel with a telescope and multi-spectrum electromagnetic scanner. That is, when one knows *exactly* where to look for it.

"You see, the approaching spacecraft has just sent us a digital, coded, electromagnetic message, four times in succession, about half a day apart between the repeats.

The message was sent using the same frequency that our recent deep-space probe had used. We won't tell you how we figured out the digital translation code. That's a secret.

"The message was in English, and incredibly, all it said was, '*Here we are*'."

Doctor O'Shea paused for a moment to allow the others to internally process this rather shocking information. Then he added quietly, "And we have also determined that the alien spacecraft is on a trajectory that traces back to the outermost section of the ring around the gas-giant planet Rasmussen, which is the seventh planet in the Sol-system. Of course, that does not mean we now know for sure where the spacecraft originated, or where these alien creatures actually live. In fact, I *strongly suspect* the alien astronauts have deliberately charted and followed a convoluted trajectory to make it difficult if not impossible to figure out their *actual* point of origin.

"Oh, and they don't seem to be in much of a hurry to get to Addy! But if they hold to their present course and speed, they can put themselves into orbit around our moon without prolonged or extreme periods of deceleration a couple months ahead of our scheduled meeting date.

"I think we can *now* field some questions from these highly-intelligent young people, General Kepler. That is, if we have a bit more time available today?"

It was General Kepler's turn to be lost in thought. But he cleared his throat, looked at his watch again and said, "Yes, as it happens, I can spare a few more minutes. So, who's first?"

"Have we selected the launch vehicle, spacecraft and lander combination, sir?" asked Major Weismann immediately and bluntly. There were *obviously* lots of questions, and the general's compressed time schedule was puzzling to Weismann, and a bit aggravating.

"Yes, we will be assembling and using a Megathrust II-B three-stage, hydrogen-LOX rocket booster, a Nebula X-treme command capsule, and a spherical Osprey IV lander," replied the general loudly. Then he growled, "All proven designs from Earth's Moon-Base era. Most systems are automated, but there will be manual override capabilities. So, an *expert* crew will be needed. And this specific booster-spacecraft-lander combination has been used successfully *many* times before, as you no doubt know, Major Weismann."

"And when will our training begin, sir?" asked Colonel Knudsen pleasantly. He was angered as well by the general's brashness, but he really was an experienced, professional officer, and he could keep his emotions well-hidden when that was required to be effective.

"That will start *tomorrow*, after you all have signed a secrecy agreement, and receive a more comprehensive briefing," snapped the general in reply. Then he added sternly, "And you will be in *command*, Lieutenant Colonel Knudsen! And Major Weismann, you will be *second* in command. Those are *direct orders*."

"Yes, sir!" replied Colonel Knudsen and Major Weismann immediately and at exactly the same time.

There was an awkward prolonged pause, then Francis said quietly, "I am a *civilian*, General, and I know virtually nothing about flying airplanes, let alone spacecraft and moon landers. What will my duties be, and why do you want *me* to be part of this team?"

"Your specific duties will be decided by your Commander, Doctor Maldonado!" barked General Kepler. Then he stared hard at Colonel Knudsen and asked, "Well, *Commander*, what will her duties be?"

Colonel Knudsen took a long, slow, deep, breath, then he said calmly, "Everyone here knows New Earth has never had a manned space program of our own, not since we left the *Second Chance* generation spacecraft that brought our species here from Earth. And we then lost the *Second Chance* when a fire started up inside of her.

"We will be depending heavily on archival information to plan this mission, design and conduct simulations, and prepare ourselves properly for success. From what I know right now of Earth's orbital and lunar missions, I believe there will be *lots* of things Doctor Maldonado can do for us, with only three of us in the crew. But we'll figure all of that out during our training sessions. And there will need to be *many* simulations and practice sessions, with a lot of practice troubleshooting potential problems.

"Judging by Professor Maldonado's academic background and expertise, I sense that you mostly want her to come along with us to coordinate and manage our direct engagement with these alien creatures?"

"Yes, that's it, exactly!" interjected Doctor O'Shea loudly, before the general could answer. Then he smiled and said quietly, "That's because we have *no idea* what these creatures are like. But we want to learn as much as we can about them, in very short order. We might have to do that by just, say, listening to the way they talk, or observing their mannerisms and the way they interact with us, and with each other. We have to know *how* they think, as well as *what* they think. We have to communicate with them effectively, and bottom line, we have to know if they are friends or foes. This is a very tall order, no doubt!

"Now, Doctor Maldonado, you just pointed out to us that you are a civilian. So, you cannot be *ordered* to complete this mission. But the Privy Council believes you are *exactly* the right person to round-out this crack team of professionals.

"And Prime Minister Wong has fully agreed with the Council's recommendation, and he is now asking you, through us, to willingly take on this obviously risky but *extremely important* task. So, will you do it for us?"

"I would not miss it for the world," replied Francis immediately with a captivating smile. Colonel Knudsen and Major Weismann then smiled back at her. They both would have immediately volunteered as well, if they had not been given the direct order by General Kepler.

7

Major Asher Weismann followed two young lieutenants he did not know into the Air Force officers' club. They did not bother to hold the door open for him, but he figured they were in a hurry for some reason.

It was early on a Friday evening after another gruelling week of intense mission training. Weismann's wife, Patricia, had just arranged a babysitter for their two kids, and she was going to meet up with him in an hour or so.

Weismann and his pretty, energetic wife usually liked to start their weekends off this way, and then hop in a cab to go off base together to explore a new restaurant. They loved their kids dearly, but they also enjoyed their once-a-week getaway. And their kids did not seem to mind their occasional break from routine. They really hit it off well with Jill, their regular babysitter. Jill was a responsible teenager, and the daughter of a sergeant on the base. She was also artistically creative, and a natural entertainer. But a pizza delivery and a jug of chocolate milk always helped to make Jill's job a lot easier.

Weismann was going to make his way over to the bar, but one of the two lieutenants he was following suddenly stopped right in front of him to block his way. When Weismann tried to walk around the rather rude young man, the other lieutenant quickly turned around and said, "Sorry, sir, but our orders are to take you to see General Kepler, and right now. Please follow us, sir. The general is waiting for you in a booth at the back of the club."

Weismann then had a closer look at the two young lieutenants. They were both wearing basic Air Force uniforms, but they were not wearing unit identifiers or insignia of any kind, and they did not have name tags. So he snapped, "You lieutenants will both show me proper identification before I follow you *anywhere*."

The lieutenants did not seem angered or surprised by Weismann's abrupt challenge. They simply pulled out plastic-laminated photo-identification cards and showed them to him. The cards indicated they were attached to a branch of military intelligence that Weismann had never heard of before. But the cards looked to be genuine. So, Weismann simply shrugged and said, "Okay, then lead on, gentlemen."

The two lieutenants then escorted Major Weismann past the busy bar and into a section of the hall that was filled with crowded tables. There were cosy booths along the walls in the hall that offered a bit more privacy. Some of Weismann's friends were sitting in one of the booths on the far-left side of the hall, and they tried to attract his attention by waving at him, and by directing a few high-pitched whistles at him over the background din inside the club. But Weismann quickly decided it would be best this time to pretend he did not see or hear them.

They made their way over to the very last booth on the right side of the hall. The general was sitting in the booth by himself, and he was talking on his cell phone. When he saw the three officers approaching, he put his left hand up in a stop sign, and continued talking quietly into his phone.

The two lieutenants then asked the two full colonels that were sitting in the adjoining booth if they would mind moving somewhere else for their private meeting. The two senior officers were visibly angered by the effrontery of the two junior officers, until the lieutenants flashed their identification cards under their noses. Then the two colonels simply slid sideways along the cushioned bench seats in the booth, stood up abruptly without comment, and made their way over to the bar.

The two lieutenants sat down on one side of the now empty booth and motioned for Weismann to sit down on the opposite side of them. Both of the lieutenants then pulled out cell phones and held on to them. Then they all sat there silently for five minutes or so, until the cell phone of one of the lieutenants started to ring.

The lieutenant put the cell phone to his ear, listened for a few moments, and then simply said, "Yes, sir."

Then the lieutenant stared hard at Weismann and said, "General Kepler is ready for you now, Major Weismann. We will stay right here, close by, in case we are needed."

Weismann then made his way over to the adjoining booth. General Kepler simply motioned for him to sit down on the other side of the empty, polished wooden table in the booth.

A waiter in an immaculate white uniform then immediately appeared and asked, "Can I offer you gentlemen a drink this evening?"

"Rasmussen twelve year old scotch, on the rocks," General Kepler growled. Then he added politely, "Major Weismann, have a drink with me, please. My treat, of course."

"All right, thank you very much, General Kepler," replied Weismann calmly. He was rarely intimidated by top brass. The usual struggle was trying to avoid getting visibly pissed-off with them. He smiled at the waiter and said, "The same for me, my good man, only add a splash of still water, please."

The waiter bowed his head slightly and quickly left them so he could immediately place their drink order at the busy bar.

General Kepler started the conversation by saying gruffly, "We *knew* we could find you here, Major. You should vary your routine, you know, to make it just a bit more difficult for people who want to follow you, or to accost you. Actually, consider that a new standing order. Vary your routine, Major!

"Now, I'm meeting you here, in this way, for security reasons. I haven't been in this place for months. That makes it a good venue.

"I have some important matters to discuss with you. Our brief discussion should not interfere with the date you made with your wife. Again, we know about that, too. That's part of our job.

"First thing, and this is *top secret*, the alien spacecraft has just landed on Addy. We managed to get a fairly close look at it with an orbital space telescope. It doesn't look like any spaceship that human beings have ever built. It's asymmetrical, and sort of shaped like a silvery, short banana with four legs.

"We watched the bizarre-looking craft descend and then disappear down the crater on Addy. I'm talking about the crater where the aliens have been flashing a discrete infrared beacon at us for months. Colonel Knudsen has just been told about this milestone event as well. We will follow up next with Professor Maldonado.

"This means, of course, that the aliens are now getting ready for our meeting with them on Addy. We *hope* they understand it takes us time to launch space missions. But they may not know, of course, that we have not conducted *any* manned space missions ourselves since we arrived here on New Earth.

"We certainly do not want the alien delegation to get bored or frustrated waiting for us. So, staying on our schedule, or even *accelerating* our schedule, is now critically important.

"The good news is that we *should* be able to launch you and the other two ambassador-astronauts thirty-two days from now. As you very well know Major, that would place you on Addy about thirty-six days from now, assuming we don't experience any serious technical glitches.

"But I want you to know, Major, *most emphatically*, that in spite of our pressing need for haste, I will not hesitate to delay this mission if I have any doubts *at all* about crew readiness.

"Now, Lieutenant Colonel Knudsen has told us he fully believes his crew is ready, *right now*, for this mission. But, I want to hear your frank opinion as well, about crew readiness, *right now*. And you are under a direct order to reply, Major.

"Start by telling me if you believe *Colonel Knudsen* is ready for this mission."

Major Weismann was stunned by the question. He struggled very hard to restrain his immediate anger, but he knew he was under order to reply. So he said with a waver in his voice, "General Kepler, in my opinion, Colonel Knudsen is *more* than ready for this mission, sir. And so is Doctor Maldonado, sir. And so am I, sir, for that matter."

There was an awkward silence for a few moments. Then the waiter suddenly arrived with their drinks. The impeccable timing was suspicious again to Major Weismann. He wondered if the waiter could be an out-of-uniform officer in military intelligence. Weismann noted for the first time that the waiter had a small, discrete, flesh-coloured circular device lodged in his right ear.

The waiter placed their drinks on the table in front of them without comment, and quickly left without mentioning the tab.

Then General Kepler took a long, slow sip of his drink while looking the whole time at Weismann over the rim of his glass. Major Weismann decided to follow suit.

Eventually, Kepler put his glass down on the table and said quietly, "Look, Major, something does not jive with us. You're happily married, we know that, and that's really great. But on the A Team we also have a handsome, intelligent, single lieutenant colonel and a beautiful, intelligent, single civilian.

"Both parties are known to be heterosexuals. I won't tell you how we know that. That's unimportant. And both parties have been working together, in very close proximity, *for months now*. And from what we can tell, both parties seem to be totally disinterested in each other. Everything has always been strictly professional between them.

"Now, are we missing something? To be blunt, are these two crewmates of yours *more* than they seem to us? Furthermore, and right to the point, are they *conflicted* in any way?

"And you are still under orders to reply, Major."

Major Weismann really was angry now, and it showed on his face. He took a quick gulp of his drink and wiped his dripping mouth with the back of his left hand. Then he put his glass down hard on the table, and forced himself to take a long, slow, deep breath while carefully studying General Kepler's face. He was surprised to see that Kepler suddenly seemed to look embarrassed, and very uncomfortable.

In a flash, Weismann concluded the general really *was* sincerely concerned about a possibly 'conflicted crew'.

Major Weismann then found the inner strength to calmly reply, "General Kepler, my two crewmates really are professionals, just like I am. After our first full day of training, Lieutenant Colonel Knudsen met with me privately, just like we are meeting now, in a booth on the other side of this hall, actually.

"He confided to me that he was, quote, '*Completely nuts* about Francis Maldonado', and he said he knew she felt the same way about him. I didn't ask him how he knew that, because that's none of my damn business.

"But then he wanted to *assure* me that they had worked it all out so the mission would not be affected or imperilled *in any way*.

"They agreed to have their first *real* date back on New Earth *after* the mission is successfully completed. And as far as I can tell, that's exactly how it sits right now, and how it will continue to sit.

"That is definitely all A-OK with me, sir. And I truly hope that it is now totally A-OK with you too, sir."

General Kepler slowly leaned back against the cushioned back rest, and he smiled broadly. Then he quickly downed the remains of his drink in one gulp, slid off the bench seat, stood up abruptly and said with obvious relief, "Thank you very much, Major Weismann. Please enjoy the rest of the evening with your wife. I think we can forgo following you around for a while. And I wish you, and your two crewmates, the very best of luck on your upcoming, *critically important* mission!"

The general then waited one more second for Weismann to respond on cue. Weismann recovered his senses and leapt to his feet. Weismann came to rigid attention and saluted the general smartly. The general returned the salute with equal formality.

Then the two escort lieutenants suddenly reappeared, and the general followed them out of the club.

After a long moment, Weismann slowly sat down again. He badly needed someone to talk to about what had just happened, but he knew that was not possible. He hoped that his wife would be along shortly to help take his mind off the upcoming mission, with all of its very human complexities.

8

The three astronauts were now living and working inside both parts of the linked *Nebula-Osprey* spacecraft.

Until a few hours before, they had been confined to the *Nebula* command module. But they had successfully fired a chemical-rocket thruster to accelerate their spacecraft out of New Earth orbit and redirect the small craft at the 'window' in space that would place it in orbit around New Earth's moon, Addy. The astronauts now knew that in less than three days' time, with the help of a decelerating nudge from their main rocket engine, they would successfully go through that distant but approaching orbital insertion window.

It was therefore time to start checking out all of the many complex systems in the *Osprey* Lander Module.

However, just prior to beginning that critically important and rigidly methodical work, all three astronauts participated in a protracted, scheduled, communication session with First Town Mission Control back on New Earth.

During the scheduled call, crew promotions were announced. Nils Knudsen was now a full Air Force

Colonel, and Asher Weismann was now an Air Force reserve Lieutenant Colonel. The two officers were very glad to hear the news, but they knew it was mostly being done in the interest of 'political optics'. It seemed that high-level politicians felt that the voting population back on New Earth would have far more faith in higher-ranking officers. And the media was fully supportive of their changes in rank.

Of course, the politicians and the members of the media really had no conception of the many really difficult, intensely stressful situations that both officers had successfully managed during their busy careers. And very few people back on New Earth had any idea what exactly lay ahead for the three astronauts. But those were moot points, from the political perspective.

The politicians had also insisted that Francis Maldonado should be commissioned as an officer in the Air Force reserves. Surprisingly, the politicians openly admitted this was *definitely* required for 'political optics'. The military had quickly agreed with their suggestion, but for a different reason. They wanted to further solidify and clarify the chain of command on the spacecraft.

So, Francis Maldonado was now officially a reservist Air Force Major. She, of course, had no say in the matter. But she had politely responded that she was pleased to hear the news.

After Colonel Knudsen flipped the switch to terminate the communication link with First Town Mission Control, he quietly said to his two crewmates, "We should probably have our own chat now about what we just heard from First Town, guys.

"As you know, I have command prerogative to conduct private conversations from time to time. I think we can stay on our tight schedule if we keep this discussion short."

The three astronauts were sitting side-by-side, with Knudsen on the left, Weismann in the middle and Maldonado on the right. They had been on a strictly 'last name basis' since their mission began. Knudsen generally wanted to keep all of their conversations strictly professional, and to the point. He also wanted to reinforce his belief that they were a cohesive team, and every crew member was essential to the success of the mission. It was not a democracy, but Nils was a very good listener, and a very good leader, and he would frequently ask for opinions from his crewmates.

"So, we just heard the aliens have sent New Earth another message, only this time without a preceding code translation table," Knudsen summarized calmly. "The code they gave us last time still worked fine, it seems. And somehow, the aliens have managed to acquire high proficiency with New Earth English.

"Let's take a minute to consider the message transcript that mission control just sent to us. Again, the most recent alien message read, and I quote:

'*We see that you are now on your way to meet with us. That is good. We have cleared the vertical entrance chamber. It will be well lit up to assist with your safe arrival. Land your space-travelling vehicle exactly in the middle of the circle. Then relax and remain in your space-travelling vehicle. We will manage the logistics of our meeting from that point forward*'.

"So, as you just heard, I agreed with mission control that accordingly, we will now change our approach and descent plan. Specifically, rather than using hover or forward motion to traverse the plain surrounding the crater prior to landing, we will now plan to align vertically with the centre of the crater during our descent.

"On the positive side, this will increase our fuel reserve. That will provide more of a cushion should we have to abort because of a malfunction, or should we decide we do not like what we see directly below us, for some reason. However, this change *does* mean that we will now be on manual control from about one kilometre above the landing target. But thankfully, we did practise a few simulations that closely approximated what we are about to do.

"Weismann, do you have any concerns about this new plan?"

Weismann hesitated a moment, and then he said quietly, "I have *lots* of concerns, Knudsen, but I think we all share them. Visibility could be a *huge* problem when our main thruster stirs up dust inside of that crater. And there *will* be dust accumulation in that moon crater, even with only one-eighth New Earth gravity. The aliens said that they have 'cleared the chamber', but I suggest that probably did not include a sweep-up and a nice vacuum cleaner job! I mean, how could a vacuum cleaner work within a *vacuum*, anyway?

"They *still* have been completely unable to see down into that cylindrical chamber from New Earth. The only thing we know about it is that it's completely dark and presently unlit, and about five times wider across at the top, or at surface level, than the diameter of the *Osprey*. And if it's significantly deeper than the height of the *Osprey*, we will lose our line-of-sight communication link.

"Also, I don't like the idea of giving up on our original plan to do a scouting fly-by around the crater first. I agree the change of plan will increase our fuel reserve, but by foregoing an inspecting fly-by, we could miss something really significant that might help us make a critical decision. I'm specifically thinking about something that might make us think twice about fully descending into the crater, or into the 'chamber' rather.

"That's about it, Knudsen. I don't mean to sound too critical."

"Yes, Weismann, I understand and appreciate your concerns," replied Knudsen crisply. Then he sighed and said, "I guess it does come down to a risk trade-off. Giving us more fuel reserve presumes our landing site will actually be clear and level.

"But Earth's pioneering Apollo astronauts had even less of an idea about where they were going when they travelled to their planet's moon. In the last few seconds of descent, they had to avoid boulders and craters, and they sometimes came close to having to abort because of their mandatory requirement to leave a five percent fuel reserve at touch down.

"As we originally planned, as we complete our descent, Maldonado will eject an antenna module on to the surface of Addy. It will be connected to us by a spool of thin copper wire that will be good for about a hundred metres or so. That way, after we touch down at the bottom of the chamber, we should still have a working communication link with New Earth via the orbiting *Nebula* command spacecraft.

"Also, Maldonado will be looking around for us while you and I manage our descent, and evaluate the landing site. And we will have four cameras looking to our sides continuously as we descend. The video records of the surrounding surface terrain can subsequently be studied at length, by us and by the mission control folks back on New Earth.

"Maldonado, can we glean anything more about who our 'hosts' are from their latest message to us?"

"Well, Knudsen, obviously they are telling us *again* that they are a whole lot smarter than we are," replied Maldonado calmly. "They obviously know a lot about our moon, or at least a certain 'chamber' in it. They seem to know a lot about us, and we still know virtually nothing about them. They have mastered our language, somehow, and from afar.

"On the plus side, I think they have anticipated our concerns about landing inside of their chamber, and want to allay some of our fears. And they obviously still want to meet with us, and if they truly *are* smarter technologically, then maybe the chamber really has been cleared properly? That is, well enough to see the 'circle' on the bottom that they talked about?

"But I think they are also warning us right up front that they will be controlling every aspect of this upcoming meeting, not just the logistical matters."

The astronauts sat quietly for a few moments with their own thoughts. Then Knudsen said calmly, "Thanks, guys. I think our discussion just reinforced the reality that our mission still has a lot of unknown risks.

But we can't do much, if anything, about those, unfortunately. So, let's just deal with the *known* risks that we trained so hard to mitigate.

"Okay, it's time to fire-up all of the systems in the *Osprey* lander, and make sure everything works okay. Come on, let's get started."

9

Weismann: Okay, altitude 400, down at 7 per second, 4 per second forward.

Knudsen: No problem.

Weismann: 350 altitude, down at 4.

Weismann: Okay, you're pegged at zero horizontal velocity.

Weismann: 270, 2 down.

Knudsen: Okay, how's the fuel?

Weismann: Twelve percent.

Weisman: 120, 1 point 5 down. You're looking good.

Weismann: 30, 1 down. Ten percent fuel remaining. Quantity Light just came on.

Knudsen: Lights just came on in the chamber. There's a circular target, centre is marked with crossing lines.

Weismann: 10 altitude, ½ down. You're on the crosshairs down there. Radar shows 50 metres depth.

Maldonado: Antennae module ejected. Our shadow is out there. All clear, nothing of note.
Weismann: Zero altitude, 1/2 down. 300 seconds until Bingo call on the fuel.

Weisman: Minus 20, 1/2 down. Picking up some dust. Right on the crosshairs.

Knudsen: Visibility good now.

Weismann: Minus 40. I see our shadow.

Weismann: Drifting forward just a bit, that's good.

Weismann: Contact light.

Knudsen: Shutdown.

Weismann: Okay. Engine stop.

Weismann: Mode Control, auto. Descent Engine Command Override, off. Engine arm, off.

Mission Control: We copy you down, Osprey.

Knudsen: Copy you First Town, engine arm is off.

Knudsen: First Town, Addy Base here. The Osprey has landed.

Mission Control: Roger, Addy Base. We copy you on the ground. We didn't crack-up on our end, but it was close. Thanks a lot.

Weismann: Thank you too.

Knudsen: Okay. Let's get on with it. First Town, we're going to be busy for a few minutes.
Knudsen: First Town, do you copy?

Knudsen: First Town, do you copy?

Knudsen: First Town, if you can copy, we are no longer receiving you. Our communication system checks out as nominal. Source of difficulty unknown. We will monitor your transmissions. If you copy us, we will broadcast again in one hour. Out.

10

The three New Earth astronauts worked efficiently as a team to complete their post-landing checklist in about twenty minutes.

The astronauts were not missing the zero-G environment of space. Okay, it was not exactly like New Earth on the surface of the little moon. But a gravitational force of about one-eighth of New Earth 'normal' was certainly better than nothing.

They were very pleased to confirm everything was working properly within the *Osprey* lander. They also determined that the electrical circuit was unbroken to the wire antenna they had shot out and unravelled on the surface of Addy while they were completing their descent.

So, the antenna *should* have been working, but it was not. And that was rather unsettling.

The cylindrical, subsurface chamber that they had landed in was still illuminated. The wall of the chamber appeared to be perfectly smooth towards its base, where the *Osprey* had come to rest. The wall appeared to morph into a natural, rough-looking rock surface towards the top of the chamber.

The white-light illumination inside of the chamber was provided by vertical, flush-mounted strips that were imbedded in the circular wall.

There appeared to be the outlines of two large doors on opposite sides at the base of the chamber, but the doors looked to be sealed tight.

The mysterious and alarming communication blackout they were experiencing was weighing heavily on their minds. But Knudsen kept everyone busy. They immediately began readying their spacesuits for some extended Extra-Vehicular Activity, or EVA.

At precisely one hour after touch down, Knudsen tried again to hail First Town Mission Control. In response, they first heard a high-pitched squeal, and then nothing but silence.

Then, after another a minute or so, they received an analogue transmission over their primary communication frequency. They distinctly heard in a monotone, contralto or tenor voice:

"We are blocking your transmissions. Stay in your space-travelling vehicle. We will now move it to a place where your normal surface planetary environmental conditions will be precisely replicated. Again, please relax and be patient."

During the incoming transmission, Maldonado had been looking out of the little starboard-side window to the right of her seat. Suddenly she gasped, "Guys, there is a door opening on this side of the chamber! It's a big, one-piece door! It's sliding away! Okay, it's fully open now. The portal looks to be big enough for our lander to pass through easily."

Then they all felt a shudder and a slight vibration. Then they could see and *feel* that the lander was being moved sideways.

Weismann was scanning all of the outside-looking video displays, and he said calmly, "We landed on what we thought was just a raised circular platform. But it actually must be a *cart* of some kind, riding on rails, or maybe on wheels. It is now moving us inside another lit-up chamber on the other side of the open door. And as you can see, the lights inside of the landing chamber just went out."

After about ten minutes, the cart stopped moving. The *Osprey* had been moved about twenty metres beyond the doorway into a well-illuminated chamber. Then the door started to close. In the vacuum of space, there was no sound to be heard as the door was being closed.

When the door had fully closed, they noted that the *Osprey* was now in a chamber that resembled a barrel vault. It was a horizontal tube with a flat bottom. The tube looked to be about sixty metres long, and about twenty metres high.

The circular wall and roof of the chamber appeared to be made of perfectly smooth, grey rock, or a form of concrete. But the vertical, far end of the tube was flat, and it looked to be made of some kind of dull metal. It was also light grey in colour.

There looked to be the outline of a human-sized door in the flat-wall side of the chamber, but if so, it was a door without any handle, or visible hinges.

There was a dull, dark, flat panel imbedded in the metallic wall beside the outline of the door. And there was a simple-looking metallic bench pushed up against the wall beneath the panel.

After a few minutes, the *Osprey* crew started hearing a soft hissing sound. "It's coming from outside, I think," suggested Knudsen with wonder in his voice.

"Yes, Skipper, that's right," Weismann agreed. Then after another quick instrument scan, he added, "The pressure is gradually increasing outside. And so is the temperature. It's too early in the pressurization process to analyse the gas composition properly."

"Right, then let's get our EVA suits on now, folks," ordered Knudsen. "We don't know what might happen next, but let's be ready for *anything*."

Just then, the radio crackled, and they heard in a clear, monotone, soprano voice:

"The only way we will talk to you point forward is by means of compressional sound waves, in your language, outside of your vehicle. Sit on the bench facing the wall panel. The atmosphere we are creating will be comfortable for you. If we had wanted to hurt you in any way, we would have done so by now. That may sound threatening, but it is meant to calm you. You must try to trust us. We simply desire a friendly discussion with you. This is the last electromagnetic transmission we will make."

Knudsen looked in horror at Maldonado and Weismann, and said, "Holy shit, guys! They expect us to trust them *implicitly*! And we *still* know nothing about them!

"Well, we actually know a few more things about them, Knudsen," replied Maldonado quietly. "They are obviously technically advanced, probably much more so than we are. They seem to know a lot about this facility. They may have actually *built* this strange place, way in the past. And they probably *could* have killed us by now! They have obviously heavily invested in the effort to learn our oral and written language, somehow. And they must have travelled a great distance to get here. So, I think we should take them at face value. They probably *do* just want to talk to us, at least initially."

"They seem to know all about the air we like to breathe anyway, and what a 'comfortable environment' probably means to us," offered Weismann in support. He was busy scanning a suite of instruments. Then he explained, "The hissing sound has stopped, obviously. It's up to one hundred and one kilopascals of pressure out there, and it is a comfortable twenty-one degrees Celsius.

"And the motion of the air is subsiding. They have even given us some water-vapour humidity, about seventy percent relative or so. The gas chromatograph is showing a composition very near to that of New Earth's air!

"There are no obviously toxic contaminants or pathogens showing up on the biological threat detector, not yet anyway. Of course, that rather complicated device is only looking for threats it *knows* about."

"Right," replied Knudsen while thinking rapidly. "Your combined input really helped me out, guys, thanks.

"So, revised decision, we won't fully suit up. We'll just wear our coveralls and a jacket. We know we can't talk through masks very well. But let's each of us take a filter mask along, and an air pack too. That might buy us enough time to get back into the *Osprey* if they suddenly decide to do something, ah, *unfriendly*.

"We'll open up now and climb out of the *Osprey* when we confirm things have been stable out there for say, twenty minutes.

"Weismann, put a microphone and camera on your head, and put a recorder pack under your jacket. I don't see any reason to try to hide our effort to record what transpires. We should assume we won't be able to download then upload any data we acquire until we're back in the *Osprey* again. Or, maybe not until we are back on our own again, in space? Who knows?

"Okay people, let's get moving."

11

The bench in the alien's inner, subsurface chamber on Addy looked to be a familiar design to the three New Earth astronauts. It had simple, tubular, metallic legs, and a thick cushion that was covered in a material that looked and felt like vinyl. Although the bench did not provide back support, it proved to be form-fitting, and very comfortable.

The three astronauts decided to move the bench a couple of metres away from the metallic wall, and they kept it directly aligned with the dark panel on the flat, vertical surface. The bench seemed to be almost weightless in the low gravity field of the little moon.

Then the astronauts took turns to carefully sit down on the bench so they would directly face the dark panel. Unconsciously, they sat down in the same prescribed arrangement they always followed in the *Nebula* and the *Osprey*, with Knudsen on the left, Weismann in the middle and Maldonado on the right.

When they were all seated, they found their eyes were at about the same height as the centreline of the rectangular panel.

They had only been seated a few moments when they clearly heard the question, "*Do you have a leader?*"

The voice was baritone, and it closely resembled that of a human male, except it was also a rather unnatural monotone. It was not clear where the sound was coming from exactly. Actually, it seemed to be coming from *all* around them. The acoustics in the chamber were obviously very good. There was no echo, and the volume of the sound at their location in the chamber was conversational.

"I am the overall leader of our mission," replied Knudsen calmly in his normal speaking voice. "We have been sent by our government to meet with you. We call ourselves 'human beings'. I am a military human being. We have two sexes. I am a 'man', or an adult 'male' by sex. I am also an aircraft and spacecraft pilot.

"My name is Colonel Nils Knudsen. My second in command is beside me, directly to my right. His name is Lieutenant Colonel Asher Weismann. He is also a military man, but he is also a scientist.

"Our third in command is Major Francis Maldonado. She is sitting furthest to my right. She is a woman, or adult female by sex. She has only recently joined our military ranks to be able to participate in our mission to visit with you. She is a linguist, and an expert in human cultures. She will function as our leader while we talk with you."

There was a short pause, then they heard the same baritone voice say, *"Let us proceed this way then, human beings. We will ask you a question, and then we will listen to you, and consider your answer. Then you will ask us a question, and you will listen to us, and consider our answer. Now, what is your first question?"*

Knudsen and Weismann both leaned forward to look at Maldonado. Knudsen nodded and gave her a thumbs-up sign, and Weismann flashed her a big smile, and a supporting nod as well.

So Francis asked in a strong voice, "You obviously are able to hear us, and you can probably see us, quite well. But we can only hear you. Why is that?"

There was a longer pause this time. Then they heard a soprano monotone voice say, *"We have survived many generations by being what you might call intelligent and reclusive beings. We do not equate our secretive behaviour with cowardice, but other intelligent alien lifeforms have in fact perceived us that way. We are not ashamed of ourselves, nor do we consider ourselves vastly superior or 'god-like'.*

"We are an isolated clan of an ancient race that has lived in many places in our galaxy. We will not tell you what we call ourselves. The less other intelligent beings know about us, the better for our security. We live secret lives in secret places. We do that because we have been pursued and persecuted by the alien race of exploitive

bullies we know you call the 'Masters'. That strikes us as an appropriate name for those monsters.

"We can see that you are not like us, physically. Your appearance is frankly disturbing to us. But our appearance would no doubt be disturbing to you as well.

"So, we can probably have a better discussion meeting in this manner, where you can only hear us, or rather hear our machine-translated voices. For now, please accept as fact that there are three of us, directly facing you now, on the other side of the dark panel.

"Now, our studies lead us to believe you may resemble us to some degree with respect to basic life principles and guiding values. You seem to get along reasonably well with each other, and you seem to be respectful of your environment. That gives us some hope that we could possibly align with you on certain shared concerns, should both sides perceive mutual benefit.

"You see, we have been monitoring your electromagnetic transmissions since you arrived on the neighbouring planet. On the positive side, that is how we have learned so much about you, and about the language we are now both using. But on the negative side, through your ignorance or arrogance, you are frankly reckless with your transmissions.

"So, now for our question. Are you unaware that indiscriminately broadcasting your presence, radially

out into space in all directions, puts us all at great risk?"

Francis looked nervously at Knudsen and Weismann, and they both looked a bit confused, and a bit scared. After a moment, she said with a bit of a waver in her voice, "Perhaps we are unaware of the risk you are talking about.

"We have used electromagnetic frequencies to communicate with each other for eons. We find it an extremely useful technology, and very efficient. The practice originated on our home planet that we called Earth. It is about one hundred and six of our light years away from us. Perhaps you may know this, but we define a year as the length of time for the planet we live on to complete an orbit around its star.

"We note that you have communicated with us using an electromagnetic frequency. Why was that not a reckless act as well?"

After a short pause, a baritone monotone voice replied, *"It was a risk we thought we must take to achieve this meeting. We did in fact send you ten very short messages. There will not be any more, and you will not be allowed to make any more while we are on this moon together.*

"We will see to that with our more advanced technology. Our ten messages were not broadcast radially, rather they were sent to you in a very tightly

confined and directed beam. The messages were all sent in your language. The digital translation code was only sent to you once. If any of the messages were heard by other advanced, intelligent beings, they will almost certainly conclude you were just talking with yourselves again, in the way you always do.

"Let us presume that you just asked us, 'Why does this matter?'

"The reason is we intercepted a digital electromagnetic message shortly after your species first settled on the neighbouring planet. It was definitely not meant for us, or for you. It was broadcast both radially, and highly directionally with great power, along a discrete and purposeful vector. It was sent using the high energy available on a 'Master' exploration, generation spaceship, as it was departing from this solar system. You see, we also know the language of the Masters, and how to decipher the many codes they use.

"The message said, 'We have confirmed the failure of our first attempt at colonization on the planet. Expect to encounter an advanced, competitive, probably hostile alien civilization when you get here. The ecosystem of this planet is toxic to us right now, and will no doubt be far worse after generations of further alien intervention and contamination. Annihilation of the entire planet is therefore recommended, if you have the technology.'

"The message also included the exploration vessel's scouting trip logs, and a full genome description of your species. That description confirms you are not like us. Your genetic material is very different from ours. We will not elaborate.

"Now, for our next question. What do you know of the Masters?"

Francis paused only briefly before saying, "Our only direct knowledge comes from a very brief encounter with a single living Master scout, presumably from the exploration spaceship you just mentioned. We exchanged samples of hair with that scout, peacefully. Subsequent analysis confirmed that the Masters are quite different from us, certainly in the genetic sense. The scout said it was sick, and it also said it was in a hurry to get to another location on our planet to recover an ancient Master exploration, data-log cache. It was using a sophisticated, tilt-wing aircraft to travel around.

"We have subsequently determined that this scout must have been heading to another southern continent on our planet. Furthermore, we believe it destroyed itself, and its aircraft, with a small thermonuclear device, very near a far more ancient and mysterious pyramid that we suspect you may know something about.

"Our indirect knowledge of the Masters is sketchy. We believe they tried to colonize our planet about six thousands of our years ago, but they did not survive the attempt for some reason. They left scattered ruins in a few places, of buildings, airstrips and plantations. And they left optical digital records in some places, on plastic strips. We were able to learn their written language by analysing those strips, and we were actually able to have a conversation with their scout using hand-written symbols. We seemed to have greatly surprised their scout at our ability to learn their language without direct contact.

"The Masters seemed to have been gene-splicers. It appears they deliberately modified plants and animals on the neighbouring planet to improve their usefulness. We are benefitting from some of their genetically-modified domesticated plants.

"But on the negative side, they also seem to have genetically modified an intelligent, quadruped, native, hominid species, to manufacture what they considered to be more useful slaves. We find the resulting hominid hybrid to be a kindly, peace-loving, family-oriented creature. We live in harmony with this intelligent species. But the species told us they felt threatened by our different ways, and by our advanced technology. So, we helped them all to resettle on the vast, arctic and sub-arctic, northern continent on our adopted planet.

"So, we believe the Masters were also slave masters, a practice we find abhorrent. Using slaves simply does not to fit into our notion of acceptable behaviour for an advanced, intelligent species.

"Our species is by no means perfect. In our distant past, we too engaged in slavery, and other abhorrent practices. Historically, we have had many horrible battles amongst ourselves, and harmed and killed many people and many animals, and damaged our fragile environment. Ultimately, a long sordid history of bad behaviour led us to want to leave our home planet.

"We arrived on the neighbouring planet about four hundred of our years ago. Our overarching mission continues to centre around the goal of getting things right this time, with respect to living in harmony with ourselves, other species, and with our new world. We view this fresh opportunity as a very fortunate 'second chance', and we doubt that we will get a 'third chance'.

"But we believe that our success as a species largely stems from a strong, innate desire to survive, and to form stable, family and community-oriented, nurturing relationships. Our culture is ultimately what distinguishes us from other animals. Our culture is the means by which we get progressively smarter.

"We learn from each other within our societies, and we build upon the learnings of our ancestors. When we get it right, a nurturing, dynamic culture provides us with the time and security to think and to create, to critically ponder ourselves, and to try to rationalize our existence within the physical universe.

"In our present day culture, we actively use the scientific method, and we apply the scientific knowledge we accumulate to make our lives better. The method is basically to first theorize, then experiment, then observe, then analyse, and then either conclude that a theory is now a proven, scientific fact, or develop a new or revised theory.

"Now, to segue back to our prior discussion, the results of an intensive scientific or archaeological study of a mysterious ancient pyramid induced us to send a probe to a distant moon around a gas-giant planet in this solar system. As we all know, you destroyed our probe, and then initiated verbal intercourse with us.

"We also know the impressive, ancient pyramid is emitting two strains of viruses. These are parasitic, very primitive lifeforms that may create diseases in other, multi-cellular species by forcing them to host their procreation. Fortunately, these viruses and their mutations have very little, if any, effect upon us or the other native and imported creatures on our adopted planet.

"We have also estimated this pyramid is about one hundred and twenty-nine thousands of our years old.

"Now, for my next question to you. Did you, or your ancestors, build this pyramid in the very distant past, and if so, what is its purpose?"

After a much longer pause, the tenor voice said, *"Yes, our ancestors built a pyramid on the planet you are now occupying. Your construction date estimate is approximately correct. That greatly impresses us.*

"We built the pyramid for a number of purposes.

"Our clan was fleeing the Masters. Other clans fled in different directions, and we have subsequently lost contact with them. It seems we do not make willing or useful slaves. And the Masters view us as competitors. So when they encounter us, they try to kill us.

"We suspect they now view your species in the same way.

"At the time of our arrival, the neighbouring planet was perfectly suited to us. But it was also perfectly suited to the Masters. So we decided to use it as part of an elaborate deception plan. We hoped the Masters would conclude we had been there, but then we had decided for some reason to move on to another solar system.

"We have always been pyramid builders. We will not elaborate. And we have always been hopeful that we can meet up again with other clans of our species, or with another peaceful, intelligent, alien species. We hope you

will fall into the latter category, but that has yet to be determined conclusively.

"We carefully placed a 'pointing device' in our pyramid, one that only an advanced, intelligent species could decipher. As you know, it pointed at a distant moon around a gas-giant planet in this solar system. We reasoned that if a species discovered the clue, and then was able to send an investigative probe to that distant moon, then that species would be ready to talk with us about a defensive alliance.

"We developed two virus strains to directly attack the Masters. Our intense fear and hatred of the Masters drove us to temporarily break our rigid rules against tampering with genetic material. The two viruses were specifically tailored to the Masters' far different genetic material. In fact, the viruses actually unwind their double-helix genetic molecule.

"The two virus strains mutate quickly as they evolve, and travel down different, unpredictable evolutionary paths. But most of the mutations are equally as deadly to the Masters. The induced diseases can therefore take many forms, which adds to the terror they induce in the Masters. We are carriers of the viruses, but like you, they do not appreciably affect us. We will not elaborate.

"The pyramid contains a virus-generating device. We are pleased to hear that it is still working. We do in

fact build things to last for eons, just like this facility we are both now using.

"We reasoned that if a scouting team of Masters managed to discover the secret of the 'pointing device', they would not be alive long enough to explore the distant moon, or this moon for that matter. And as you have probably guessed, the distant moon is itself a deception. We do not live there, but we closely monitor what is occurring there. And what is occurring there is wonderful, and must not be interfered with, by you or any other alien creatures.

"Now, we are finally moving closer to the heart of what we really want to discuss with you.

"You see, while we were living on the neighbouring planet, or your new planet, we were also establishing our standard defence system. We built this facility, and hid it very effectively. It is much more than you know right now. We may get to that in time.

"But then we had a very intense, protracted conflict within our clan. One faction suggested that doing the same things we always did while expecting a different result was either stupidity, or insanity. The rebel faction argued that we must stop our endless cycle of re-settling and re-building in a new place, only to flee again when the Masters re-discovered us.

"We are not gene-splicers. We believe you are not either, although we know you cross-breed domestic

species. We consider even that practice immoral. But we may be able to overlook that practice. We know we are not perfect either, and we at least strive not to be overly judgemental.

"Now, let us return to our clan's highly significant historical incident. Thankfully, the rebel faction won the argument. We knew our bodies could adapt to different environs to some degree, especially over a number of generations. So, we chose to complete our deception, and complete this defence facility, and then move elsewhere in this solar system, to seemingly inhabitable and hostile places.

"We will not elaborate, other than to say we find the gravity field on this moon completely comfortable, whereas you are obviously struggling to even stay seated, and you might even be feeling a bit ill.

"But the subsequent self-induced evolutionary changes have weakened us. We now would be unable to survive very long on the neighbouring planet. And space travel for us must be made without prolonged periods of elevated acceleration or deceleration. We will not elaborate."

There was a short pause, and then the soprano voice said, *"You apparently know the Masters are totally selfish and lack any form of empathy. And you have determined correctly that the Masters are 'gene-splicers'. But they are in fact much worse than you fear.*

"They genetically modify their own species!

"The Exploration or Worker variant of their species, the only type that you have encountered, is designed for optimal communal living in space, and for performing most of the societal tasks in their everyday lives. They are hermaphroditic clones.

"When they successfully establish a new planetary colony, they create two other variants of their species.

"One is a taller, debatably more handsome, Ruling caste, with two sexes and a slightly longer lifespan. This variant may have equal intelligence, but that is also debatable. But of greater interest, the Ruling variant probably approximates the Master's original form.

"The Warrior caste is the other variant they create when they have fully established a colony. They are brutish eunuchs, with much greater size and strength. They are also able to be placed into hibernation for eons. That is a very useful trait for a long space voyage, with some sort of physically demanding battle waiting for them at the end of that voyage.

"When they explore from their mother planet, or from a fully established colony, they select prescribed trajectories that target a series of prospective planets. They always send two generation spaceships along each trajectory, first a pioneer ship, and then a follow-up ship. They seemingly try to space the ships about six thousands of your years apart. But that depends upon

many factors, and the actual gap varies considerably. The ships travel at about one-twentieth of light speed.

"Their two-ship exploration strategy is designed to either support successful pioneering colonies, or to identify new threats to their species when one of their colonies is found to have failed.

"When they find us, or some other perceived serious threat to their galactic expansion effort, they alert the closest fully-established Master colony. They use electromagnetic radiation to communicate, at light speed of course, using digital codes.

"All three variants of their species are arrogant, and they all believe no other intelligent species in the galaxy can break their codes, or ultimately defeat them.

"The alerted colony is obligated by their culture and overarching expansion strategy to send out battlecruisers full of hibernating Warriors to destroy the perceived threat.

"They always send out seven Warrior ships in an attacking Armada. Seven is the most important number in their culture. The reason for that is debatable, and moot for the purpose of this conversation.

"The Warrior ships are powerful and massive, but only half as large as their exploration generation ships. They function as motherships for smaller attack vessels. They employ mostly beam energy weapons, but they

also have thermonuclear, high-energy kinetic and chemical, explosive weapons."

The three astronauts were really struggling to stay seated suddenly. They were looking at each other with horror, and they were all clearly very uncomfortable. Then they heard the baritone voice say, *"By your dramatic change in disposition, we suspect you are now reacting emotionally to the information we have just provided to you. You have reacted quite appropriately, and that pleases us.*

"That is because you should be very concerned, and actually very afraid. We believe it is almost certain that seven Warrior battlecruisers are now either enroute to destroy you, or will soon depart when their colonial mother planet becomes technically capable.

"The only unanswered question is when they will arrive.

"Now, we may be able to help allay your newfound fears. If we choose to help you, we may also help ourselves. If we choose, we can provide you with the means to fight the incoming Warrior ships. And we have a well-developed, highly-detailed follow-up plan we can share with you so you can also find and attack the Warrior's home planet. We have had many eons to develop this plan.

"We are no longer physically suited to such a struggle. We lost that ability many generations ago. But

we deduce that you are physically capable of withstanding the high physical and mental stresses that will almost certainly occur during the upcoming battle. And we suspect you have the intelligence and technical awareness to learn to fully utilize our more advanced technology, through the use of language interface devices that we will provide."

There was another prolonged pause, then the soprano voice said, *"In conclusion, we have determined that you may be able to make use of the sophisticated physical assets located on this moon, and some selected but restricted aspects of our technology. If you use these gifts to save yourselves, we also may be able to continue living in peace and solitude.*

"Bottom line, we want to coexist with you, but secretly, forever.

"And so, we have just decided to offer you some technically-advanced treasures, as gifts.

"But we have a few conditions that you must first agree to meet.

"Firstly, you must never talk about us on any electromagnetic frequency, or make any written or electronic records of us, or try to find us, ever.

"Secondly, you must openly claim within your society that the technologies we give you are your own, and that they were developed organically, with your own intelligence, and on your own initiative.

"And thirdly, you must never go back to the distant moon where you sent your probe.

"So, now for our final and most important question. Do you want our help, subject to our conditions?"

The three astronauts were now holding on to each other, and to the bench, which through their unintended motions was noticeably wobbling around in the low gravity field.

Maldonado looked carefully at Weismann and Knudsen. They both looked as worried as she felt. But after a few anxious moments, Knudsen forced himself to relax a bit. He attempted to smile back at Maldonado, and he flashed her a thumbs up sign. Then Weismann quickly and simply nodded in agreement.

So, Francis Maldonado answered for the team, and for New Earth. She said with a waver in her voice, "Yes, *of course* we would like your help! And thank you very much for asking us!

"But we three human beings are just emissaries. We will need the leaders on our adopted planet, that we call New Earth, to somehow confirm acceptance of your magnanimous offer, and its three conditions. And furthermore, we hope they will authorize us to start learning your technology, and begin working within your defence plan."

After a moment, the tenor voice said, *"Yes, we had greatly hoped that would be your answer. It pleases us immensely.*

"We observe that you have been digitally recording our conversation. That is very useful. Now, let us discuss how we can best inform and engage your leaders, subject to our constraints..."

12

Lieutenant Colonel Asher Weismann had been alone for three and a half days. To help keep himself mentally occupied, he had brought along his computer tablet from the *Osprey* lander. He could recharge its battery by clipping it to an alien device with a glassy surface. The induction coil beneath the glassy surface was able to sense and adjust the voltage required for optimum recharging.

Weismann's tablet was filled with interesting technical and pleasure reading material, and also with his favourite music. Still, the tablet had proven to be a very poor substitute for human company, and he had been bored most of the time. He had also slept more than was normal for him.

But he knew the long flight home was finally about to get *really* interesting.

He was the sole occupant of an alien, lifting-body spacecraft. Everything about the highly-advanced craft was alien, but obviously also fully functional and very efficient.

He had been warned by the aliens not to meddle with *anything*, and he could only guess at what the controls actually did. The symbols and labels on the instruments were incomprehensible. But thankfully, the systems were fully automated, and they had been carefully set by the aliens to deliver him safely on to the main runway of First Town airport.

The retro-rockets had just fired, and he could see by a graphical flight-path tracking instrument that he was now in a transverse, seemingly stable orbit around New Earth. The artificial intelligence built into the spacecraft was now firing attitude-adjusting, chemical-reaction thrusters to further refine the orbital path.

He knew there was a manual override that he could choose to activate for the final stages of touchdown. He had been told the need for such intervention was highly unlikely, but the aliens had also told him which button to push to engage the override system.

Since the craft was essentially a glider, there were no throttle controls, but there was a small fly-by-wire joystick that could be engaged to manipulate aerodynamic control surfaces. There had been no time, or the means of course, to practice real or simulated landings with this combination spacecraft – aircraft. So trying to fly the thing manually would be a final act of pure desperation, especially without the benefit of familiar instruments to guide him.

Weismann had left Knudsen and Maldonado in the alien subsurface facility on Addy. The aliens had offered the astronauts the use of the one-person spacecraft as a means to communicate directly with the human leaders on New Earth. In fact, it was the *only* means of communication that they had provided, or allowed.

Weismann had been ordered by Knudsen to make the solo trip back to New Earth. But the decision was a logical one, and Weismann had not objected in the slightest. He was the most technically-aware member of the crew, and he had worked very hard to absorb as much as he could during his brief, four day visit to Addy. And he had been the astronaut tasked with recording everything they managed to learn about the massive, very impressive and well equipped alien facility.

The three astronauts had been guided as a group on a series of tours by the aliens. Their mysterious but polite hosts had spoken to the astronauts over well-hidden and acoustically perfect loud speakers the whole time. They still had never revealed or even hinted at what they looked like.

During his solitary confinement in the alien craft, Weismann had lots of time to reflect on the whirlwind of weird things they had experienced on Addy.

He especially sympathized with Maldonado's situation. When he had left, she was clearly frustrated. She had learned very little about the true nature and culture of the aliens. They had rigidly controlled and restricted dialogue to matters that only fostered their agenda.

And their agenda was pretty simple really: 'Help us by destroying a relatively nearby Master colony. Do what we have told you to do, and helped you to do. And leave us alone ever after.'

Maldonado had once pressed the aliens harder to reveal more about themselves, 'in the interest of improved mutual understanding'. The response had been a blunt refusal, and a stern reminder that the *aliens* had the overwhelming superior power in the relationship. They had tempered their rebuke by assuring her that they were not bullies like the Masters. They said they were truly peaceful, and always chose to remain unseen and unheard until they were directly threatened.

The cockpit of the alien spacecraft also did not provide many clues about the physical form of the aliens. The single seat was just an amorphous blob when the machine was empty. But when Weismann had sat down on it, it had adjusted itself to become a form-fitting, highly-supportive contour seat.

He also found that during acceleration periods the chair had G-suit attributes. It would wrap around and squeeze his body's extremities to help keep blood within his brain and delay the onset of a 'blackout'.

There were three circular, flat, presumably thick-glass viewing ports that allowed Weismann to look straight ahead, and directly to either side. He reasoned the aliens must have hand-like and finger-like appendages, because there were many buttons and levers, and touch-control screens. Most of the controls were located where he could reach them without having to leave his seat. So, he also reasoned the aliens might be about the same size as human beings, but of course, he had no way to be verify that theory.

Weismann had brought food and water supplies along with him from the *Osprey*. He was wearing his light, non-EVA space suit, with hoses and cables attached to a small EVA support unit that he had placed behind his seat. The aliens had told him how and where he could vacate his bodily waste accumulations. The cockpit itself was pressurized, so he had decided to leave his helmet and his gloves off, but carefully placed beside him, close at hand.

He had brought a lightweight headset with him to connect to his tablet. The aliens had told him how to also connect it to the communication system built into the spacecraft. Knudsen had helped him do that with a set of hand tools from the *Osprey*.

But he had been told by the aliens that he would only be allowed to use the built-in radio to assist with landing safely. So, he had asked them to set the two-way radio to the emergency frequency of 121.5 'megahertz', or megacycles per New Earth second. That way, he thought he could alert a no doubt startled New Earth airport traffic controller about his location, and about his intentions, after first declaring a 'Mayday' alert.

Weismann knew he would be moving very fast in the streamlined lifting-body, even during the final flare manoeuver. The aliens told him there would be a series of relatively high G-force turns to help slow the aircraft down in the atmosphere, and to properly align with the active runway. An assumption had to be made about which runway would be the active runway. It was presumed that the active would be pointed into the prevailing wind direction. Furthermore, the aliens assured Weismann that the lifting-body could compensate for a moderate cross-wind.

Weismann and Knudsen had expressed a concern to the aliens about mid-air collisions, and they had mentioned the use of transponders on New Earth as aircraft safety devices. The aliens understood the concept, and remotely adjusted a device within the spacecraft to receive interrogations from ground-based surveillance radar on a frequency of 1030 megahertz, and to 'squawk back 7700' on a frequency of 1090 megahertz.

About an hour before Weismann had departed, he had joked quietly to Knudsen, "Well, sir, with me leaving and all that, you might as well consider this your first real date with Francis Maldonado."

Colonel Knudsen had initially frowned in anger at Weismann's wisecrack, but then he had calmed down, laughed and mumbled, "These alien guys, and or gals, or whatever they are, are watching *everything* we do, Weismann, you know that! Maybe we *will* have our first date on this moon, but it will definitely be after the aliens leave."

"Okay, Skipper, no offence intended," Weismann had replied sheepishly. Then he had added in a whisper, "Please believe me, sir, that I sincerely wish only the very best for both of you.

"We had no idea what we would encounter up here, including, ah, other *opportunities* that might arise. So, you'll find a wrapped-up present for you inside the back-up inertial guidance cabinet on the *Osprey*. When you open it up, you'll see that I smuggled a couple hundred condoms on board for you. The weight and balance technicians knew all about it, and accounted for the package in their calculations, don't worry. It was a well-intentioned conspiracy, Skipper, I swear. You have a lot of secret friends."

Knudsen had first looked shocked at the news. Then he had simply smiled, and patted Weismann on the back without further comment.

Maldonado had kissed Weismann on the cheek when he was about to enter the alien spacecraft, and she had wished him the very best of luck, too. Knudsen had shaken his hand vigorously and said with a waver in his voice, "Everything depends on you now, Asher. You must *convince* them that forming this strategic, secret alliance is absolutely essential for the survival of our species.

"You are a very brave man for confronting yet another highly significant and unknown risk. You are also a highly intelligent fellow, and absolutely the *right person* for this job. So, good luck to you, Lieutenant Colonel Weismann, and please enjoy the imminent reunion with your family! I am sure they will be surprised as *hell* to see you come home announced, and so soon!"

Weismann had barely managed to choke out the reply, "Thanks a lot, Skipper. And please don't worry about me too much. I *will* be coming back here, you know, come hell or high G-force!"

13

First Town airport was used by commercial and military aircraft of all types. Ordinarily, it was a quiet, rather boring place.

On most days, the airport traffic consisted mostly of electric-powered drones, and autonomous and human-piloted electric-powered helicopters. The airport also handled a few electric-powered airplanes on daily, local, scheduled flights. The airport only handled a couple of long-distance flights every week. Those large, LNG-powered turbo-prop and high-bypass turbo-fan aircraft travelled to and from other continents on New Earth.

The nature of airport traffic reflected the cultural norms that had evolved on New Earth. People mostly preferred getting around on the ground by efficient, electric-powered trams and buses, and a few autonomous electric cars. LNG-fuelled, motor-assisted sailing ships, electric-powered trains and electric-powered trucks handled most of the long-distance cargo transportation needs.

Even though it was not an especially busy place, there were always four controllers in the First Town airport control tower. They took turns managing landings and take-offs, the movement of aircraft on the ground, and the regulated movement of aircraft travelling on filed flight plans, and within control zones.

The controllers were sipping coffee, and discussing recent team-sport results, when they heard a distress call in their headsets. It was hard to make it out precisely, but through some rather loud static they thought they heard, "Mayday! Mayday! First Town Tower, unregistered glider, repeat glider, no power. About 100 kilometres east at about 50,000 metres, inbound for emergency landing, no flight plan. Flashing 7700."

"Holy shit!" yelled lead flight controller Philip McTavish, while spilling coffee all over himself. Then he barked, "Vic! Vic! Divert the inbound Second Continent flight to Holding Pattern 'B'!

"Marsha, notify the brass at Government House about what's happening! Tell them we have a UFO, and it's probably theirs!

"Wu, order the emergency crews down to the end of runway two-four! And get down there yourself, right now!"

Then McTavish turned on his headset microphone and said calmly, "UFO glider, active runway is two-four, winds light and westerly, altimeter one oh one point two five. You are cleared to land. What is the nature of your emergency?"

The reply came instantly and more clearly. "Inbound UFO has no power. Undergoing automatic hypersonic high-G turns." There was a long pause, then the controllers heard what sounded like a groan or a grunt, then, "UFO is a lifting-body, with brakes and a 'chute, I hope. Coming in really hot! Better clear everything out of the way!"

"Roger, UFO glider, we will be ready for you, good luck," said McTavish calmly.

After a few minutes, controller Vic Champlain said, "Phil, its transponder is flashing on radar now. It's moving really fast! Now about forty kilometres out. Glide path looks very steep, but acceptable. Making tight S-turns."

A few minutes later the controllers heard a sonic boom. Then they heard on the radio, "First Town, inbound UFO glider is on final approach. Now have visual on runway two-four. Glide path is steep but looks about right."

"Roger, UFO glider, we can see you now visually."

The controllers watched with fascination as the strange-looking, silvery craft completed its high-speed approach. The craft had only the slightest hint of wings. It was shaped a bit like a flattened arrowhead. The streamlined fuselage itself was providing the lift it needed. There were three fins at the back, and the one in the centre was pointing straight up. The other two tail fins angled to the sides.

They could see control surfaces on the fins working hard as the craft started to nose-up into a flare. A tricycle type of wheeled landing gear suddenly appeared on the bottom of the craft during the flare manoeuver. The flare extended a long way down the runway due to ground effect until the two rear wheels touched down with a quick puff of smoke. A tiny drogue chute, and then a large parachute, ballooned out behind the aircraft. When the nose wheel had gently touched down, smoke appeared around all three wheels due to obvious hard braking.

The controllers watched intently as the strange craft slowly turned right at the end of the long runway, before coming to a complete stop on a holding ramp.

Then McTavish said calmly, "Vic, the active is obviously clear again. So, bring down that waiting, incoming bird." Then he said on the radio, "Well done, UFO glider pilot. Are you all right?"

After a short pause, the controllers heard, "Roger, First Town Tower. What a ride! Now, please, send someone out to get me, and take me to your leader!"

14

General Jorge Kepler and Doctor Abdul O'Shea were immediately ushered into the prime minister's office when they arrived in the reception area. Prime Minister Wong hurried over from his cluttered desk to greet them just inside his office door. Then he led them over to the adjoining lounge area in the large suite.

Resource Minister Patricia Hernandez had arrived a bit earlier for the impromptu meeting. She had been scanning through a thick document, but she rose from a comfortable-looking leather chair to greet her two colleagues with firm hand shakes. Then she sat down again behind a large laptop computer that she had placed on a coffee table in front of her chair. The coffee table was overflowing with stacks of thick file folders.

When everyone was settled, Wong said, "Thanks for coming over on such short notice, fellows. Minister Hernandez and I have just been reviewing the composite recording, and the mission log transcript. All fascinating stuff!

"But obviously, also a matter that must be kept absolutely secret. That's my first and foremost concern.

So, have we managed to keep what happened secret, Jorge? And if so, can we keep all of this astounding *information* secret?"

General Kepler suddenly looked a bit uncomfortable, but he cleared his throat and said calmly. "Well, unfortunately, the cat may be *partially* out of the bag, so to speak, Prime Minister.

"You see, lots of people heard and saw the totally non-conventional and frankly weird-looking lifting-body make its successful landing at First Town airport. Sonic booms are a rare thing, as you know, and the ones that occurred helped bring a great deal of attention to the aircraft.

"We towed the alien lifting-body into a secure hangar right away, with Lieutenant Colonel Weismann still inside of it. Nobody saw him. We are sure of that.

"But the press managed to obtain some amateur digital still shots of the lifting-body, and a rather wobbly and fuzzy video recording of the aircraft that was taken by a civilian with a smart phone.

"We are sticking to our story that this is one of our secret, experimental, robot-controlled aircraft that got into a bit of difficulty. We keep telling them that we cannot tell them anything about it, because it is all part of a government project currently classified as 'Ultra Top Secret'. So far, they seem to be buying our cover story.

"So, bottom line, no one knows Weismann was in the strange aircraft. They think he is still up on Addy with Knudsen and Maldonado.

"But everyone knows we lost radio contact with the Addy astronauts right after their lander disappeared down a moon crater.

"Most people fear the three astronauts are dead, and that the mission was a complete failure. We have been feeding trivial story lines and sound bites to the media, and they are now running human interest bits about the lives of the three astronauts."

"As for Weismann, he is physically and mentally in remarkably good shape. Doctor O'Shea and I have just spent half a day debriefing him. But he is *really pissed* that we will not let him contact his wife and family.

"He understands we have genuine security issues, but he also thinks we should be able to work out *some* sort of arrangement whereby he and his family can, quote 'sort of have a life together again' unquote. I think he's right about that, but that's ultimately your call, Prime Minister, of course."

Prime Minister Wong shook his head and looked sad for a moment. Then he said, "Okay, let's park that rather awkward and sensitive matter for a moment. But I'm sure we *can* work something out to help the poor man.

"Now, what did you guys learn from talking to Lieutenant Colonel Weismann?"

Kepler flashed a quick glance at O'Shea to indicate he should field the question. The eminent Doctor of Science looked very tired suddenly, and was showing his advanced age. O'Shea carefully adjusted his thick glasses, and then he said in a hoarse voice, "First of all, Prime Minister, Weismann believes we may only have a day or two to either accept or reject their offer. We pressed him for supporting facts to back up his belief. He eventually admitted he had nothing definite to offer us, just a 'gut feeling'. He acknowledged that the aliens had never specified a hard, time deadline.

"Still, General Kepler and I believe that we cannot indefinitely delay our response to their offer. And, if we choose to accept what the aliens have offered us, Weismann believes we will also have to accept *all* of their conditions. He said they actually *insisted* upon that, multiple times. So, no 'gut feeling' on that issue.

"Weismann also believes the aliens are peaceful, intelligent creatures. But now Maldonado and Knudsen are essentially their hostages. They were still being treated well when Weismann left Addy. But who knows how the aliens will react if we delay our response, or worse yet, *reject* their offer, or some of their terms?

"If we say 'no', Weismann thinks they *may* let Knudsen and Maldonado live, but they will undoubtedly destroy the Addy subsurface base, completely, just to keep it out of reach of the Masters."

Prime Minister Wong suddenly looked very grave, and deep in thought. He closely studied the faces of his three visitors again. Then he nodded slowly, and asked, "So, how do we indicate our decision to them?"

O'Shea nodded at Kepler to answer this time, so Kepler said, "Prime Minister, Weismann and Knudsen suggested to the aliens that we could use a signal in visible light, say green for a complete 'yes' response, and red for a 'no' response to their proposal, or to some of their conditions.

"The astronauts know we have the *Sprite* missile in our stores. It's used for scientific research, and to launch small suborbital satellites. They suggested to the aliens that we could launch an explosive charge with a *Sprite* missile, and use an upper atmosphere 'fireworks' display, if you will, to convey our message with visible light.

"We would have to make sure the explosion happened in line- of-sight with Addy. That just requires timing the explosion properly. And we would have to tell the public and the press that it was yet another 'experiment' that went awry.

"But that's no big deal. Those things actually *do* happen, unfortunately.

"So, Prime Minister, in summary I think the Knudsen and Weismann idea has great merit."

"So how long would it take to send up such a missile?" asked Minister Hernandez. She also wanted to ask how such an obviously *ad hoc* launch would be funded, but she bit her lip instead.

"The missile could probably be ready to launch in say twelve hours or so, weather and other factors permitting, Minister," replied Kepler immediately. Then he added quietly, "Or maybe a bit longer. Unfortunately, it's kind of hard to say.

"But of course, we first need to know what *colour* we want our 'Roman candle' to be! In the lab, we have produced both a red and a green variant in suitable payload packages." Then he looked a bit embarrassed, and added, "We didn't want to be on the critical path, that's all. We were not trying to jump the gun or anything..." He trailed off and looked hard at Wong for a reaction.

Wong smiled back at Kepler, and asked quietly, "And what colour would *you* like our fireworks display to be, Jorge?"

"Why, *green* of course, Prime Minister!" Kepler growled immediately and loudly. Then he explained, "I believe the threat of a Master attack is very real, unfortunately. We will need all the help we can get to fend it off!

"And we could *really* make use of a moon base! We could make a giant leap forward in the breadth of our technology, in many fields, by accepting their many gifts. The possibilities are truly mind boggling! And I don't see *anything* to lose by saying 'yes', frankly."

"Yes, I thought that's what you would say, Jorge," replied Prime Minister Wong with a nod and a slight hint of a smile. "Thanks for providing your reasons, too. So, Abdul, what do you think?"

O'Shea took a deep, raspy breath, and said, "I totally agree with General Kepler, Prime Minister. We just *have* to send up a green signal! And right away, too."

"Right, thanks, Abdul," replied Wong with a broader smile. He wished his visitors would pick up on his less-than-subtle messaging to speak informally in these settings, but old habits die hard, he mused to himself.

Then Wong looked directly at Hernandez. She was methodically searching through the stack of file folders on the coffee table. When she apparently found the one she wanted, she started to open it up, but then stopped herself. She looked around at the others, and then she looked slightly embarrassed. Wong then asked quietly, "Patricia, what are you concerned about?"

Hernandez shook her head, and then she said angrily, "I'm thinking about the deep *political hole* we are digging for ourselves, Prime Minister, of course! So, say we *do* send up a green flare. Then what? Where is this headed, and how do we pay for it, and how can we *possibly* keep it all secret?"

Wong winced at her angry tone, and then looked hard at Kepler. Kepler was looking a bit 'steamed' suddenly. In contrast, O'Shea still looked calm and composed, so Wong decided to ask him, "Abdul, do you offer any suggestions about our best way forward beyond the, ah, green flare signal?"

O'Shea slowly took off his glasses, and removed a soft cloth from the inside pocket of his old, frayed, tweed sports jacket. He methodically used the cloth to clean the thick lenses, and then he put his glasses back on. As he was carefully putting the little cloth back in its assigned inner pocket, he said calmly, "Yes, Prime Minister. General Kepler and I have just talked at length about this very matter with Lieutenant Colonel Weismann.

"We were very pleased to find that Weismann had thought this through at great length, ahead of our interview. Actually, he had tested his ideas with Maldonado and Knudsen before his departure from Addy, and they had both agreed that it all sounded pretty good.

"Weismann is a very bright, highly capable guy. We're fortunate to have him on our team." Kepler grunted and nodded in support, so O'Shea continued, "As soon as we send up our green flare, Weismann believes the aliens will leave Addy immediately. But they will hopefully leave Knudsen and Maldonado behind on the moon with clear and elaborate instructions on how to make full use of their incredible base, and all of the *space vehicles* that have been carefully stored away inside of it.

"I'll come back to that new, no doubt startling revelation in a minute.

"Weismann believes Maldonado and Knudsen can *easily* hold out for a year or so on their own. They can synthesize what appears to be nutritious food using machines the aliens modified for our use, and make use of the raw materials and fresh water the aliens have stored in their base.

"Now, I don't think we should ask our two stranded astronauts to stay on Addy much longer than that, however. Weismann says they are effectively shielded from radiation in a vast network of converted lava tubes. But the low gravity on Addy will negatively affect and degrade their bodies over time. We're not sure exactly how they will adapt to their new diet either, but they have a large supply of vitamins and supplements in the *Osprey*.

"General Kepler believes we can send another lander up to Addy within a year. We won't need an orbital component this time for communication and support, since we already have the *Nebula* command module in orbit around the moon. And the *Nebula* is not going anywhere, and can stay fully operational on its own in robot mode for a couple of years.

"And Weismann says there are *four more* lifting-body vehicles in the base that can be used for returning people to New Earth! Two are one-person designs, and two are bigger, possibly three-person designs. I think we will want to replace those rather handy little vehicles in time with our own copies.

"So, we can use a bigger, shuttle-type lander for the next mission. The manufacturing and logistical systems are in place now, so constructing another proven launch system will be relatively straightforward, although admittedly, we know it will be costly.

"I think we can tell the public that this will either be a rescue mission, or a mission of scientific investigation. You know, to find out what exactly went wrong up there, if the worst has in fact happened.

"We'll only need two additional astronauts for this next mission, because Weismann wants to go back, rather badly I might add. And General Kepler and I think he *should* be allowed to go back, but only secretly.

"We think we should make a big, public deal about only putting *two more* brave young astronauts at risk. In other words, very few people should know that Weismann is also going on the second mission. *We* will know, and so will the other two astronauts, of course, and only a few other essential support people who must be sworn to total secrecy.

"So, to carry on with this idea, when the second team of astronauts land on Addy, they will make an *amazing* discovery! They will find that Knudsen, *Weismann* and Maldonado have somehow managed to survive!

"We will be able to use our radios then, with discretion. The astronauts will claim they never met any aliens in person, but they discovered this fantastic and complete ancient base, and amazingly, it could be as old as the pyramid the aliens probably also built on New Earth!

"And we will then announce this base is *filled* with exciting advanced technology, with many potentially beneficial and commercial applications.

"We will then permanently inhabit the moon base, and justify the ongoing, high operating expense by demonstrated, publicized, indisputably beneficial contributions to our Resource Development Plan."

O'Shea stopped to catch his breath, and stared hard at Kepler. He then nodded to suggest that the general should continue with the joint proposal.

Kepler looked really excited now, rather than angry. But he managed to say calmly, "Meanwhile, Prime Minister, in parallel, we want your permission to start quietly and discretely assembling and deploying a fleet of alien-built spacecraft!

"Weismann says they are *incredible* machines! There are twenty-four of them altogether. They're stored in vertical tubes, in two sections per vehicle. The two sections are launched separately, using dry-chemical boosters, and they meet up in New Earth orbit, automatically. The launching operation is relatively straightforward, due to the low gravity, and the lack of an atmosphere around Addy.

"One launch payload is the cylindrical fuselage, with the engines, weapons and support systems. The other payload is a tubular section that becomes the part of the completed spaceship where the control systems and the crew resides. That section *bends itself* into a torus! It then mates with the cylindrical section to form an integral, complete spacecraft. Connecting tubes along the side of the cylindrical section are automatically deployed, and they work like the spokes of a giant bicycle wheel! The completed spacecraft spins around the long axis of the fuselage to provide some gravity for the crew that normally live and work in the toroidal section.

"Now, these *remarkable* alien spacecraft can also be operated remotely! The main thrust system they use is similar to the magnetoplasmadynamic system that was used on the *Second Chance* generation spaceship that brought our ancestors to New Earth.

"Only, there are a few significant and beneficial differences. Weismann says the main thrust system is *way* more powerful, and *way* more sophisticated! For instance, a number of different fuel options are available, in slurry form, to power the fusion reactors.

"Now, the aliens have suggested we first deploy *six* of these spacecraft to work as deep-space sentinels, and our first line of defence. Four would go out at right angles to each other in alignment with the Sol-system orbital plane. The other two would go out at right angles to the orbital plane, only in opposite directions…" He trailed off when he noted that both Wong and Hernandez were looking very confused and very anxious. Then he looked sheepishly at O'Shea for some help.

Doctor O'Shea smiled at everyone in turn. Then he said calmly, "We are truly sorry for this barrage of startling new information, Prime Minister Wong, and Minister Hernandez. There is still a *lot* to work out, of course. But I believe General Kepler has just provided us with a pretty fair, high-level overview, at least of the initial plan beyond sending up a green flare.

"Bottom line though, and *miraculously*, we suddenly have found, at our finger tips, a cornucopia of astounding and powerful, very advanced technology! We could soon have the means to defend ourselves against a far more advanced aggressor. And we could also use these amazing discoveries to make our everyday lives a whole lot better too, and there can be no doubt about that!

"All we have to do to start down this path towards accelerated enlightenment is to send up that green flare. And we will want to send up a very *bright* green flare, one that can be clearly seen by all of the creatures living on the near side of Addy, that is, the side that always faces New Earth."

Wong nodded emphatically, and then stared hard at Hernandez. She at first avoided his stare. But after a few moments, she reluctantly made eye contact with him. Then Wong said quietly, "I entirely agree with these rather fired-up two guys, Patricia. I *really* want to send up that green flare, and right away. But what do you say? Are you with us?"

Patricia Hernandez took a deep breath, sighed quite audibly, and said, "Yes, I'm with you guys. This is obviously going to be a risky, *expensive* investment. But okay, I hear you, it is one with tremendous potential upside. I get that! But even if all this ends up doing is to help us to *survive*, it's actually a no brainer, isn't it?"

Wong then looked hard at Kepler and O'Shea. They both looked visibly relieved, and they were smiling broadly back at him. So Wong slapped his thigh, laughed heartily, and said loudly, "Right then! We are *fully* agreed! It *is* a no brainer, damn it! And I haven't had one of those for a very long while!

"So, start the fireworks display for us, General! That's an order! Only, please make damn sure you send up the *green* payload, and not the *red* one! Okay?"

15

It was now almost six days since Lieutenant Colonel Asher Weismann had left the other two astronauts on Addy, and departed on his own for New Earth.

Major Francis Maldonado and Colonel Nils Knudsen had been living mostly outside of the *Osprey* lander, however their ability to move around the alien base was still very restricted. In fact, they had been confined to the *Osprey* hangar area, and a single room nearby.

They had not been offered any more remotely guided tours by their secretive alien hosts since Weismann had departed. But the aliens had provided them with two tablet-like devices that allowed them to interface with the massive main-frame computer system and database that were built into the facility. The hand-held devices came equipped with an easy-to-use English language portal. Maldonado and Knudsen were therefore allowed to keep exploring the base in a virtual, but still very limited, manner.

Otherwise, the aliens had left them completely on their own.

The additional, cube-like room that they were allowed to make use of was mostly open plan, and apartment-like. There was a small enclosed space in one corner of the room with a toilet of sorts, and a sink with running hot and cold water. They used their sampling kit from the *Osprey* to confirm that the tap water was almost pure, with a few dissolved ionic compounds. It looked safe enough to drink, so the astronauts were drinking it.

The toilet outwardly resembled what one might find in a well-built outhouse back on New Earth. It was an enclosed bench with a hinged cover over a circular hole. Waste disappeared down a chute, and the flushing process was automatic. All of their waste went down that chute. There was no paper for cleaning up afterwards, but there was a rubber-like hose nearby with an adjustable water jet.

Their 'apartment' had a well-concealed door that led back to the hangar where their *Osprey* lander was hibernating. They simply had to place the palm of a hand on an adjacent glossy-black panel to open or close the door.

A square metal table was positioned in the centre of the apartment. Two cushioned metal benches allowed the astronauts to comfortably make use of the table while sitting down.

There were also six, rather amorphous-looking 'blobs' arranged around the room in pairs. They were covered with a soft, synthetic fabric. The astronauts discovered that the blobs became very comfortable form-fitting lounge chairs when one sat down on them. There were also two flattish blobs that became comfortable beds when one laid down upon them.

The two astronauts also discovered food preparation machines, cleaning appliances and cleaning supplies located in cupboards and on shelves around the apartment. The furniture and appliances in the room were coloured in various soft hues of green and blue. The pleasant, complementary colour scheme extended to glass and ceramic bowls, and metal utensils, which were also provided for them. The utensils were odd-shaped things, but a few of them were useful. The astronauts supplemented the alien houseware with selected items from the *Osprey*. But the *Osprey* stuff was all designed for use in a zero-G spacecraft, and therefore not ideally suited for their new environ.

The walls, ceiling and floor were all a uniform, warm, comforting, linen colour.

It all made for a surprisingly pleasing interior space.

The two astronauts were about to sample what they hoped would be a reasonably tasty, hot dinner. The aliens had concocted a number of 'safe' recipes for them to try using a human genome map, and descriptions of what types of foods the astronauts said they liked to eat. They had also provided instructions about how to adjust the settings on the food producing devices to vary colour, texture and flavour without creating poisons. So far, the results had been less than exciting, but there had been some gradual improvement. The food they were making was about on par now with the various packaged pastes, crumbles and slurries they had brought with them from New Earth.

"Not bad at all this time, Francis," Knudsen mumbled appreciatively between mouthfuls. "Maybe it's a *bit* too salty and spicy. No, I take that back. It's just about right! Say, you're not a bad cook, or kitchen chemist I guess, for an anthropologist!"

"And you're a much better *pilot* than a food critic!" laughed Maldonado. But she really liked receiving the compliment.

She smiled at Knudsen as she watched him eat. After he had washed down a last mouthful of food with some water from a plastic bottle, he smiled back at her.

They were very much in love. But they had somehow managed not to show it. At least, they *thought* they had hidden it well.

Their passionate emotions were tightly coiled, however, and straining to explode. They *hoped* New Earth politicians would sensibly agree to the alien proposal, and that the aliens would soon depart.

But sometimes, there was just no accounting for the whims or schemes of politicians. Or for the secret schemes of aliens, for that matter.

They were in an information vacuum, and they were finding the wait and uncertainty very frustrating, and a bit stressful.

There was a large, flush-mounted, dull-black rectangular panel on a wall in their apartment. Maldonado and Knudsen had assumed it was a one-way window of sorts, which they imagined was used by their hosts to closely observe what they were doing.

Suddenly, for the first time, the panel turned a dull blue colour. Then a very high-resolution image of New Earth appeared. They could see about one-eighth of the New Earth orb. The image filled the bottom centre of the panel. It was then obvious to the two astronauts that the panel was actually a sophisticated projection screen, or a high-definition television-like device.

Then they heard a tenor monotone voice say, "*Sorry to interrupt your dinner, Maldonado and Knudsen, but we thought you would like to see what just happened. Please observe the viewing screen carefully.*"

After a few moments, an intense green flash in the form of a starburst appeared in a localized spot over a brown-coloured land region on New Earth. The green starburst then slowly dissipated over the course of a minute or so.

The fact that the starburst was very distinctly green, and not red, did not go unnoticed by the two astronauts.

Then a soprano monotone voice said, *"We believe that green-coloured explosion is a clear signal to us from your leaders on New Earth. We conclude that they have just fully accepted our contractual proposal. Do you agree with our assessment?"*

Knudsen smiled broadly at Maldonado, and then he nodded quite emphatically at her. She looked back at him first with an expression of disbelief, but as acceptance grew, she visibly relaxed, and smiled back at him. Then she said calmly, "Yes, we *totally* agree. It looks like our New Earth leaders have just fully accepted your offer, and all of your conditions."

Then they heard a baritone monotone voice say, *"That is very good. So, as a result, we will be leaving you soon.*

"We have found the only comfort we can find in this immense and dangerous galaxy is the support we derive from each other. That may sound overly cynical to you. But we have noted that similar sentiments have been expressed in your historical literature. And meeting with you has not been as difficult to bear as we had feared. All of this gives us hope, for you and for us.

"You will not know when we leave, and you will not be able to observe our departure. We will not elaborate.

"But exactly one of your New Earth days after our departure, your computer interface devices will become fully functional. You will hear a high-pitched tone in this room, and a passcode will appear on this viewing screen. The passcode will remain on this screen until you determine how to change it. To begin accessing the full computer database, copy the passcode, exactly, into the access port on one of your interface devices, and then change the passcode to one of your own. Then this entire facility will become yours in every respect.

"We urge you not to use electromagnetic communication devices for intercourse with your friends and leaders on New Earth until we are, say, a month away on our long journey home. We realize that will be hard for you. But we ask you to respect this last request."

Knudsen nodded to Maldonado, and whispered, "Go ahead, Francis. Tell them about our security plan."

Francis nodded in response, and said calmly, "We promise to maintain complete communication silence until an expected 'rescue' team arrives. Hopefully Lieutenant Colonel Weismann will be part of that rescue team. We do not yet have a reserve of suitable spacecraft to call upon to expedite such a mission. A suitable vehicle will have to be constructed using ancient Earth plans stored in a secure archive.

Therefore, the arrival of the rescue team might be a year away, or more.

"Our hope is that the people on New Earth will believe we are dead, until our rescuers 'discover' that we are still very much alive. Then we will claim we never met you, but we discovered this wonderful place. In addition, we will say our communication system failed for some reason, and we were unable to communicate with people on New Earth until our rescuers arrived.

"Our government will then control the messaging to the people of New Earth, so we can subsequently fully exploit this fantastic facility and everything in it. Eventually, we will no doubt turn it all into our own 'human-like' base.

"Now, before the arrival of the rescue team, Weismann suggested we could turn the infrared light on and off in the crater every ten days or so, in long and short pulses, to show the highest leaders on New Earth that we are actually still alive, and in control of this facility.

"We have been thinking that we might flash the letters 'M' and 'K' in an old, simple system known as 'Morse code'. Those are the first letters of our last names, of course.

"Will that be possible, and does all of that sound all right to you?"

There was a long pause, and then the soprano monotone voice said, "*Yes, you can do anything you want with this facility after we leave. And thank you, your infrared light flashing plan introduces very little additional threat to us.*"

There was another pause, and then the soprano voice added, "*We believe you would make a very compatible mated pair. You clearly like each other, a lot. We hope you truly enjoy your year or so alone together.*"

Knudsen reached for Maldonado's hand. She squeezed back hard, and looked him straight in the eyes. Her eyes were suddenly tearing-up, so Knudsen gulped, "Yes, we are quite sure we will enjoy being alone together. But it is with some regret that we must say good-bye to you now. We will never forget you. Thank you for everything!"

After another pause, the baritone voice said, "*Good-bye, and we wish you good fortune. All of our futures depend upon it.*"

16

Ibrahimović: Minus 15. 1/2 down. Picking up some dust. Right on the crosshairs.

Chamberlain: We still have a good com-link with First Town.

Weismann (interior sound only, no radio microphone): Visibility good.

Ibrahimović: Minus 40. I see our shadow. Lights still on in the crater.

Weismann (sound only): Drifting aft a bit, that's good.

Chamberlain: Contact light.

Weismann (sound only): Shutdown.

Ibrahimović: Okay. Engine stop.

Weismann (sound only): Mode Control, auto. Descent Engine Command Override, off. Engine arm, off.

First Town Mission Control: We copy you down, *Stork*.

Ibrahimović: First Town, Addy Base here. The *Stork* has landed.

First Town Mission Control: Roger, Addy Base. We copy you down on the ground inside the crater. That was a really nice bit of flying.

Ibrahimović: No sweat, First Town, thanks. No sign of the *Osprey*. No extra room in this crater anyway.

Weismann (sound only): Okay. Let's get on with it. Weird. Place looks exactly the same. Still clean too.

Ibrahimović: First Town, we're going to be busy for a few minutes. No reception committee. Not unexpected I guess. Sad though. We will holler at you again when we can. Out for now.

The three astronauts then went about methodically completing their elaborate post-landing checklist.

The *Stork* was about the same diameter as the *Osprey* lander. It was egg-shaped however, and about seventy percent taller than the spherical *Osprey*. It was an old Earth space-station to Moon shuttle design, originally intended for six occupants. Since it had only arrived with three astronauts, it was carrying a lot of additional supplies.

The *Stork* had been assembled from three modules that had been sent separately into New Earth orbit. The three astronauts had to travel in a separate, smaller spacecraft to reach the *Stork*'s primary module. They had put on their EVA suits and transferred to that module. Then they docked it with the secondary and tertiary modules to form the completed, fully operational *Stork* spacecraft.

They had left the smaller spacecraft in New Earth orbit in robot-mode. It could be used again to take returning astronauts back to the surface of New Earth. But by design the *Stork* could only function as a shuttle craft, working between New Earth orbit, and the surface of the moon, Addy.

Colonel Weismann was technically in command of the mission, but *officially* he was already on Addy, and presumed dead.

Lieutenant Colonel Eduardo 'Ted' Ibrahimović was officially in command of the rescue/investigation mission from an 'optical perspective'. He was the only astronaut on the team that had been allowed to communicate with New Earth. He was an accomplished

Air Force pilot, and very fit. He was short and stocky, with a fair complexion. When he was a kid he had been covered in freckles. He had always sported a military-style brush cut, and it looked good on him. He was thirty-five years of age, but he could have passed for twenty. He was single, and once divorced.

Major Mustafa 'Musty' Chamberlain was a forty-two year old Air Force reservist, and a computer hardware and software specialist. He also had a couple thousand hours of flying time. But like Colonel Asher Weismann, he also had a PhD, and was a full Professor of Applied Mathematics and Electrical Engineering at Abubakar University. He was about average in height, and lean, with dark skin and short, black, curly hair. He had recently become a widower. His sister and her husband were currently looking after his teenaged son.

About twenty minutes after they landed, Chamberlain glanced out of a small circular window in the *Stork*, and said, "Hey, guys, a big door has started opening up out there on this side."

Weismann moved over beside him to take a look himself, and said, "Yep, and it's not the same one the *Osprey* used. It's a bit taller, and on the other side of the crater. I bet there's a hangar in there that can be pressurized, and we're about to get moved into it on a sliding cart like last time. I'm sure glad we landed smack dab on the crosshairs. Just by eyeballing it, it looks like we're properly centred, and can get through that door okay.

"So, how are your checklists coming along?"

"I'm done with mine now, Skipper, and all is A-OK," replied Chamberlain with a big grin. "That's why I was looking out of the window."

"I am too," replied Ibrahimović, also with a grin. "Everything is also A-OK, Skipper. I just started double-checking things, actually, for no good reason."

Weismann then smiled back at both men, and said, "Guys, I think the timing of the door opening is highly significant. Let's take it as more confirmation that Colonel Knudsen at least is still alive and well in this subsurface complex. He was always a stickler in mission simulations for fully hibernating the *Osprey* lander in twenty minutes or less. And he gave us exactly twenty minutes! He *must* be the same guy that I knew so well, and that is truly a hopeful sign.

"And we did get another Morse code letter 'M' and letter 'K' flashed at us during our descent! So, hopefully that means we'll also be seeing Major Maldonado again shortly, too."

After a few minutes, the astronauts felt a slight vibration, and through the viewing ports they could see that their landing platform was indeed moving the *Stork* through the now fully open hangar door.

"Skipper, should I notify mission control what is happening?" asked Ibrahimović quietly.

Weismann paused for only a second, and then he said, emphatically, "*No*. Definitely not! We have to start working with our cover story now.

"Firstly, and hopefully, we will soon *discover* that both of our astronaut friends are still alive and healthy, and that I am in the same condition, and that I have been with them all along. And then we will 'spill the official beans', so to speak, with a prepared speech that I've brought along with us for this occasion. Actually, those are my direct orders, and those are now *your* orders, too."

Chamberlain and Ibrahimović quickly glanced at each other, and then they barked, "Yes, sir!" almost at the same time.

It took about ten minutes for the cart carrying the *Stork* to complete its transit from the base of the cylindrical crater to a parking position inside the hangar. Then the hangar door slowly closed.

Chamberlain watched a suite of instruments intently, and after another minute he declared, "We just lost our com-link with New Earth. I suspect the closing of the hangar door has severed the cable to our antenna that we shot out on to the surface of Addy on the way down."

"Right, but that's okay, I hope," replied Weismann calmly. "Knudsen and Maldonado may know how to use the alien's communication system by now.

"You know, that hangar door obviously has to be airtight when closed, so I guess the seal must be metal-to-metal, and easily able to cut a thin wire.

"We should start seeing some pressure build-up outside of the *Stork* shortly. Yes, you can hear a faint hissing sound now. Keep your eyes on those gauges for us, Chamberlain."

After about thirty minutes, Chamberlain declared, "Everything has been fairly stable out there for five minutes or so now, Skipper. Looks like it's a New Earth standard atmosphere, with a temperature of about twenty-one degrees Celsius."

"Thanks," replied Weismann. He went back to looking out of a viewing port. He noted again that the hangar was similar to the one that the *Osprey* had been moved into. It was a barrel vault, or a horizontal tube with a flat bottom. As they had found within the other hangar, there was a flat wall on the far side of the chamber, opposite the hangar door. This hangar was clearly longer than the other hangar however, and perhaps eighty metres in length.

Weismann could vaguely make out the outline of a human-sized door in the flat wall, beside a dark, flat-black, flush-mounted rectangular wall panel. He figured the panel was a combination one-way window and television-like viewing screen. He had observed many similar panels on his 'guided tours' of this elaborate, fascinating subsurface facility.

"Okay, guys, a door in the flat wall is opening now!" Weismann announced loudly. Then a moment later, he somehow said more calmly, "And there is Colonel Knudsen entering the hangar area, wearing just his astronaut coveralls. God, it's really great to see him again! And there is Major Maldonado now, right behind him. And now they're both waving at us!

"Okay, guys, it is high-time time you met a couple of *really* great people! Open up the hatch for us, Chamberlain."

17

"First Town Mission Control, this is Air Force Lieutenant Colonel Ibrahimović calling from Addy Moon Base, do you copy? Over."

There was no reply to the verbal, analogue, standard-frequency radio query. After exactly one minute, Ibrahimović followed up more loudly with, "Mission Control from Addy Moon Base, do you *copy*? Over."

"Roger, Addy Base, First Town reads you five by five!" came the immediate and excited reply. "Boy, we're sure glad to hear from you guys again! Your signal is actually incredibly strong! Ah, can you start by relaying your current status? Over."

"Conditions at Addy Base are nominal, First Town," Ibrahimović replied with restrained excitement. "*Much* better than that, actually. You see, we have found that our three predecessor explorers are all *alive and well* up here!

"So, with that bit of astounding news out of the way, I will now turn our end of this radio exchange over to our ranking Base Commander, *Colonel Nils Knudsen*, who will provide a brief report for you."

There was a short pause, and then Knudsen said calmly, "This is Knudsen. Chamberlain, Weismann and Maldonado are listening in, as is Ibrahimović, obviously.

"Everyone is in excellent shape. Our two lander radio systems are inoperative for different reasons, but otherwise both landers are in nominal shape. They are safely tucked away in separate pressurized hangars within the alien facility that we discovered up here.

"The subsurface facility we are in is completely abandoned. It must have been this way for a very long time. But most of the stuff inside of it seems to be working okay, amazingly! In fact, we are using the alien communication system to talk with you just now.

"This facility is truly incredible, and obviously life-sustaining. But we will not elaborate over this unsecure radio link. Instead, we will first upload a new code-deciphering algorithm for you to use, that links to our own Air Force top-secret code number twenty-four. Then we will upload in code our full report to you. Will that be acceptable? Over."

There was a long pause, and then the five astronauts heard a different voice reply, "Roger, Addy Base. We are so glad to hear this truly *fabulous* news!

"We copy and approve your proposal to upload two files. Agreed you will start with the decipher algorithm, then your status and update report. Ah, please give us about twenty minutes or so to get ready for all of that. We will need to get some code people over here in a hurry. And it's not your fault, of course, but you caught us between shifts, as it *is* midnight around here. Over."

Knudsen replied, "Roger, First Town, we will start uploading file number one in exactly thirty minutes. Over."

Knudsen then took his headset off and set it aside. He looked carefully at all of the others in turn. They were all smiling back at him, so his stern expression quickly melted into his own broad smile. Then he started finding it really hard to stay composed.

But he cleared his throat, and managed to say, "Major Maldonado and I have been waiting a *very long* time for this day. We're just *so damn glad* you guys got here okay!"

Francis Maldonado wiped a tear from her eye, and laughed quietly while nodding in support. She looked radiant, and very healthy. Knudsen looked just a bit older, but equally as healthy.

Weismann then forced a cough and asked, "Ahem, so, can you give us an overview of what's in your report, Skipper?"

Knudsen paused for a long moment to subdue conflicting emotions, and to organize his thoughts. Then he said with some lingering excitement in his voice,

"It's the daily log of our entire stay here, guys. And it will *definitely* stir them up down there, believe me!

"This place really is incredible! *Everything* is governed by artificial intelligence. The alien machines can all think independently. But they also work in unison within an overarching, controlling architecture. It's a bit like our very best quantum, parallel computing technology, only on steroids. A *lot* of steroids!

"And the aliens have given it *all* to us! Chamberlain especially should find this place truly fascinating.

"As for our status, well, we've got things pretty well ready for the next operational phase. We just need the 'go' order from New Earth to launch the twelve modules that will self-assemble into our six 'sentinel' spacecraft. We held off on that deployment operation as part of the secrecy 'conspiracy', if that's the right word for it.

"And the modules for another *eighteen* alien spacecraft all check out okay! That in itself is astounding, considering how incredibly *old* everything is around here! Our alien allies really knew how to build things to last, and how to protect things from radiation, et cetera."

"I think we'll get the 'go' order to construct the six sentinels immediately, or at least after the government issues a few well-crafted press releases," offered Weismann. "And I know you both are about to be promoted again, Colonel Knudsen to Brigadier General and Major Maldonado to Lieutenant Colonel. Actually, I heard the promotions will be retro-active to the day I left you both here. So, you've earned a bigger wad of back-pay than you might have expected.

"I also think they will want you back on New Earth right away, for face-to-face debriefings. But, is that possible? I mean, the leaving *soon* part? And if it is, have you thought about a handover process? And how long that might take us to accomplish?"

Knudsen looked at Maldonado, and nodded for her to answer. So in a clear, strong voice she said, "Yes, we have given that a *lot* of thought.

"There are some domestic things we should run through with you all right away, like how to prepare food properly, so you won't poison yourselves. And how to manage waste disposal. Everything is automatically and safely recycled here, including human waste.

"We've made a lot of e-notes for you, but we probably should do some structured, hands-on mentoring to help you get properly familiar with the base, and the myriad of strange things inside of it. It took us a *year* to get where we are, and we know we have really only just scratched the surface!

"Ultimately, deciding when we should leave will probably be your call.

"As for promotions, Colonel Nils Knudsen is a career military man, but I'm a civilian at heart. I want to get back to my academic career, but maybe stay on as a reservist. We'll see, I guess.

"That's because we also have an, ah, an *announcement* to make. We want to get married, right away…" She trailed off as her eyes met Knudsen's. She looked embarrassed by the thought that she may have revealed far too much personal information in their military setting.

But Knudsen laughed with joy, and said, "Well, we had to tell them our news *some* time, Francis! We made no reference, of course, to our currently common law marriage in our report, but I'm sure there has been some speculation back on New Earth by the few people in the know?

"No matter though. It is strictly our business. And as the aliens liked to say to us, 'We will not elaborate'. Just know that there has *never* been any conflict of interest up here."

Weismann smiled and said, "Yes, it is *entirely* your own business, of course! But I know for a fact that the few people 'in the know' back on New Earth were hoping it would work out that way for you two! Your fan support includes General Kepler, remarkably.

"And strictly speaking, you have both officially been 'presumed lost' until just a few minutes ago, just like me, of course. I am really looking forward to having a conventional family relationship again!"

Knudsen nodded with sympathy and understanding at Weismann, and said quietly, "Yes, we figured it has not been easy for you either, Asher. Thanks again, by the way, for doing what you did. Now, what can you tell us about it?"

Weismann looked sad for a moment, but he caught himself, and forced a smile. Then he said quietly, "I guess it was not that bad, really. They decided to risk bringing a supply sergeant on the base into the inner-circle security loop. His name is Staff Sergeant Jefferson, a really nice guy with lots of useful, discrete, logistical connections. He secretly went to work converting my secure holding area on the base into a two-bedroom apartment.

"Then the security people brought my wife and two kids over to live with me. The surprise reunion was pretty dramatic, as you can probably imagine, with lots of tears and laughter at the same time.

"Fortunately, Sergeant Jefferson's daughter, Jill, has always been out favourite babysitter, and she was brought into the top-security loop, too.

"Our kids, a boy and a girl, Sam and Trish, are ten and eight, respectively. My wife, Francine, had been working as a high school English teacher. But she adjusted easily to our new, rather surreal family situation, and multi-tasked as mom, personal teacher and tutor to our kids.

"The two Jefferson's, father and daughter, really helped us out, a lot, by fetching the stuff we needed, and helping to keep up our morale.

"I had the easy bit, of course, being able to leap right back on the career horse again, so to speak, and start secretly training for this 'rescue' mission with Ibrahimović and Chamberlain.

"I also was actively involved with the top-secret, reverse-engineering study of the lifting-body spacecraft that took me back to New Earth. We have been making good progress, but we are still a *long* way away from understanding how the artificial intelligence system in that weird, highly complex machine works.

"But we had a reasonably normal family life in the evenings. And now things can get back to normal again for my wife and kids. I'll be away again for a while, of course. But that's happened before. And whenever they have been asked about what I do exactly, they have always just replied that it was 'top-secret stuff' and explained they could not talk about any of it. If their friends won't accept that, well, they immediately become ex-friends. That's just the way it has to be in our line of service. And I know you guys know *all* about that harsh reality, too."

Maldonado was crying now. Weismann's mostly heart-warming story had brought back many repressed memories of her own family and friends back on New Earth. She remembered she had been terribly lonely at times, even while her romantic relationship with Knudsen had blossomed into the real deal. She abruptly leaned over to give Weismann a hug. Weismann was caught completely off guard by the spontaneous gesture, but after a moment, he heartily returned the hug. Knudsen just shook Weismann's hand again without trying to say anything.

Then a few long moments elapsed as the five astronauts struggled with their own thoughts about home, and friends and family.

Then Knudsen suddenly put his headset back on and growled, "Okay, I'm now the yet-to-be-confirmed Base Commander again everyone, until they make me a desk-jockey, a New Earth General, or whatever they're going to do with me. So, let's get ready to upload a couple of important files to our friends and colleagues down in First Town Mission Control!"

18

Patricia Hernandez was sitting behind her massive, ornate, antique desk, and uncharacteristically, she was daydreaming.

It had been another long, frustrating day. Unknowingly, she was an incurable perfectionist trying to lead a large, bureaucratic government in an imperfect world.

She was still undecided if she would call for an election, and run for her third term as Prime Minister. She was proud that the economy was growing at a record pace, mostly through the introduction of all the amazing, incredibly advanced technology that Addy Moon Base had provided and was still providing. And she was also proud that she had finally made a few inroads into curbing the illicit black market.

But she also knew that a huge chunk of the economy was still functioning outside of the centrally-controlled, highly complex and overarching Resource Development Plan. In her mind, fuelling the problem were some revolutionary, step-change initiatives championed by her predecessor, Phillip Wong, over his long tenure as Prime Minister.

Early in his first term, fulfilling a campaign promise, Wong had re-introduced electronic and paper currency for all transactions. And then, for the first time on New Earth, he started allowing wage differentials to widen between different jobs and professions, and even within those job families and professions, based upon merit and experience.

But Hernandez knew it would be political suicide if she tried to reverse those fundamental policy and macro-economic shifts.

They were proving to be just too damn popular.

On the flip-side of populism, Wong had also introduced a very unpopular five-tier income tax system, and a value-added tax on all sales and services. But the resulting hard currency revenue flow to government coffers made it all work, and that just *had* to continue.

Hernandez was thinking in a fuzzy way about a possible beach vacation when the telephone on her desk rang. She was tempted to ignore the incoming call, even though she could see by a glowing yellow button on the hard-wired, ultra-secure device that the call was coming from her office administration assistant. She let the phone ring three times, then she snatched up the handset, and snarled angrily, "Yes, what is it *this* time, Marge?"

There was a brief pause, then her receptionist replied meekly, "I am very sorry to disturb you, Prime Minister, and I know this is against your scheduled meeting protocol. But, General Knudsen has just arrived in reception! And he has two members of the Privy Council with him, ah, Francis Maldonado and Asher Weismann. They say they have an *urgent* matter to discuss with you. They will not tell me what they intend to discuss with you, or why it is all so urgent. Should I send them away?"

Prime Minister Hernandez considered blowing off the brash intrusion, but she realised with a bit of shame that she had been indulging in selfish, useless time wasting. So instead she answered, "No, as it so happens, I can spare a few minutes for them right now. Please show them in, Marge. Oh, and I'm sorry I barked at you just now."

"Oh, that's okay, Prime Minister," Marge replied brightly. "Okay, here they come now."

The prime minister rose from her desk and formally greeted General Knudsen just inside her office door. The general's handshake was as firm as ever, and Hernandez noted with lustful approval that he was still a handsome devil. She had a quickly fleeting thought that it was too bad he was married. She remembered that his wife certainly did not deserve a failed marriage because of an affair.

Knudsen's hair was still blond with no sign of grey. He had held the top post in the combined military and security force for two years now, since General Kepler had retired with full honours. Knudsen seemed to have adjusted well to the high work load and elevated stress level that went with the outrageously difficult Minister of Defence and Security role.

Knudsen's wife, Doctor Francis Maldonado, was following right behind the general. Hernandez took a moment to carefully study her face as they shook hands. Francis had a few more wrinkles around her eyes, but otherwise she was still very pretty. She was the mother of two healthy and bright kids, a boy and a girl, but her figure was still quite youthful. She was also the Chancellor of Abubakar University, and her supporters within that politically-powerful and highly-innovative academic institution were many.

Following right behind Maldonado was Doctor Asher Weismann. He was dressed in a smart-looking, dark grey suit. He was no longer in the professional military and security force. Actually, he was no longer even in the reserves. Hernandez noted that he was also ageing well. He was wearing expensive-looking, wire-rimmed glasses, which suited him far better than the black-rimmed, plastic, antique clunkers that he used to sport. He was now the Dean of Astrophysics and Space Engineering at Abubakar University.

The prime minister motioned for everyone to take a seat in the adjacent lounge area in her cavernous office. When everyone was settled, Hernandez barked, "Well, isn't this interesting? Judging by this *elite* cast of characters, and our shared, rather turbulent history, this must have something to do with *aliens*? Am I not mistaken?"

Knudsen cleared his throat, and said calmly, "Yes it does, Prime Minister. Unfortunately, our concern today is not with our secret friends, you know, the benevolent kind of aliens."

Knudsen leaned back for a moment, and had a quick glance at his wife, and his close friend, Weismann. They both looked grim, but they nodded back at him for support.

"If you recall, Prime Minister," Knudsen continued while leaning forward again, "We sent six alien robot sentinel spacecraft radially away from New Earth, or more precisely, radially away from our star, Sol. They are now all about half-a-light-year away from Sol. That puts them in the inner reaches of the Sol-system equivalent of Earth's Oort Cloud."

"I recall the staged deployment of the six alien-designed spacecraft, but I am at a complete loss to remember anything about an *Oort Cloud*," admitted the prime minister. "What is it, exactly?"

Knudsen nodded at Weismann to field the question, and Weismann answered in the manner of an experienced lecturer. He first covered his mouth with his right hand, and quietly coughed to clear his throat. Then he said, "The Oort Cloud, Prime Minister, is a region of relatively small, icy and primordial objects at the very edge of our solar system. It is the most likely source of the comets we occasionally observe from New Earth. Infrequent, close interaction between the ice balls can redirect them towards Sol, causing comets.

"Something like the Oort Cloud probably surrounds every solar system.

"So, our Oort Cloud surrounds Sol, all of the planets in the Sol-system, and the Sol-equivalent of Earth's intra-system asteroid belt. Our limited surveying from afar suggests it is indeed composed of mostly icy planetesimals, but we suspect there may be a few rocky bits within in it as well.

"Our Oort Cloud seems to be nothing like that which surrounds Earth's Sun, but it is still highly significant. Our Oort Cloud is a spherical shell, whereas the Sun's Oort Cloud has both a spherical shell, and a disc-shaped region in the orbital plane. Earth's Sun seems to have been a bit of a space-junk magnet in our peripheral region of the galaxy, and as a result, it has a much higher density of objects in its Oort Cloud.

"But for perspective, the *Second Chance* generation spaceship that brought us to New Earth did not slow down while traversing and departing through Earth's, or rather, the Sun's Oort Cloud. And its original, professional crew did not pay any attention to the many planetesimals they knew were within it.

"And many generations later, another *Second Chance* crew did not concern themselves with the Sol-system Oort Cloud. The risk of collision was deemed too small to worry about. And that crew had *lots* of other things to worry about. They were frankly amateurish, but still, they managed to complete the long journey, and get us successfully re-settled on New Earth.

"That being said, the *Second Chance* spaceship *did* hit something in interstellar space, well outside of Oort Clouds. Even so-called 'outer space' presents many risks to human beings, and many unknowns."

"Okay, but I still don't see why we would *want* to position our sentinels, or first line of defence spacecraft, inside such a seemingly hostile place as an Oort Cloud?" asked the prime minister rather aggressively. "Why are *we* so unconcerned about a collision with one of these, ah, 'planetesimals', icy or otherwise? They must still be big enough to cause catastrophic damage to a relatively small, fragile, quickly-moving object, like a robot spacecraft?"

"Yes, we are concerned about that remote possibility, Prime Minister," replied Knudsen respectfully. "But the Oort Cloud provides a number of natural defences for a scout ship, that is, if one does not want it to be detected.

"A spacecraft within the Oort Cloud could easily be confused with a natural object, such as a planetesimal, from far away.

"And a spacecraft guided by artificial intelligence can intentionally position itself behind an actual planetesimal, to hide itself from an object of interest that it is monitoring. That is an especially useful tactic to employ if the object of interest could be *hostile*.

"We believe the risks are well worth taking to gain a significant tactical advantage.

"But we are mostly here today, Prime Minister, to alert you to the recent discovery of what we believe is an *approaching force of hostile spacecraft*!

"We are fairly certain now that there are *seven* alien spacecraft travelling towards us in close proximity to one another."

The prime minister's facial expressions then went through a rapid series of fascinating and dramatic transformations. Her visitors watched with sympathy and understanding as she first recoiled with shock. Then she looked to be in total disbelief. When Hernandez noted that her three visitors were grim-faced and obviously very serious, she looked fearful, and perhaps even on the edge of panic.

Then after another long moment, Prime Minister Hernandez just looked angry, and mumbled sternly through gritted teeth, "Tell me *all* about it, General."

"The approaching Armada, Prime Minister, if that is what it is, was first detected by the scout ship that we positioned to align with the Sol-system's southern celestial pole," replied Knudsen calmly. "The Armada has now also been detected by four other scout ships, the closest ones to the southernmost scout ship.

"The approaching group appears to have been heading *directly* for Sol at great speed, perhaps at one-twentieth of light speed. Doppler imaging suggests the alien fleet is decelerating. That undoubtedly means that the occupants of the spacecraft intend to *visit* our planetary system, not just pass through it. It also means we probably have some time to complete our defence readiness, but not a lot of time."

"So, how do we *know* they're not friendly?" asked the prime minister abruptly. "And you used the word 'Armada' a couple of times. How certain are we that this is a *hostile* force?"

"As certain as we can be, Prime Minister," answered Maldonado quietly. Knudsen and Weismann both nodded at her for support, so she added more emphatically, "You see, Prime Minister, the hermit-like alien race that gave us the Addy Moon Base and our existing deep-space fleet, also told us exactly what to expect, based on their direct historical experiences.

"We know there are seven approaching spaceships. That is significant in itself. In addition, there is a central ship, which our friends told us will be the command or 'Flagship'. The other six ships appear to be precisely arranged around the Flagship in a hexagonal pattern. That also agrees with what we were told to expect.

"So, all of this means the approaching spacecraft are almost certainly piloted by Masters of the Warrior caste.

"Warriors are not explorers, or ambassadors. They are probably under orders to *totally annihilate* us as a species. Saving some physical assets in our Sol-system for future use by other Masters may be a secondary consideration to them. Then again, it may not."

"And what do we know about this, ah, 'Warrior caste' of Masters?" asked the prime minister with a waver in her voice. She was still reeling a bit from this startling development. But she was also a tough, pragmatic leader. And she actually had great respect for Knudsen, Weismann and Maldonado. Asking their advice was not in the least bit demeaning.

"We know nothing directly about them, Prime Minister," replied Maldonado immediately. "We have never encountered this variant of the Master species before. Our second-hand information suggests they are a bit like warrior ants, using an Earth insect analogy. They apparently always fight to the death. They never surrender. But they are also not suicidal. They fight for glory, and they want to experience the societal glorification that comes after victory in battle."

"That's not much to go on, now is it?" asked the prime minister with a touch of sarcasm.

"No, but it is probably enough, Prime Minister, to give us a strategic edge, and formulate effective tactical attack plans," replied Knudsen firmly. "The *friendly* alien race, or our hermit-like allies, also provided us with the nucleus of an overarching plan. And we want your permission now to flesh-out that plan, in appropriate detail, and then put it all *immediately* into effect. Please let me elaborate a bit for you.

"Firstly, we want to make our Addy Moon Base our command centre. General Ibrahimović will be the overall frontline commander, reporting directly to me.

"Secondly, we want to immediately manoeuvre the four robot scout spacecraft that I mentioned earlier into tactical holding positions near planetesimals much closer to the Sol-system celestial South Pole. They will form our spearhead attacking force, together with the robot scout spacecraft that made the initial discovery of the approaching Armada. And *that* spacecraft will become the control centre for our very remote, totally independent, artificial intelligence network.

"Are you okay with this so far, Prime Minister?"

"Yes, of course," replied the prime minister bluntly. "Consider those actions approved, and *right now*."

"Thank you very much, Prime Minister, we will immediately comply with your order, of course," replied Knudsen formally. Then he seemed to relax a bit. He took a deep breath, and said, "Thirdly, we will mobilize a naval battlecruiser and our first Space Ranger commando unit from Addy Moon Base. Now, here is our overall battle plan…"

19

The Warriors did not consider themselves a sub-Master, servile caste. Rather, they believed they embodied the *true* nature of their successful, galactic, domineering, highly-intelligent and tri-variant species.

Outwardly, the Warriors resembled large, male, beardless, human beings. Anatomically and behaviourally, however, they were considerably different.

The Warriors possessed vastly different internal organs and genetic material than human beings. They were aggressive, fanatically brave, athletic, muscular and physically attractive to each other and the other two variants of their species. They were also cloned eunuchs, but they perceived that reality as a simplifying and empowering *advantage*.

And the Warriors were always tasked with the really difficult, physically demanding jobs that the hermaphroditic Worker and Explorer caste, and the heterosexual Royal caste, could not handle, or were afraid to handle. They were simply infantry 'grunts', and they were *damned* proud of that fact.

But the Warriors were in fact sincerely revered by the other two castes. Their rewards for victory in martial or species-elimination operations were *glory*, and the opportunity to fight again.

The Warriors also believed that doing one's very best in the line of duty would bring immortality in the afterlife. Like the pagan Viking raiders in Earth's history, they believed that dying in battle was a noble act. But they also believed it was always better to survive, to enjoy the fruits of plunder with your mates, and celebrate a victory well-won.

In other words, to a Warrior, it was better to let some other poor bastard die for its race than to die yourself.

The language that the Warriors used was the same as that employed by the other two Master castes. But their voices were pitched much lower, and their words would seem harsher sounding to a human ear, rather like choppy, guttural grunts.

Warriors had to earn promotions in rank through proven success in operations, especially combat operations. Officers were therefore especially well-seasoned blokes. And a Commander, well, a Commander was a truly *formidable* fellow.

In practice, however, they found that most of their battles were against unintelligent but often fierce lifeforms that the Master Ruling caste had officially deemed to be a threat, or unsuitable for genetic modification. But occasionally, they encountered truly worthy, semi-intelligent and cunning opponents, which always made for excellent sport, and possibly a feature role in a new legend.

There were seven ships in the Warrior Armada, arranged in a precise hexagonal pattern around the central Flagship. The ships were separated by the Masters' displacement unit equivalent of about ninety-one kilometres.

The seven vessels were identical in every way. The fuselage was a long, slender cylinder, and it contained the plasma ion-drive engines, fuel tanks, storage bins and most of the vessel's life support and weaponry systems. The Warriors lived and worked in a separate toroidal section that was connected to the bow of the fuselage by cylindrical spokes. These spokes contained service conduits, service elevators and ladders for emergency or back-up access.

The original total crew compliment on each vessel was one hundred and one Masters, all of the Warrior caste. Each spaceship rotated around the long-axis of the fuselage section to provide the Warriors in the toroidal section with a comfortable artificial gravity generated by centripetal acceleration.

Each vessel also was equipped with seven, highly-sophisticated, heavily-armoured, single-Warrior, combination attack and scouting vessels. These vessels were parked on the outside of the central section of the fuselage, and they were only accessible by airlocks.

The Armada Commander on the Flagship was standing alone in the middle of a small, hexagonal, darkened chamber. A single, low-intensity light was positioned directly above its head. Suddenly, at exactly the set time, holographic images of the six Ship Captains sprang up around the circumference of the chamber.

"Greetings, Ship Captains," growled the Armada Commander. "As always, I will report first. Conditions aboard the Flagship are nominal. One half of the Warriors on this vessel are still in hibernation, and I have decided those Warriors will remain that way to provide the Armada with a reserve of replacements, if that should prove necessary.

"Point forward, for you to declare a nominal readiness status, *all* of your Warriors must be awake, fully alert and completely fit for duty! Your vessel must also be *fully functional*, in every way!

"Now, does anyone need to confess to a *sub-optimal* condition?"

There was a long moment of silence, then the commander said, "Right, Ship Captains, so I will now conclude that we are at one hundred percent battle readiness, and I will officially log our combined status as such.

"Standard deceleration will continue for another, ah, zero point three five home planet years. You will now begin drilling everyone according to the training and re-training manuals.

"Furthermore, we will continue to manoeuvre in a coordinated, disciplined fashion at battle-readiness speed when we have penetrated the expected outer solar system region of icy planetesimals. Our long-rang scanning indicates the density of outer planetesimals appears about average for a yellow dwarf star system.

"Our primary target has become quite clear to the command staff. It is a rocky and watery planet, and the third planet orbiting the target star. The planet has a moon. Both the planet and its moon are practically *glowing* with unnatural, organized electromagnetic emanations! A lifeform on the planet and its moon may prove to be relatively intelligent, but this lifeform is also incredibly *foolish and arrogant* to reveal itself so blatantly! Still, we will assume it is a worthy opponent, and we will proceed on that basis.

"Our battle plan will be refined as we gather more information. You will all be asked to contribute and comment on each new draft of the battle plan in an expeditious manner. Consider this task as equally important as commanding your vessel and crew! Give it your *full* attention!

"Are there any questions or comments at this time?"

As expected, there was another prolonged moment of silence, and then the Armada Commander said sternly, "Right then, Ship Captains, today's meeting is therefore *completed*. Resume your individual command duties!

"We will meet again at the same time tomorrow."

20

Including commissioned and non-commissioned officers, there were one hundred and twenty highly-trained, elite commandos in the First Space Ranger Company. The Company consisted of two Assault Platoons, and one smaller Special Weapons and Equipment Platoon. The Assault Platoons each had three squads, and each of those squads was led by a sergeant.

Each platoon was under the command of a lieutenant who reported to the company commander, Captain Fitzpatrick. Fitzpatrick was assisted by an executive officer, First Lieutenant Sweetwater, who was *de facto* second in command.

The senior and very experienced First Sergeant McIlroy also assisted and advised Captain Fitzpatrick. McIlroy was so respected by the Ranger Company that when he simply *suggested* someone should do something, all Rangers, including officers, would treat his proactive suggestion as a direct order from Captain Fitzpatrick.

The members of the entire Company were now standing at rigid attention in a long, single row inside of an airtight, structurally-reinforced and smoothly-panelled lava tube deep within Addy Moon Base.

Colonel Mustafa 'Musty' Chamberlain had just been transferred to the newly-commissioned Space Navy service. Chamberlain had been commissioned as Captain of the *Indefatigable*, the first combined troop carrier and space battlecruiser.

The name *Indefatigable* had been used before on Earth. The name was first assigned to a British Navy, 64 gun, ocean-going, sail-powered, ship-of-the-line. Later, the name was assigned to a British battlecruiser in the iron-ship dreadnought era. Then later still, the name was assigned to a British fleet aircraft carrier.

So, everyone knew the illustrious history of the ship's name, and they loved it dearly.

Captain Chamberlain stood at rigid attention directly facing Captain Fitzpatrick, who stood with equal rigidity at the extreme right-end of the long line of Rangers.

The Addy Moon Base Commander, General Ibrahimović, had decided to start his close inspection at the far away left-end of the assembled Company.

General Ibrahimović did not rush through his inspection routine. He considered this final inspection of the assembled Company very serious business. He stopped directly in front of each Ranger, and studied every facial feature, and every aspect of uniform and deportment.

He also thoroughly examined every weapon. He even looked at hair trim and fingernails because he perceived precise grooming as a key indicator of proper discipline and high morale. He finished each individual inspection by staring the targeted Ranger directly in the eyes for thirty seconds or so, with his face close enough to smell the breath of the now fully scrutinized Ranger. And bad breath was something else that he simply would not tolerate.

Captain Fitzpatrick was the last member of the Company to be inspected. He was put through exactly the same routine. After the final eye stare 'test of character', the general took two smartly-executed steps backwards. Then he slowly scanned backward and forward along the long line of Rangers, and declared loudly so everyone in the Company could clearly hear, "I can find absolutely *no fault* with you or the men and women in your Company, Captain Fitzpatrick! Well done!

"Proceed now with the boarding operation! You have *exactly* two hours to get totally sorted-out! Then I expect you to directly report to me that your Company is *fully ready* for immediate departure.

"Make your report to me in my office. Bring your executive officer, First Lieutenant Sweetwater, with you. We will also be conducting a final mission briefing, with Captain Chamberlain in attendance as well.

"Now, dismiss your Company, Captain Fitzpatrick, and get moving!"

Everyone in the Ranger Company then came to attention and saluted the general. General Ibrahimović and Captain Chamberlain smartly returned their salute.

Then Captain Fitzpatrick ordered First Sergeant McIlroy to quick-march the Company to the boarding ramp of the *Indefatigable*. When McIlroy barked out the order, everyone in the Company smartly pivoted and quick-marched away up the long lava tube tunnel. The high precision of their coordinated movement was especially impressive in the low gravity field.

Exactly two hours later, Captain Joachim 'Mad Beast' Fitzpatrick and his executive officer, First Lieutenant Heidi 'Akela' Sweetwater, arrived in the Addy Moon Base Commander's office reception area. They found that Captain Chamberlain was waiting for them there. They were all immediately ushered into the general's office by an attending staff sergeant.

Chamberlain, Fitzpatrick and Sweetwater came to rigid attention just inside the office door and saluted the general. General Ibrahimović rose from his immaculately well-ordered desk, strolled over to stand in front of the three officers, and casually returned their salute. Then he said pleasantly, "At ease, Captain, Captain and First Lieutenant."

General Ibrahimović was considerably shorter than the two Ranger officers, and just a bit shorter than the lean, black-haired and dark-skinned Chamberlain. Ibrahimović carefully studied them all again for a moment.

The two Ranger officers were both in their early thirties, and incredibly fit and muscular. They also both had brush cuts, and that seemed appropriate.

Fitzpatrick was hairy everywhere, and he had a blemish-free, olive-coloured complexion. His face had been closely shaved, but it still looked like he needed a shave. He was a tactical genius and a superb organizer. He had started his career at the top of his military college class.

In contrast, Sweetwater was fair-skinned, and even freckled a bit, like Ibrahimović. The general guessed she would either be a blonde or a redhead if she let her hair grow. Until a month or so ago, she had been a reservist. She was also a medical doctor and a psychiatrist. And of course, she was also a crack commando.

The forty-eight year old Captain Chamberlain was an all-around genius, especially in electrical and computer engineering. He knew everything about the alien spaceship he would be commanding. And he knew everything about the nine 'naval' crew members that he had personally trained to help him run it.

They were three very smart and determined-looking officers.

Brigadier General Eduardo 'Ted' Ibrahimović also proudly sported a brush cut. At sixty years of age, he had a lot of grey hair now. He had never left Addy Moon Base since he had arrived eleven years before, and he had been the only official Base Commander. He had been promoted *in situ* as the facility had grown in size, complexity and strategic importance.

"We all know we have to keep this short to stay on our demanding schedule," growled the general. "So, cutting right to the chase, we are completely ready to go, *right?*"

All three of the officers that were under 'final, final' inspection barked loudly in unison, "Yes, General!"

There was an awkward pause as the general continued to intently scan the faces of the three officers standing in front of him. Then he smiled, and said quietly, "I *knew* that would be the case. You are the best we have, and so are your people.

"This is really my last chance to wish you good fortune, and to formally empower you. You have a *huge* responsibility! The *survival of our species* probably depends upon the success of your mission! That is a *hell* of a lot to ask of one hundred and thirty people!

"Cutting to the chase again, we will no longer control anything you do from Addy Moon Base, and by extension, from top Defence and Security command back on New Earth.

"The five robot frigates are now in full 'AI Mode'. You will be directly able to monitor their activity of course, just like we can do from here. The robot ships know their mission, and they can adjust properly to an evolving situation, intelligently, referring at all times to our overarching strategy.

"But *you* will have full override capability, Commodore Chamberlain! Yes, you heard me right! You are now a *Commodore,* equivalent in rank to a Rear Admiral, or a Brigadier General, the same as me.

"Your command will include the First Space Ranger Company. I suppose we might have called them 'Marines' to make matters easier or clearer for everyone, from an historical perspective. But that was a decision made higher up the ladder. We all must take our orders, and we must not question them. However, good executive officers always suggest alternatives for consideration.

"But, I apologise, I digress.

"So, back on point again! We have to *fully empower* you, Commodore, because of the time lag associated with being about half-a-light-year way from us when you directly encounter the enemy. And we do not want to reveal *anything* to the enemy until we absolutely must! So, there will be no electromagnetic communication, with the five robot ships, or between us, until that is *absolutely necessary*! Is that quite clear, Commodore Chamberlain?"

"Yes, General Ibrahimović, that is fully understood, sir!" barked the newly promoted Commodore. His facial expression and overall demeanour remained stoic, and revealed nothing about the inner turmoil that was suddenly boiling up deep within his gut.

Chamberlain had suspected that the chain-of-command arrangement would be something like this, but the magnitude of his responsibility had finally been driven home. He was glad that the general had made the order so clear. And even better, the order had been made in front of the key, Ranger, now officially subservient officers.

"Good!" yelled General Ibrahimović immediately. Then he moved over to stare Captain Fitzpatrick once more in the face.

He paused a long moment, and then he barked, "Your commanding officer is Commodore Chamberlain, Ranger Captain Fitzpatrick! You heard that clearly! There already is a chain of command on *his* battlecruiser. If he should die in action, or otherwise, overall command will move to the next *naval* officer in the ship's crew. So, one of the commodore's primary duties will be to ensure that the people under him are ready at all times to move up the ladder of naval command, should that prove necessary.

"And the same applies to *you*, Captain! Make sure *all* of your people know *exactly* what the mission is, and what everyone else's role is! People *die* in combat. That has always been the case. But we really have no *freaking idea* what the *hell* we will be encountering out there!

"So, everyone in your Company *must* know what everyone else does, exactly, so they can take their place if necessary! That extends right from the most junior buck private in the Company up to its Commander.

"Now, thankfully, you will have about two-and-a-half years to get everyone up to speed. That is because the alien spacecraft, now your troop carrier and the commodore's *Indefatigable* battlecruiser, cruises at one-fifth light speed.

"So, now you know how you will keep *everyone* completely occupied, and *everyone* physically and mentally fit for action. Because we must *win* this battle, decisively, so we can proceed to the next attack objective!"

General Ibrahimović then slowly stepped sideways to stare First Lieutenant Sweetwater in the face. Again, he waited an awkward long moment, and then he barked, "And *you*, First Lieutenant Sweetwater, are going to help your Captain, and your Commodore, in *every way that you can*! You will be *fully ready* to take Captain Fitzpatrick's place at any time as commander of the Ranger Company. And you will monitor the mental and physical health of *everyone* on the vessel, treat the sick and injured people, and proactively suggest ways to keep everyone in *top mental and physical condition*."

Then General Ibrahimović took two steps backwards, saluted smartly, and barked, "That is all, Assault Force commanders. Now, do your duty and make us all proud!

"You are dismissed."

21

The five robot ships were finally all in attack position within the Sol-system Oort Cloud. They were identical in all aspects, and each of them possessed independent, super-human, artificial intelligence. They could indeed function independently, but their human masters had ordered them to obey the coordinating instructions from the designated 'Alpha' robot ship.

Spatially, the Alpha ship had remained radially-aligned with the celestial South Pole of the Sol-system. It had hidden itself behind a rather large planetesimal.

The 'Bravo', 'Charlie', 'Delta' and 'Echo' scout ships had also found suitable planetesimals to shield their whereabouts from the approaching Warrior Armada.

The human masters on Addy Moon Base had also fixed the hierarchy of command. The Beta ship would coordinate the attack in the event the Alpha ship was disabled or destroyed.

The Alpha ship decided it was time for the attack to begin. The seven Warrior battlecruisers were still cruising in a hexagonal formation, with the presumed command ship, or Flagship, in the centre of the hexagon.

The Warrior Armada had just completed an impressive, perfectly coordinated course adjustment as it picked its way carefully through a particularly dense section of the Oort Cloud. A small one-Warrior scout ship was about ninety-one kilometres out in front of the Armada. It was one of the seven scout ships that were directly and permanently assigned to the Flagship.

So, it would be a battle of five New Earth robot frigates up against seven Warrior battlecruisers. This meant that two Warrior battlecruisers, and the small, leading scout ship from the Flagship, would survive the initial barrage.

There was no way around that physical reality. Each robot ship could only direct a near light-speed, high-energy, particle beam and gamma ray burst at one target at a time. And it would take roughly three minutes to re-arm and re-aim the weaponry on each robot ship to launch another attack.

The Alpha ship selected a target, and then it assigned each of the other robot ships a separate target. It chose the Flagship as its target. It also pre-assigned the expected targets for the second barrage.

In the second barrage, Bravo and Delta robot frigates would both aim at one of the remaining Warrior battlecruisers. Charlie robot frigate would aim at the small, leading scout ship. And Echo robot frigate would aim at the remaining Warrior battlecruiser.

All the robot ships had been playing a sort of 'peek-a-boo' game of hide-and-seek to avoid detection. They now manoeuvred to expose themselves just long enough to fully bring their weapons to bear on their assigned targets.

At the instant when all was ready, the Alpha ship started a three second countdown.

All five robot ships fired simultaneously. Bravo, Charlie, Delta and Echo fired at maximum intensity. The focused blast was the equivalent of an interstellar gamma ray burst. The blast was designed to completely obliterate a target, and that was in fact the spectacular result.

The Alpha ship fired a far less intense burst at the Armada Flagship. The goal was to destroy the lifeforms within that ship, but not the ship itself.

It appeared to have worked. The Flagship outwardly appeared to have been undamaged by the attack, and it remained on the same course and at the same speed.

In contrast, the two remaining, undamaged Warrior battlecruisers, and the small advance scout ship, began a wild series of obviously uncoordinated and rather frantic evasive manoeuvres.

After half-an-hour or so, the captains of the two remaining Warrior battlecruisers decided their best course of action was to leave the site of the attack at maximum acceleration, even though they were still within the Oort Cloud. The two Warrior captains selected different trajectories for their high-speed retreat manoeuvre.

The Alpha ship then refined its sensing analyses, and performed a rapid series of iterative, four-dimensional, pseudo-spherical-triangulation calculations. When the fleeing Warrior ship trajectories were established with precision, and the weapon batteries on all of the robot ships were fully re-charged, the Alpha ship began another three second countdown.

The second barrage was completely successful. The two fleeing Warrior battlecruisers and the small scout ship were all blown into space dust.

But there was an unexpected twist. Just before the second barrage, two small scout ships had separated and moved away from one of the fleeing Warrior battlecruisers, and another small scout ship had undocked and escaped from the other Warrior battlecruiser. The three scout ships quickly accelerated away in a darting fashion, and soon became completely lost from view within the Oort Cloud.

The Alpha ship decided that the three escaping scout ships were probably piloted by living creatures. According to the covert intelligence provided by Addy Moon Base, the scout ships would have vastly superior manoeuvring capability compared with the battlecruiser motherships. But the intelligence also indicated that the scout ships would also have a significantly shorter range of operation, and a finite, albeit significant, life support capability.

The Alpha ship had been pre-ordered to stay in close proximity to the disabled Armada Flagship at all times. The Flagship was still moving through space, and it might be necessary for the Alpha ship to clear or deflect a planetesimal out of its way to prevent a catastrophic collision.

But the Alpha ship quickly devised a comprehensive plan to systematically seek out and destroy the three remaining scout ships. Then it assigned detailed orders to the other four robot ships, and a new battle mission began.

The Alpha ship also decided to risk sending a narrow, directed-beam message to the manned *Indefatigable* battlecruiser that it knew was approaching the battle site. The approaching battlecruiser was still over a year away. But the Alpha ship figured the commodore on the approaching battlecruiser would want to know *exactly* what the robot frigates were all doing.

22

Ranger Captain Fitzpatrick and his 'exec', First Lieutenant Sweetwater, were sitting together in an isolated corner of the mess hall of the *Indefatigable*. They were quietly sipping some tea after eating their noon meal.

They were also sitting in the 'highest' part of the hall. The bend in the floor was quite pronounced everywhere in the living area of the battlecruiser. Fitzpatrick and Sweetwater could only see people at the neighbouring tables in the hall for thirty metres or so before the ceiling blocked their view.

The mess hall was in the toroidal, full-gravity section of the *Indefatigable*. So, it was a bit like sitting on the inside wall of a very large donut that was spinning around its centroid to induce artificial gravity. No one could 'feel' the spinning motion, but they could certainly feel, and they greatly appreciated, the centripetal acceleration that forced them towards the floor.

By now, everyone was fully acclimatized to the artificial environ of the large spaceship, strange as it had originally seemed to them.

The space in the galley was limited, and meals had to be taken in shifts. The naval crew members and the non-commissioned Rangers always chose to sit apart from their officers. But Fitzpatrick and Sweetwater could not help overhearing their mostly cheerful banter in the relatively close confines of the mess hall.

The two officers were hearing the usual crude jokes, which they chose to ignore. But they were also hearing a few interesting, animated stories. These stories were mostly anecdotes about the wild antics of kids and teenagers, and some adult 'shore leave' adventures.

Fitzpatrick took a long moment to carefully study his exec. He had realized long ago that they were two vastly different people, and could never truly be friends. They certainly could never be romantically involved, even if military service allowed that, which it definitely did not. Any Ranger that wanted to pursue such a thing would have to quit the service. And Rangers that got caught in intra-service sexual relationships were immediately dishonourably discharged.

That fixed reality greatly simplified things. Still, Fitzpatrick had immense respect for Sweetwater's abilities as an officer, professional soldier, and medical doctor.

They were now past the midpoint of their journey to intercept the Warrior Flagship. The commodore had just briefed them on the distant battle in the Oort Cloud that had been won by their robot scout ships.

Fitzpatrick mostly believed his long list of tasks and responsibilities were well in hand, but he had some lingering doubts. He also knew that one of his character flaws was overly-harsh self-criticism.

Fitzpatrick just could never feel completely satisfied with any situation. His superior officers had always viewed that trait as a strength, not a weakness. But it sometimes ate him up emotionally.

He thought that what he really needed now was someone to share his inner feelings with outside of the command structure. But any kind of fraternization with subordinates while on this mission was not something he could engage in, no matter how tempting it sometimes felt. He could not risk degrading his hard-earned authority in any manner.

But he had observed that Sweetwater had the amazing ability to put aside her professional role for a few minutes to listen to *anyone*, objectively and sympathetically. Her advice was always sought out, even by the commodore. And he had heard it was always kept in the strictest confidence, and forgotten about as soon as normal duties resumed.

She was also a bit psychic, as well as empathic. While staring fixedly into her mug of tea, she said quietly but bluntly, "What's bugging you, Skipper? Is there anything I can help you with?"

Fitzpatrick reacted immediately with a disapproving grunt, and was about to blow her off. But then he thought for another long moment, and realized this was probably a really good time for the chat he been wanting to have with someone he could trust.

So he said quietly, "Okay, thanks for asking, First Lieutenant.

"Look, I think we're doing okay with our morale and our combat readiness. But I just can't shake this *feeling* that won't go away. I'm wondering all of time if I'm missing something really important.

"And I *hate* that feeling! So, I guess I would like to hear your thoughts now.

"Specifically, should we be doing more, or less, of some aspect of the training program? And are we too harsh with the Rangers, or not harsh enough?

"And, I hear the rumblings in the ranks. You can't miss them!

"Do the members of this company *really* hate me?"

Sweetwater looked up, and said bluntly, "Don't worry, they just hate your guts, sir."

When she saw Fitzpatrick recoil in shock and then look a bit hurt, she laughed and said, "Sorry, old joke, Skipper! But I just couldn't resist!

"Actually, if you truly want my assessment, for what it's worth, I believe these people are now ready for just about *anything* you can throw at them.

"You are definitely not loved, but nor should you be! They will do *anything* you ask of them, because they greatly respect you, and they feel great pride in being part of this elite company. They do not want to let you down, or to let their buddies down. That is their biggest motivator to be professional, and brave.

"You know, I think our biggest problem is maintaining our current state of high readiness.

"With over a year to go on our journey, boredom will now be harder to overcome. Most of the company are heavily into self-improvement courses. The medics are practically doctors now, for instance. They are certainly all very good nurses! And I'm sure we now have a few junior engineers in the Special Weapons and Equipment platoon, no doubt about that.

"But I think we need to keep encouraging people to stay intellectually sharp, and to get even sharper."

Fitzpatrick nodded, and sat quietly for another long moment. Then he looked around and said quietly, "Thanks, that's what I've been thinking, too.

"And I've been thinking pretty hard about what we might have to face in combat. We *think* the Warriors have all been killed with a radiation blast from the Alpha robot ship, but we don't know that for sure of course.

"We only have a few high-velocity kinetic energy weapons with us because we don't want to damage the captured Warrior battlecruiser, say by shooting holes in the exterior hull, or some other vital piece of equipment! Our 'special weapons' are mostly energy blasters, as you know. But they can do some *serious* damage as well, if they happen to miss a flesh-and-blood target, or ricochet off armour.

"The Rangers are all Jeet Kune Do martial arts experts. The fighting, if there is any, might be hand-to-hand, because our foes likely won't want to damage or destroy their battlecruiser either. And the conflict might occur in a weightless or nearly weightless environment.

"So, I think we need a tactical edge that we probably don't have right now."

"An 'edge', as in what exactly?" asked Sweetwater with growing interest. "Everyone has trained extensively with knives, and bayonets."

Fitzpatrick nodded, and after a moment he decided to elaborate. He said quietly, "Don't laugh, but I'm thinking about making and issuing weapons like axes and maces, stabbing swords and Taser-tipped spears, repeating crossbows and maybe even a few longbows," replied Fitzpatrick.

He was pleased that Sweetwater did not immediately laugh at his idea. Instead she looked even more interested.

So, Fitzpatrick added, "If we had some relatively lower-energy but nevertheless *lethal* weapons like swords, or bows and arrows, and we became experts with the use of such ancient weapons, we might just have our useful edge."

"I think you're on to something really good with that idea, Skipper," replied Sweetwater slowly. "It would also add another new and interesting aspect to our physical training. And every Ranger *loves* caring for their assigned weapons, and I don't think having a few more in our arsenal will upset anyone.

"And I think the Special Weapons platoon would really enjoy making these other weapons for us. I know we have the materials on hand, and well-equipped workshops. And we have a complete Earth and New Earth historical database with us. We can find out how to properly make the weapons, and how best to use them.

"So, to summarize, I think this is a *very exciting* idea, Skipper!"

Fitzpatrick smiled and nodded. Then he looked around, and noted that some of the Rangers that were sitting nearby had stopped talking. He realized with horror that they might have overheard some of what the two Ranger commanding officers had just been discussing.

So, Fitzpatrick stood up abruptly, loudly cleared his throat, and barked, "Draft an implementation plan along those lines *immediately* for my consideration, First Lieutenant!"

Sweetwater jumped to her feet as well, and stood to attention. Then she saluted smartly, and yelled, "Yes, sir, Captain Fitzpatrick!"

Fitzpatrick smartly returned the salute, and said in his normal voice, "Then carry on, First Lieutenant. Dismissed."

23

Commodore Chamberlain was pleased that he could have a few moments alone to gather his thoughts before what he believed would be an especially important, shift-handover, command staff meeting.

They always met at midnight for this recurring, daily meeting. Of course, the selected scheduled time for the meeting was irrelevant, since they were now far away from New Earth, and rigidly *incommunicado* with higher command. The members of the twelve-hour night shift faced exactly the same workload as the folks on the twelve-hour day shift. And the darkness of surrounding space never varied.

No one was missing any daylight because of the shift they were on, because there was none.

The command staff used the small meeting room adjacent to the bridge of the battlecruiser for these mostly information-sharing meetings. The room was well equipped with highly useful gadgetry, even if it was also totally *alien* gadgetry.

All nine members of Chamberlain's naval crew on the *Indefatigable* battlecruiser were now as familiar as he was with the ship's intricate and alien systems and instrumentation. That was by no means a trivial accomplishment. Almost every device on board had an artificial intelligence component that was linked into an overarching, 'mentoring', computerized architecture.

Mentoring was probably close to the right word, but not quite right.

The alien builders obviously had a different way of thinking, and of solving problems. But ultimately, logic was logic, and that had helped the human naval crew steadily work their way up a very steep learning curve.

Holistically, the ship was operated by a mostly self-controlling and almost self-aware system. It basically functioned as a Chief Engineer. It made sure every device was working properly, and every device had what it needed to fulfil a specific request or task. It told the naval crew exactly when something needed to be repaired or replaced, and exactly where to find the right spare parts in stores.

At the highest-level, the robot-like 'controller' on the vessel wanted to maintain the security and full-functionality of the battlecruiser at all times. Thankfully, it worked extremely well, and it allowed the non-machine, human crew to focus on other important things, like getting ready to fight battles. And the AI controller had quite willingly and completely changed its allegiance from its alien builders to the human crew.

Chamberlain was spending his free time by taking another hard look at the latest holographic, highly-detailed, three-dimensional image of the disabled Warrior Flagship. The disabled craft was nearby now, and moving through space at a speed of 53,214 kilometres per hour. The *Indefatigable* was holding a relative position of about twenty-one kilometres away from the equally massive, Master-constructed vessel. Thankfully, the Warrior Flagship still appeared to be quite inert.

Four New Earth robot scout ships, or frigates, were positioned much closer to the Warrior Flagship. They were radially spread apart, and holding relative positions of about one kilometre away from the Warrior vessel.

The robot scout ship search-and-destroy mission had been protracted, but in the end, successful. However, one of the New Earth robot frigates had been completely destroyed, and two others had been moderately damaged. It had all come to a climax about three months before.

The three small, presumably one-Warrior, attack ships had proven to be immensely powerful for their size, and impressively nimble. But they each had been under independent control by a living, mortal creature. Thankfully, New Earth's robot frigates were collectively smarter, and they had worked in close coordination with each other.

The commodore and his naval staff had noted with great interest how closely the tactics employed by the frigates had resembled those used by wolf packs on ancient Earth. Also, the Warrior 'prey' must in the end have been completely exhausted. The last Warrior counter-attack appeared to have been one of pure desperation.

The three command staff officers all arrived for the handover meeting at the same time. In addition to Ranger Captain Fitzpatrick, and Ranger First Lieutenant Sweetwater, the command staff included the commodore's executive officer, Naval Commander Yamato.

Fred Yamato was a good natured, rather short and swarthy fellow, in his mid-thirties. He had short, immaculately trimmed, jet-black hair. He was also a computer system genius.

As the three officers took their seats, Chamberlain froze a static holographic image of the Warrior Flagship over the centre of the circular table, which was itself positioned in the centre of the darkened room.

There was a ring of flush-mounted spot lights in the ceiling near the circular wall of the room. Chamberlain dimmed those lights to enhance the clarity of the holographic image.

Then Commodore Chamberlain performed his usual routine of carefully studying in turn the face of each of his command staff officers to confirm they at least *appeared* to be fit for duty.

Then Chamberlain said loudly and bluntly, "Commander Yamato, please provide us with your watch report."

"Yes, Commodore!" Yamato barked. "Our situation is nominal, sir! We have no impairments with any of our systems. There have been no changes of note with the condition of the Warrior Flagship. We have had no incidents of note, either with naval crew members or with Ranger personnel.

"Oh, one trivial item can be noted, I suppose. The coffee maker in the bridge had to be repaired. It gets a lot of use, of course.

"That's about it, sir."

"Okay, nothing is ever wrong with nominal and boring, of course, Commander," answered Chamberlain with a quick smile. Then he frowned, and said quietly, "But our well-established, comfortable routine is about to be *broken*, of course."

Chamberlain then took another closer, harder look at the two Ranger officers. To someone who did not know them, they might have appeared calm and relaxed. But he could tell they were a bit tense, and eager to talk about something. He thought he knew what that was, so he asked, "Captain Fitzpatrick, are you closer to recommending a final tactical attack plan for our consideration?"

"Yes, Commodore, we have settled on a plan, and we are pleased to report that we have also obtained full concurrence from our platoon leaders," Fitzpatrick replied immediately. Then he added for explanation, "Strictly speaking, sir, platoon leader concurrence is not required, of course. We only need *your* concurrence. But I thought you should know we involved Commander Yamato, and all of our officers and non-commissioned officers, as we put our tactical plan together, and we now have their complete buy-in."

"Acknowledged, Captain," replied Chamberlain without any sign of emotion. His muted reaction was not especially concerning to anyone, because the commodore was usually inscrutable. Then Chamberlain ordered, "Provide us with an overview of the tactical plan now, Captain."

"Yes of course, Commodore," replied Fitzpatrick crisply. "Lieutenant Sweetwater will work with your holographic image, while I do the talking, if that is all right?"

Chamberlain simply grunted in reply, and slid a keyboard over to Sweetwater. He had guessed correctly that the image of the Warrior Flagship might prove to be useful in today's meeting.

"Okay, sir, our first problem is entry," Fitzpatrick began in a confident-sounding voice. "Our primary, overarching goal, as you have clearly defined for us, is to determine where the Warrior Armada originated. We believe that means we need to obtain full access to the computer systems controlled from the bridge, which we know is located in the toroidal section of the vessel. And for those alien computer systems to work properly, we will first have to restore power to the crippled ship, or at least to key, controlling sections of the ship.

"As you know, the Flagship is moving through space, and we are currently keeping pace with it. It is still rotating around its long axis, so there will be artificial gravity in the toroidal section. However, the centripetal acceleration will be slightly lower than what we are used to, at about 8.9 metres per second squared. But that's no big deal.

"Because the Flagship is disabled, the vessel has unfortunately taken on another very slight toppling spin around its centre of mass. Currently the bow of the vessel is pointed at about eighty-two degrees to its direction of travel. However, we believe we can successfully accommodate for this awkward reality. Of course, we *must* successfully compensate for the complex spinning motion to be able to successfully dock with the vessel. Commodore Yamato tells us that successful docking will require a tricky but manageable 'space dance manoeuvre', so to speak.

"There appear to be seven, relatively large hatches arranged around the outside of the torus. There are also seven similar hatches around the circumference of the main body or fuselage of the ship. But we suspect none of those hatches were used very often.

"They might just be escape hatches, but more likely they were only used to move machinery, waste and supplies in or out of the vessel during construction and re-fitting operations. They probably all have elaborate, electronic, password-protected security systems. And we also believe those security systems are now locked, as the power systems on the ship are down.

"But there *may* be an accessible hatch, where a scout ship used to be docked. As you know, six scout ships are still attached to the Flagship, which can also be viewed as a 'mothership'. The missing scout ship was destroyed by one of our robot ships a few months ago.

"The hatch of interest is located on the after-body of the cylindrical section of the ship, just forward of the engine compartment. Thanks for pointing it out for us, Lieutenant Sweetwater. Now, maybe you can rotate the image and zoom in a bit so we can have a closer look at it? Thanks again, First Lieutenant.

"As you can see, Commodore, this hatch is much smaller, and less substantial than the other hatches we think we can see. But the structural frame around this particular hatch is flat, metallic and smooth, which introduces an ingress opportunity for us.

"The first part of our tactical plan is to attach a work module to the Warrior Flagship right over this hatch. Commander Yamato will pilot this module remotely for us, from this room actually. After docking, we will have to depend on a glue-like sealant and electromagnets to remain attached to the metallic skin of the alien craft until we can get some lag bolts and proper welds in place.

"Our work module will have a working end that is sort of like a caisson. And it will have a docking end too, which will include an airlock. We will use the docking end later, to attach our transport ferry when we are ready to send over the Ranger boarding party. The transport ferry only holds the two-person naval crew and up to ten passengers, so we'll have to make, ah, *twelve*, trips with it in total.

"A partial, spearhead squad of specialist Rangers will travel with the work module. They will work within the module to either open the hatch, or more likely, force entry into the vessel by cutting their way through the hatch.

"To be more precise, there will be four Special Weapons and Equipment Rangers in the 'caisson' work party. Those Rangers will be Lieutenant Clayton,

Sergeant Ngubo, Corporal Mitterrand and Private Klopp.

"We have no idea really what conditions will be like on the other side of the hatch. We hope there will be some kind of atmosphere, and a bit of pressure. It will be really cold, no doubt, but we are not sure *how* cold exactly.

"So, the work party guys will probably be fully suited-up for a long time. It will be awkward and uncomfortable for them, but they have been training really hard for this critically important operation. I believe they are now fully ready for the challenge.

"So, the first step will be for the work party to drill a small hole, either through or beside the hatch. Then the specialist Rangers will push a cable-mounted probe through the hole to measure and assess whatever we can. If things inside the vessel look okay, or okay enough, then they will open or cut away the hatch. We know that all sounds a bit fuzzy, but there will have to be a judgement call or two made during this phase of the operation, as we will probably have to work with insufficient information.

"If there is an atmosphere inside the Warrior Flagship, and if it is not too cold inside of it, we will then deploy a drone for initial interior surveillance.

"Commander Yamato will fly that drone, steering it from this room. I know I do not have to attest to his competency with you. The commander will want to fly the drone everywhere it can go to obtain as full a threat and condition assessment as possible. He will then seek my concurrence before we co-present to you a full discovery report, and a detailed forward recommendation.

"Our recommendation might be just to proceed as currently planned, or to proceed with a modified plan. Bottom line, however, we will not enter the Warrior Flagship and start deploying the Ranger boarding party, until we get the final go ahead from you.

"The next step in the current plan calls for Lieutenant Ghandi's platoon to make its way to the bridge. Commander Yamato and Lieutenant Sweetwater will go with Ghandi's platoon, as will Sergeant Gonzalez from the Special Weapons and Equipment platoon.

"Gonzales is a computer systems expert. Commander Yamato is no slouch either in that regard, as you well know. And I want Lieutenant Sweetwater on board but well away from me at all times. We do not want to risk being, ah, taken out, together. Sweetwater will have to assume frontline command, of course, if something should happen to me.

"First Sergeant McIlroy and I will be with Lieutenant Yang's assault platoon. Our job will be to eliminate any threats we discover, search through every nook and cranny in the vessel, and visually assess its overall condition.

"The second, overarching goal that you have given us is *salvage*. The first part of the salvage operation will be to find out everything we can about the vessel. Also, we want to know more about this Warrior caste of Masters. All of that investigative work will take time, which we might not have. So, that part of the plan is *especially* fuzzy, but we cannot improve upon it until we gather some first-hand information.

"Okay, Commodore, that's about it, sir. We apologize if our plan seems uncomfortably nebulous in a few places."

Commodore Chamberlain shook his head slightly. Then he scratched his chin, sighed, and said quietly, "No, thank you, Captain, I understand the data-gap issues, and the inherent risks with this operation. I think you have all done very well.

"Bottom line, I agree with the plan. When can we be ready to start?"

Captain Fitzpatrick smiled for a very brief moment, then sat bolt upright in his chair and barked, "The equipment we need is all ready to go, sir! I would like to give the caisson module work party, ah, six hours to grab some more shut-eye and a full, hot breakfast. Would that be acceptable to you, sir?"

Commodore Chamberlain abruptly stood up, and the others followed his lead. Then Chamberlain said loudly, "I concur fully, Command Staff! Consider the plan you have outlined as *my* plan now, and I *order* you to carry it out. Everyone knows how important this mission is to the survival of our species.

"Failure is not an option! Now, do your duty, and make us all proud. Dismissed."

The staff officers then came to rigid attention, and saluted smartly. Commodore Chamberlain returned a snappy salute, and the meeting was adjourned.

24

There was a bit of a jolt when the troop-carrier shuttle craft docked with the caisson module. But there actually *needed* to be some momentum transfer to ensure the dogs on the docking mechanism were all properly displaced, and then rigidly locked into place.

Commander Yamato was seated at the co-pilot station of the shuttle craft. Captain Fitzpatrick watched over Yamato's shoulder as he systematically reviewed all of the items in a long checklist.

After a fifteen minutes or so, Yamato turned around and said quietly, "Everything looks pretty good, Captain. As you know, with the hatch now completely cut away, they are wide-open over there. They have now fully equalized to the conditions inside the alien vessel. I'm reading an atmospheric pressure of 92.4 kilopascals, and an ambient temperature of minus 66.4 degrees Celsius, within the caisson module.

"So, we have indirectly confirmed that there is pressure integrity, and a heat source of some kind, inside that alien vessel. The atmosphere within it is as dry as a bone with respect to water vapour. That aligns with what we observed with the drone flight. Water vapour has condensed out of the internal atmosphere and become a layer of frost on everything inside.

"The atmosphere is predominantly nitrogen-oxygen, with about 31.2 percent molecular oxygen. So it's a little richer than what we're used to, but using some of your favourite phraseology, 'that's no big deal'. I don't pick up much in the way of organic compounds in the air. And I don't see any obvious toxins. But we'll have to wait to confirm all that when we get inside, and do a full suite of analyses.

"We'll also have to wait a bit to see what the air inside *smells* like. That's because we'll have to stay suited-up until we get the power back on, and straighten things up a bit in there.

"Not being able to smell the air inside right away is not such a bad thing, however. Remember, we believe that our Alpha robot ship killed quite a few Warriors in that vessel with an artificial gamma ray burst. And the air inside that vessel would not have been circulating since then, with the power off.

"Bottom line though, we'll have to equalize the shuttle craft atmosphere before we can safely open up the hatch to the caisson module. So, let me know when you've got everybody fully suited-up. And then have everyone hang tight until I give you the final thumbs-up to proceed inside."

"Will do, Commander," replied Captain Fitzpatrick in a whisper. "Thanks for reminding me about the dead Warriors over there. I hope there's a *lot* of stink in the air actually, and that they're all quite dead. But we'll assume of course that at least *some* of them are still alive, somewhere in that vast ship, until we know for *certain* otherwise.

"You know, I'll bet we'll want to leave our suits on until we pitch all of their corpses out into space, and you get the air well circulated through filters. There could also be rotten food over there, and sewage. Who knows?"

Then Fitzpatrick turned to the pilot and said with a smile, "I'm no expert of course, but I think that was an *amazing* bit of 'flying', Ensign Sarawak, if that's the right word for what you just did to get us safely docked."

Ensign Sarawak just initially smiled back from the pilot's seat. He looked very young, but actually he was a very experienced helicopter pilot. He was also a highly proficient drone pilot. All of those acquired skills helped him master the piloting of the troop shuttle. Then the Ensign said sheepishly, "Actually, the self-docking system worked perfectly. I was just ready to manually override if necessary. But thanks anyway, sir."

Commander Yamato was suddenly looking very grim, and he said quietly, "That may have been the easy bit, Captain. We hope you won't have to live up to your nickname, and become a 'mad beast' or whatever, should there be something really nasty still alive over there.

"Okay, the Ensign and I need to get back to work, and then get our own suits on, too. And you need to get your suit on and fully buttoned-up. Make sure everyone uses the buddy system we practised to double-check seals, radio connectivity, air supply, *et cetera*."

Ninety-six minutes later, Commander Yamato ordered the hatch to be opened. First Sergeant McIlroy worked two levers near the hatch in sequence. There was a very slight hiss of air for a few moments. Then McIlroy pulled on the edge of the hatch to open it fully.

The four work party members in the caisson module were all hovering inside near the open hatch. Their helmets were lightly covered with frost, but a name and rank could clearly be read on the top of each helmet.

Captain Fitzpatrick pulled himself into the nearly weightless environment of the caisson, and shook gloved hands with Lieutenant Clayton. He then snapped off a salute as best he could while wearing his bulky spacesuit.

Lieutenant Clayton, Sergeant Ngubo, Corporal Mitterrand and Private Klopp all returned the Captain's salute. Then Captain Fitzpatrick asked quietly over the radio command frequency, "Are you and your guys all right, Lieutenant? I can't see your faces very well. This frost is a real pain in the butt. Over."

"We're making out all right, Captain," replied Clayton. His voice was loud enough to be clearly heard, but it sounded a bit hoarse. Clayton paused for a moment and then he added, "You can see that we had to cut away the hatch. The edges are a bit ragged, with some sharp burrs. We're sorry about that. We did our best, but it would have required a lot more grinding in this confined space to smooth them all away. So, every Ranger will need to be especially careful when they pass through the portal we just made.

"The skin of the hull is aluminium, and the structural members are titanium and high-strength stainless steel. Thankfully we have achieved a full seal, and our bolts and welds have secured us in place very well." Clayton paused for another short moment, and then he added, "Captain, we're all a bit bushed right now, but I'm sure we'll soon get our full strength back. We can still help the company out if you need us for something. And we would sure like to do that. Over."

Fitzpatrick thought for a moment, and then he replied, "We might have to force entry into a few places in there, and if so, we'll want to do that very carefully. The rest of your platoon will be coming over in the last shuttle. As planned, attach yourself to Lieutenant Yang's platoon. He's your senior anyway, Lieutenant

Clayton, so follow his orders *to the letter*. And, ah, thanks for volunteering, again. You've all done really well. Now, stand down and out of the way for a bit until the first squad is all inside. Over."

Then Captain Fitzpatrick pushed a button on his wrist-mounted control panel, and he said loudly over the radio 'operation frequency', "Ranger Company, I'm going in now with First Sergeant McIlroy. When I give the okay, Sergeant Van Der Meer's squad will follow us inside, to conduct the initial site inspection.

"If we can open a hatch to gain entry to a spoke or shaft leading to the toroidal section, Commander Yamato may do another drone flight for us to check out what's in the 'donut' before the shuttle departs. Then, if things look okay, Lieutenant Yang will come over with his assault platoon, and bring in all of our weapons and tools. When all of the accessible areas in the cylindrical section of the ship are known to be secure, the rest of the Company will follow us.

"When we're all inside, our first priority will be to help Lieutenant Ghandi and his platoon make their way to the bridge. Commander Yamato and Sergeant Gonzales have a lot of critical work to do for us in the bridge area, including getting some power back on inside this ice box. First Lieutenant Sweetwater and I will be the communication conduit between our two groups to coordinate operations over the command frequency. Keep your radio chatter to a minimum over the operation frequency. Give everyone who might need to say something the opportunity to do just that.

"Okay, that's it for now. Let's you and I get moving, First Sergeant. Over."

25

As expected, it was pitch dark, and there was no gravity inside the Warrior Flagship. A thick layer of frost on everything inside the vessel made it especially difficult to move around. It proved awkward to get a firm grasp on things with bulky, gloved hands. And finding a firm foothold to push off or to get some useful leverage was frustratingly difficult as well.

Captain Fitzpatrick and Sergeant McIlroy were both wearing head-mounted, forward-directed lamps. The lamps helped a bit, but the narrow halogen beams also made an obviously alien and surreal place even more eerie and mysterious.

McIlroy eventually found a useful metallic flange on the lid or door of what look to be a large sealed bin. He secured a battery-powered lamp to the flange. A permanent magnet on the bottom of the lamp held it firmly in place. When he turned the high-intensity, 360 degree lamp on, he and Fitzpatrick immediately got a better sense of the environment they were in.

The interior of the fuselage of the vessel was cylindrical, and perhaps fifty metres across. The internal dimensions were hard to judge properly. There were hundreds of cubical and cylindrical containers or modules of various sizes fastened in place around the interior circumference. There no apparent order to the arrangement of anything. It all looked rather haphazard.

There was also a crooked, semi-cylindrical corridor of sorts running right down the centreline of this part of the vessel. The passageway averaged about fifteen metres in diameter. There were handles and rails everywhere on the containers and modules, presumably to help human-like creatures find useful handholds to move around a bit more easily.

Fitzpatrick concluded that it must have been a weightless environment most of the time in this central corridor. The ship was spinning, so artificial gravity would increase as one moved away from the centre of rotation. And it would be unlikely for any Warrior to have to come into this part of the ship during periods of acceleration or deceleration. If the engine compartment was anything like that on the *Indefatigable*, one would want to be well away from that part of the ship when the radioactive plasma drive was engaged.

He imagined that they would find fully-gimballed seats in the toroidal section of the ship. The Warriors could make use of such seats when hard manoeuvres were performed. Well-designed seats could provide a degree of comfort, and compensate a bit for higher, variable-vector G-forces.

"Sergeant McIlroy, this place looks like a warehouse or storage area, next to the engine compartment, which must be on the other side of that rather imposing bulkhead," suggested Fitzpatrick over the operation frequency after a few minutes of looking around. "And that looks like the outline of a closed sliding door in the centre of the bulkhead. And there is no obvious way to open that freaking door, either. Over."

"Yes, I agree, and this place is *lot* bigger than what the drone images suggested to us, Skipper," McIlroy said calmly in reply. "Thankfully, I'm not picking up any unusual radioactivity on the Geiger counter. In fact, the background radiation reading in here is a lot lower that what we would probably measure in space outside of the ship. That suggests some effective shielding is in place. And that's a pretty useful design feature if one wants to survive a long interstellar space voyage. Over."

"Okay, thanks, First Sergeant. So, it's probably safe enough to start the *real* search of this place. We're definitely going to need some more help with that effort."

"Sergeant Van Der Meer, I know you've been listening in. Come into the Flagship now with your squad. Let's first see if there's anything moving around in here, and if there's anything in here that resembles a dead body. If we cannot find any obvious threats, Commander Yamato will then join us in here too, but maybe after he pilots another drone flight for us. For that, we'll first have to see if we can find a way into the toroidal section. Then when everything checks out okay, Ensign Sarawak can start ferrying over the rest of the Company. Over."

"Roger, Skipper, we're leaving the caisson module now," replied Sergeant Van Der Meer immediately. "Over."

26

The Ranger scouting squad completed a systematic visual inspection, but it did not find any Warrior corpses in the cylindrical section of the Flagship. They also did not find anything that might pose an immediate threat to their survival.

But every Ranger knew that they had not been able to look inside what looked to be hundreds of modules, cabinets or storage bins. And it was still uncertain if some of the odd-shaped and different-sized metallic modules might contain machinery that was needed to operate the ship.

But there was no obvious way to safely force entry into bins, boxes or modules. They literally could contain anything, including hazardous, flammable or explosive materials. Everything was sealed-up tight, and Captain Fitzpatrick decided that was probably not such a bad thing, for now.

Seven structurally-essential, cylindrical 'spokes' connected the toroidal section of the Warrior Flagship to its cylindrical fuselage. The tubular spokes were all the same diameter when viewed externally. However, the scouting squad quickly discovered that four of the spokes were completely inaccessible. They were sealed-up tight. A lot of piping, and many different sized conduits, presumably for power and telemetry cables, led into those four spokes.

There were elevators in two of the other spokes. Presumably the elevators were used for moving both equipment and Warrior crew members around between the two sections of the ship. But with the power off, there was no way for the Ranger scouting party to make use of those elevators.

There was a square, metallic hatch that they thought must lead to the interior of the seventh spoke. They knew it was a hatch because there were obvious hinges along one of its edges. There was also a wheel in the centre of the hatch. When Captain Fitzpatrick was satisfied with their immediate security, he ordered the incredibly muscular Sergeant Van Der Meer to see if the wheel could be turned by hand.

Van Der Meer had to strain for only a few moments to get the wheel turning. He managed to turn it one full rotation, and then a small gap appeared at the edge of the hatch on the other side of the hinges.

"Give it a steady pull now, Sergeant, and see if it will open up some more," ordered Captain Fitzpatrick calmly over the operation frequency. "Over."

Every Ranger that was watching nearby had a spear or a stabbing sword ready for use. A blaster was not something they wanted to use in this strange, confined place, with no idea what a stray shot might hit.

Sergeant Van Der Meer instantly obeyed. He managed to widen the gap another few centimetres, but it required all of his strength.

Lieutenant Clayton and three of his Special Equipment Rangers were hovering twenty metres or so away from the hatch. Captain Fitzpatrick had seen them come out of the caisson module twenty or so minutes before. They all looked fit enough again, and profoundly interested in what was going on. So, Fitzpatrick had decided not to order them to standby somewhere well out of the way. Now he thought they might be of some immediate use. So he said, "Lieutenant Clayton, come closer, have a look at this hatch, and tell me what you think can be done to open it all the way. Over."

Clayton floated over and had a close look at the hatch. Then he said, "Turning the wheel probably retracted mechanical locking dogs, Captain. Either the hinges are frozen or corroded, or there is a hydraulic dashpot of sorts that is now working against us. Since the hatch did move a bit, I bet we can pry it open with an electro-hydraulic jack. It will probably be best to take it really slow though. I don't think we should risk permanently deforming or damaging it until we know there is no other way. Over."

Captain Fitzpatrick paused to consider the suggestion for a moment, and then he ordered, "Right Lieutenant, then get right to work on that operation. Over."

A few minutes later, Sergeant Ngubo and Corporal Mitterrand managed to insert the end of a device they called 'the jaws of life' in to the crack at the edge of the hatch. Then they hooked up a braided-metallic hose to the power unit on Private Klopp's back.

Lieutenant Clayton worked the controls on the power unit to slowly open the jaws. Ngubo and Mitterrand had to reposition the hydraulic opening device a few times to obtain the proper leverage. The hatch seemed to free up a bit as it was being displaced. The team of specialists then skilfully used a simple block and tackle to complete the job of fully opening the hatch.

Captain Fitzpatrick peered into the open hatch for a few minutes. Then he said, "The shaft looks clear as far as I can see. I can't see the other end of the shaft, but Commander Yamato said it is about one hundred and eighty-six metres long if it terminates at the near edge of the toroidal section.

"There are two ladders inside, and the tunnel appears to be wide enough for two guys moving back-to-back, wearing suits like ours. If there's a closed hatch like this one at the other end, we might have a *bigger* problem on our hands…." He trailed off with a shake of his head inside his space helmet. Then he said, "Over."

"I can check that out with this pistol-like sonar and laser device, Captain," offered Lieutenant Clayton. "It will measure the distance to the first solid reflective surface. Over."

"Okay, Lieutenant Clayton, have at it," ordered Fitzpatrick. "Over."

Clayton carefully aimed the pistol up the centre of the tunnel, and after only a few seconds he declared, "Two hundred and twenty-one metres, Captain. That means if there is another hatch down there, or up there I guess, it must be open. Over."

"Right Lieutenant, thanks very much," replied Fitzpatrick calmly, while successfully hiding his relief. Then he said, "Commander Yamato, you have probably been following all of this with the video stream from our head-mounted cameras. What do you think? Can you fly the drone up this tunnel for us, and have a look around inside the torus? Over."

The drone was parked nearby, stuck with an electromagnet to a flat, frosty metallic surface. It had six rotors arranged in a hexagonal pattern, and it was about a metre-and-a-half wide from rotor tip to rotor tip.

Yamato was back at the co-pilot seat of the shuttle craft. Without hesitation, Yamato replied, "Piece of cake, Captain. Strictly speaking, you were actually looking *down* that tunnel. So, we will have to fly looking *down* while we traverse the inside of the spoke, as there will be something close to full gravity when it gets over to the toroidal section. But that's no big deal. I'll just take it real slow and easy, if that's okay? Over."

"That's definitely okay, Commander, taking it slow and easy is appropriate," Fitzpatrick replied calmly. "We only have one drone with us, and we need to do this right.

"Okay, we will all back well away from the hatch, right now, and you can get started, Commander. Over."

27

About six hours later, Commander Yamato hailed Captain Fitzpatrick over the command frequency. Fitzpatrick did not immediately respond. He was in a deep sleep with his feet tucked under the edge of a container. He had positioned himself near the open hatch that they had confirmed provided access to the toroidal section of the massive Warrior Flagship. It had been the first time in over thirty-six hours that Fitzpatrick had felt it would be safe enough to shut his eyes for a while.

Commodore Chamberlain and First Lieutenant Sweetwater were able to hear the hail, and they both joined Commander Yamato with polite pleas for Captain Fitzpatrick to wake up. They made sure Fitzpatrick knew they were both monitoring the conversation when Fitzpatrick said he was fully awake and alert again.

"I just set the drone down in there, Captain, in a place that looks to be a bit out of the way," Yamato began. He was no doubt excited, but his voice sounded calm and controlled. He was obviously functioning well on very little sleep.

Yamato paused for a moment to converse privately with Ensign Sarawak who was sitting beside him in the cockpit of the shuttle craft. Then he said, "I know you have a small televiewer with you, Captain, but I suspect it would have been very difficult to make out what we observed during our long flight around the toroidal section. And no doubt the frost on your helmet glass is still problematic. For what it's worth, I think it's *great* that you managed to get a bit of sleep while we did our reconnaissance sortie. Hopefully it's my turn now?

"But first, I'll give you an overview of what happened. There *definitely* are corpses in there. But there is nothing especially gory to speak of anywhere. The place is frosty, but clean. The bodies just look like they are sleeping, albeit in sometimes contorted positions.

"I counted exactly fifty corpses in total, all frozen solid of course, and all fitting the outward, physical description we have for Master Warriors. It looks like they were killed instantly where they stood, or at their work stations, or in their seats or bunks, by the gamma ray burst from the Alpha robot ship.

"There are fifty fully-gimballed chairs in there too, mostly in what must have been the bridge area. There is a work station of sorts attached to every chair. It's quite an impressive, technically-advanced set up, actually.

"None of the Warriors were suited-up for space, but some were wearing what looks like a flexible kind of body armour. A few of those guys were also wearing what looks like some kind of electrical power-generating back-pack. Those guys might have been guards, as there are lances or spears on the floor near their corpses. I strongly suspect those spears may also have had an additional feature like a Taser. I'm sure you will want to have a closer look at them yourself, as I know you have similar weapons, and armour.

"The toroidal section is almost a completely open floor plan, so it was relatively easy to move around in there with the drone. There are only three private cabins. Perhaps a few high ranking officers had special status, and the rest of the company had the same rank or hierarchical status? There are sixty bunks in one area. That may mean there are more bodies to be found somewhere else on the vessel, and that Warriors did some 'hot bunking' on shifts?

"There is a kitchen with a very large pantry and freezer. It's right next to what looks like a combination mess hall and lecture hall that would seat thirty Warriors. And there is an area that looks like an exercise or training room. Also, there are what look like lounge, sitting areas in four separate places, but nothing resembling a recreational area. Recreating might not have been one of their allowed activities, perhaps? There are what must be toilet facilities spaced-out about evenly throughout the torus.

"The bridge is a fairly obvious feature, thankfully. There are a few glowing lights on workstation panels within it, probably from light-emitting diodes. So, there must be at least a *trickle* of electric current flowing in a few places on the Flagship. That is *very* good to see. I am now feeling a bit more upbeat about our ability to break into their computer systems, and hopefully get some real power back on again within the vessel.

"I suspect there are thermophotovoltaic cells onboard, somewhere. They work like solar cells, only they tap infrared energy emitted by something hot, rather than say, visible light photons from the sun. Those cells could also be the heat source that is keeping the interior space well above absolute zero. But we all know that it is still really freaking cold inside this temporary space hulk!

"In addition to the suspected, perhaps 'emergency only', radioisotope thermoelectric generators, we know from our intelligence reports that the Masters used deuterium fusion generators, for their magneto-plasmadynamic ion space-thrust drive systems, and to generate electrical power for primary weapon and life support systems. Those large power-producing units are probably all located in the engine compartment, behind some radiation and heat shielding, and probably some massive, currently closed doors.

"So, bottom line, Captain, I can see no reason why we cannot now proceed as planned. Specifically, I suggest it is now time to have a first-hand look around the toroidal section. Over."

Captain Fitzpatrick waited for only a few moments to say rather loudly in reply, "I fully agree with your suggestion, Commander.

"And therefore, Commodore, I ask your permission to bring over the rest of the Ranger Company now. I assure you that no one will actually enter the toroidal section until we are all fully assembled and fully sorted-out. That will give Commander Yamato the opportunity to enter the Flagship right now, and get a bit of sleep, too. I'd say he has definitely earned it!

"As planned, when we are ready, Lieutenant Ghandi will lead his platoon into the toroidal section using the 'spoke' we discovered with the two ladders. Commander Yamato, First Lieutenant Sweetwater and Special Sergeant Gonzales will go with Ghandi's platoon.

"Do you concur, Commodore? Over."

There was a short pause, then in a clear, strong voice, Commodore Chamberlain said, "I fully concur, Captain. Proceed as we have planned.

"Now, while the torus team is doing their thing, I know you and the rest of the Company will be tempted to try to open things up in the cylindrical section, like modules, bins or lockers. But only do that if you suspect there might be an immediate hazard that has to be dealt with. Hopefully, Commander Yamato and the bridge team will soon be able to access database and control systems that can tell us exactly what lies behind every door and hatch on the vessel.

"That might be wishful thinking, of course. But I strongly suspect the bridge team may be able to remotely open hatches and doors so you will not have to actually break into anything forcefully. We should suspect that some places might be mined or booby-trapped, until we know for certain otherwise.

"So, Captain, after marshalling your company and sorting everyone out, with the help of Lieutenant Ghandi's platoon, focus on getting all of the frozen corpses the hell out of there. We don't want them to start melting and stinking up the place. That would not just be bad for morale. The corpses may be biologically hazardous.

"But we have to do this right. Carefully strip and search every corpse. Itemize and document everything you find on the bodies, carefully. And get before-and-after digital images of every corpse.

"Seal-up one corpse in a body bag, and send it back to the command ship in the shuttle. We'll perform a comprehensive autopsy on it over here, and collect DNA and other tissue samples.

"Every other corpse should be pitched-out into space using the airlock in the caisson module. That can only be done, of course, when the shuttle is not docked there. Try to push them in the opposite direction to the vessel's trajectory so they won't bother us again.

"When all of the corpses are removed, perform a complete interior sweep for known human pathogens and toxins. When the power comes back on, and you have some hopefully room-temperature heat in there, perform the complete sweep again before you take off your space suits.

"On second thought, check in with me again for a final okay before anyone in the Company takes off a suit.

"Now, do you have any questions, Captain? Over."

Captain Fitzpatrick immediately barked, "No, sir! All fully understood, sir! Over."

"Right, then proceed as ordered, Captain," Chamberlain replied crisply. Then after a long pause, he added quietly, "And good luck to everyone. I know you will all perform your duty safely and efficiently. Over."

28

Captain Fitzpatrick found a quiet little nook to himself. He sat down on some sort of small container to enjoy a boxed lunch. He hooked his booted feet under a gap under the next container so he would not float away in the zero gravity.

He had not been able to have any real, solid food for about four days, and he was famished. The packaged food was basic, but it still tasted great. The food tube inside his space helmet had been supplying him with some liquid nourishment on demand. It had been sustaining, but far from satisfying.

It also felt great to be finally out of his damp, confining and smelly space suit. Thankfully, the two fully-comprehensive 'known toxin and pathology' sweeps had not turned up anything of concern within the interior of the Warrior Flagship.

The power had been fully restored in the Flagship for about twenty-six hours now. It was no longer a space hulk. An artificial intelligence system was once again automatically self-controlling the vessel's attitude, and this same Master-designed AI system had decided to realign the bow of the huge vessel with its direction of travel through space.

The Rangers were now all wearing flexible body armour. Each Ranger was also armed with a holstered-blaster, a Taser-tipped spear, and either a short stabbing sword in a scabbard, or a mace, or a short-handled axe holstered in a back pouch. Most Rangers also carried a half-body-length shield. Those who were without a shield had a modified Chinese Repeating Crossbow with a large attached magazine of composite-shaft arrows. And a few especially mighty, 'crack shots' had a composite long bow with a quiver of armour-piercing, composite-shaft arrows.

Use of a blaster was strictly forbidden, unless a countermanding order was directly issued by a Ranger officer. It was more certain now that there were many probably explosive or flammable threats all around them.

But the primary fear remained accidentally puncturing or rupturing the hull. There was only a relatively thin metallic barrier separating them from the vacuum of space. A shot from a blaster, or a higher-velocity kinetic weapon, simply carried to too much energy should a living target be missed, evenly partially.

There was still a large section of the Flagship that could not be accessed and fully checked-out. So, Captain Fitzpatrick had insisted upon full combat readiness. He was pleased that he had not heard any protests from within Company ranks about what could have been perceived as 'overkill' readiness.

Everyone knew by now that there was no obvious way to open the door to the engine compartment. There was some sort of intricate, multi-level, password-protected security system that was still in place. Commander Yamato and his team of computer experts on the bridge had so far been unable to crack the code, so to speak.

And if there was indeed a door in the centre of the engine compartment bulkhead, it was obviously stoutly made. Lieutenant Clayton had quite openly admitted he had no idea how to cut through it, even with the suite of sophisticated tools he had on hand. His probing, non-destructive analyses suggested that the obvious bulkhead, and the possible door, were composed of many layers of various types of metals, and probably many layers of high-tensile strength fiber mesh embedded in a tough, rock-hard polymer matrix.

The barrier was clearly more than just a radiation shield.

But the bridge team had been able to break into many parts of the computerized system that controlled the Flagship, and some parts of the immense, ancillary, data storage system. And Commander Yamato had just informed the command staff that he thought they were finally getting closer to discovering the location of the ship's log.

With that log in hand, the location of the home planet of the Warriors should be revealed. And then their primary mission would be accomplished.

Fitzpatrick had placed his helmet on the floor beside him, and loosely tied it down with a single Velcro strap around some sort of hook embedded in the floor. As he was washing the last of his meal down with some bottled water, a little red light on the top of his helmet, and another one on his wrist strap, both started flashing. The red lights indicated someone was calling him on the command frequency. Yellow lights would have indicated an incoming call on the operation frequency.

Fitzpatrick quickly untied the strap and put his helmet back on. Then he said calmly into the built-in mouthpiece, "This is Fitzpatrick, go ahead. Over."

"Captain, this is Yamato. Look, there is something strange and alarming going on behind the bulkhead door. We're not sure what exactly. We have been trying for a day or so to get the lights back on in there. We just had some of them on for a minute or two, and then we think we saw some sort of movement. But it was all a bit blurry. Then all of the lights went out again, and we don't know why exactly.

"Also, we are pretty sure all of the video cameras in the engine compartment have now been disabled. So, instead of continuing to try to open the bulkhead door, we thought it best to put our own extra layer of password protection into the Master-designed security system.

"But someone, or something, is now trying very hard to hack into that system! And the attempts are being made from somewhere within the engine compartment! If it's a living Warrior, they may succeed, as they obviously know this ship a whole lot better than we do.

"Therefore, I strongly suggest Captain that you ready your company for an imminent attack that will probably come through the bulkhead door. Over."

"We're on it, Commander!" yelled Fitzpatrick, loud enough for the Rangers around him to hear without radio assistance. "Thank you. Over."

Then Fitzpatrick started barking orders in quick succession. He had Lieutenant Yang and First Sergeant McIlroy arrange the assault platoon along the central corridor. Everyone with a shield hooked a foot under a rail and found a nearby hand-hold so they could properly defend themselves, and use a weapon.

First Lieutenant Sweetwater suggested over the command frequency that half the platoon in the toroidal section could safely be sent over to bolster what everyone believed would become the front line. Fitzpatrick instantly agreed to her suggestion, and about ten minutes later Lieutenant Ghandi arrived on the scene with twenty-nine Rangers. That increased the strength of the frontline force to ninety-six Rangers, including officers and non-commissioned officers.

Fitzpatrick positioned archers and a blaster rifle at the very end of the corridor. He left Lieutenant Ghandi in charge there. Lieutenant Yang and Lieutenant Clayton positioned themselves at the midpoint of the corridor, on opposite sides.

Captain Fitzpatrick and First Sergeant McIlroy then went forward, and took station next to each other about ten metres from the bulkhead.

And then everyone waited.

They all had their own thoughts, and their own way to ready themselves. They were all a bit scared, but no one was incapacitated by their fear. They had been well-selected, and they were all very fit and very well trained.

They only had to wait about twenty more minutes.

Commander Yamato yelled over the command frequency, "Captain, they have just broken through our extra password firewall! That bulkhead door is about to open! Over."

Captain Fitzpatrick switched to the operation frequency, and said crisply, "Get ready everyone. The bulkhead door is about to open. Brace yourselves for an attack. Over."

Fitzpatrick and McIlroy heard a hiss of air, and then the bulkhead door quickly slid fully open. Immediately, one Warrior after another propelled themselves through the door and then on down the long central corridor. It was pitch black behind the door opening. Each Warrior had a spear and a round shield. They were all wearing body armour, and helmets with face guards, and a bright, forward-directed head lamp. They flew right by Fitzpatrick and McIlroy, apparently without noticing them.

Between passing Warriors, Fitzpatrick yelled, "Keep a head count of these bastards, First Sergeant!"

McIlroy yelled back, "I'm on it, Captain! Sixteen so far!"

The once orderly scene in the central corridor became chaotic bedlam. The 'floating' Warriors would fend off blows with their shields until they could get a foot or a limb hooked into some place secure. Then they would engage in hand-to-hand combat. They were massive creatures, and obviously very fit, muscular and well trained.

But the Rangers were largely holding their own. It seemed that the Warriors were surprised by what they had encountered in the corridor. They clearly were not working to a coherent plan. Each Warrior was working independently. In contrast, the Rangers were forming up into clusters to form shield walls.

Four Warriors propelled themselves as a group to pass right down the centre of the corridor. They clearly had no intention of stopping to engage in a skirmish. They were each struck with a few arrows as they approached the far end of the corridor. That only seemed to infuriate them more.

They immediately killed three Rangers with their spears. Then they seemed to realize Lieutenant Ghandi was in charge, so they focused all of their attention on him. Corporal Simons and Private Romano formed a shield wall in front of Ghandi. They worked well together, and used their stabbing swords effectively. Coordinated timing was everything.

They remembered their training: 'Defend yourself and your neighbours with your shield, look for opportunities to hack at a spear, or better yet, to poke at a limb or a face.'

They found that the body armour the Warriors were wearing stopped or deflected most of their blows. But there were chinks in their armour where some flexibility was needed, such as around the wrist, elbow, shoulder, knee, neck and waist region. The Warrior helmet face plates also offered a small opening from directly in front.

Private Fazlutdinov worked low behind his buddies Simons and Romano. He stabbed effectively with his Taser spear at exposed ankles and knees. After a few minutes, the four Warriors stopped hitting back. They were full of arrows now, and bleeding from many wounds. The orange blood of the stricken Warriors, and the red blood of wounded Rangers, was floating everywhere in tiny, spherical globules.

Romano was unconscious and bleeding profusely from a grisly spear-thrust wound near his waist.

Lieutenant Ghandi put his blaster pistol to the neck of each of the four wounded Warriors to finish them off. The focused, particle-beam blast instantly severed their heads.

Ghandi then looked down the long, central corridor to see what was happening. Similar hellish battles were still ongoing everywhere.

McIlroy yelled, "That's fifty altogether, Captain! None have come through for over five minutes now."

The non-commissioned Rangers were all communicating verbally with shouts, which left both the operation and command frequencies wide-open for the use of the officers.

Fitzpatrick was extremely proud of the discipline and fortitude that all members of his Company were demonstrating. He yelled into his headset over the operation frequency, "Lieutenant Clayton, how are we doing up there? Over."

There was no reply, so Fitzpatrick yelled, "Lieutenant Yang, how are we doing up your way? Over."

There was a short pause, then Fitzpatrick heard between gasps and grunts, "This is Yang. Clayton is gone. Sorry, Sir.

"We are... we are holding our own... mostly. Our small shield walls are working. These bastards are fierce and very strong! They just want to kill us... don't seem to have... to have... ugh... any other goal in mind. There are ten plus Rangers wounded or killed in the middle section. But we might be starting... we're starting to get the upper hand. Over."

"Right!" replied Fitzpatrick loudly. "Keep at it, hard! Lieutenant Ghandi, report!"

"It's quiet here just now, Captain," replied Ghandi with amazing calm. "We fended off one very determined attack. Four Warriors were clearly trying to get past us to get to the bridge through the open spoke hatch. We put them all away. But Private Romano just died. He fought bravely..." He trailed off with a gasp. Then he said feebly, "Over."

Fitzpatrick paused to process what he had just heard. Their losses were tragic and staggering, but he could not dwell on that cruel fact right now.

Just then, Fitzpatrick noted someone was calling him over the command frequency. Fitzpatrick pushed the switch on his wrist, and yelled, "This is Fitzpatrick. Go!"

In response he heard, "Captain, this is Yamato. First Lieutenant Sweetwater advises that we just successfully broke into the ship's log. We now know there were exactly fifty Warriors in hibernation. They were all in a shielded chamber adjacent to the engine room.

"And we are now uploading the digitized ship's log to the *Indefatigable*! Commodore Chamberlain says they are pleased with the quality of the data they are receiving. Over."

"Right, thanks, Commander!" Fitzpatrick barked in reply. Then he added, "Can you try to shut the damn bulkhead door again? We have to contain these bastards, and keep them in a place where we can finish them all off. Over."

Then Fitzpatrick switched back to the operation frequency, and yelled, "Lieutenant Yang, we could use another spear or two down at this end, and maybe a crossbowman too. Can you spare them? This open door will soon start looking like an inviting safe haven to the Warriors. Over."

"Roger, Captain!" replied Yang immediately. "We can spare those guys now. Give me a minute, and they'll be on their way. Over."

Then Fitzpatrick switched off his microphone and yelled, "First Sergeant, your head count was spot on! That's the lot of them. And we may be getting the upper hand. That means some of those vicious bastards might try to go back to their safe little cubby-hole. So, you and I will just have to keep that from happening, now won't we? But we might get some help soon."

McIlroy just nodded, and returned his attention back to the fierce melee in the corridor.

They did not have to wait long for action. They saw an obviously wounded Warrior making its way down the corridor towards them. The Warrior was fending-off a determined charge by a huge Ranger spearman, while bouncing along between handholds. The Warrior was a huge beast itself, and it was missing the lower part of its right leg below the knee. The ugly, jagged wound was streaming orange blood and muscular gore. A crossbowman was closely following along beside the Ranger spearman, and he managed to fire a bolt at point blank range into the face of the Warrior. That ended the fight.

When the two approaching Rangers got their bearings again, and finally looked towards the open door, McIlroy yelled at them, "You two Rangers, form up right here, with us. Now!"

Captain Fitzpatrick then had a close look at the two new arrivals. They both looked highly stressed, but they were obviously very alert, and unhurt. Then he recognized them, and yelled, "Welcome, Corporal Mitterrand, and Private Klopp. Fancy meeting you two guys here."

Corporal Mitterrand was holding a repeating crossbow, and the gargantuan Private Klopp had a bloody spear in his right hand, and a short-handled axe in a back pouch. Klopp also had a shield strapped to his back.

After a moment, Corporal Mitterrand gasped between breaths, "Lieutenant Yang said... he said we should drive this one back towards Mad Dog... I mean you... sorry, Captain. This was the bastard that killed... that killed Lieutenant Clayton, Captain."

Fitzpatrick paused for a second, and then he yelled, "That's really tough to hear, Corporal. The First Sergeant and I are really sorry to hear that.

"But you guys did really well. Now, get your heads straight again. This battle is not over yet, not by a long shot. This end of the corridor will see a lot of action until we get that freaking door shut again.

"So, Corporal, get yourself wedged in somewhere handy nearby, behind a bit of cover if you can, where you can get off clear shots with that bow of yours.

"Private Klopp, keep your axe tucked away for now. Use your shield and your spear and join up with me and the First Sergeant. We are going to put up a shield wall next to the door. We can't block the door, it's clearly too big, but we must not let any Warrior get past us.

"Now, let's get set everyone!"

When everyone was in place, Lieutenant Ghandi hailed Captain Fitzpatrick on the operation frequency. He said calmly, "They seem to be forming up into small groups now, Captain, and gradually retreating your way. There are at least two dozen of them left. A lot of them are wounded. Over."

"I concur, Captain," interjected Lieutenant Yang with a growl. "Over."

"Okay, then drive the battle back this way, you guys!" yelled Captain Fitzpatrick. "We'll block the door until it closes. Over."

The struggle at the door then became extremely fierce, but no one panicked. The Warriors quickly realized they could not just move past the door with the neighbouring shield wall in place, and an obviously proficient crossbowman working as a sniper nearby. So, they focused their attention on destroying the shield wall first.

Klopp was magnificent. He stood in the middle of the shield wall, and Fitzpatrick and McIlroy protected his flanks. Klopp withstood the press of sometimes two or more Warriors at a time, while McIlroy and Fitzpatrick took opportunistic and flesh-and-bone finding thrusts with their stabbing swords. A Warrior chopped Klopp's spear shaft in half, so he brought out his axe. He quickly proved to be a proficient butcher with it.

It was brutal, gruesome, intensely physical work.

Fitzpatrick knew they could not keep up the non-stop, total exertion much longer. Determination, training and good tactics were all very good in principle. Overcoming pure fatigue was ultimately an impossibility.

Yamato knew Fitzpatrick was monitoring the operation frequency. So he used it to yell, "We just broke through the door security firewall, Captain! Do you still want us to shut that bulkhead door? Over."

"Yes, close the fucking door, Commander!" yelled Fitzpatrick immediately. "And right now! Over."

And that marked the beginning of the end of the battle. When they saw the door closing, the Warriors went back to fighting as individuals all along the corridor.

It became clear that surrender was not an option for any of them. So, the Rangers accommodated them. They continued to fight effectively in small teams, until the last of the once mighty, reawakened Warrior force was destroyed.

29

Captain Fitzpatrick was embarrassed, and astounded that he had fallen asleep. As his head cleared a bit more, he realized that he was sitting quite comfortably with his back to a box-like container of some sort. He also noted that he had hooked his booted feet under the lip of a door on another box.

He was still wearing his helmet and battle armour. The armour was heavily spattered and smeared with dried blood. Thankfully, it looked like most of the blood stains were of the orange variety.

During the fierce, long battle he had been unable to empty the urine containment sack that was built into his armoured suit. He realized with disgust that the sack must have ruptured or over-flown while he had dozed off. His under-garments were completely soaked, and he stank heavily of both urine and sweat.

He also noted that his short, battle-notched sword, and his heavily battered shield, were both floating nearby. They were tethered to his belt by slender nylon straps. The sword and shield were also heavily smeared with gore and mostly orange blood. He admonished himself for not properly cleaning his weapons, forgetting that he had literally collapsed with fatigue.

But remarkably, he was mostly unscathed. He just had a few bruises and gashes. Well, maybe two of the gashes were rather deep. Those wounds were still bleeding a bit. Lieutenant Sweetwater would probably conclude they would need to be stitched up. But unfortunately, other Rangers were in far greater need of a doctor's attention right now.

He remembered with more clarity that a few minutes ago he had ordered First Lieutenant Sweetwater to manage the first aid operation, and to start ferrying the critically wounded back to the battlecruiser nearby. He had given her full discretion to use her own judgement on who should be returned to the *Indefatigable*.

Or, had he issued those orders a few hours ago?

Fatigue had really messed him up.

Then he sensed in a fuzzy sort of way that someone was hailing him on the command frequency.

"Captain Fitzpatrick, do you read? Over!" It was Commodore Chamberlain, and he was yelling at him! Uncharacteristically, the commodore sounded a bit frantic.

"Ah, roger, Commodore," Fitzpatrick mumbled. "Sorry, sir, I must have passed out or something. I'm pretty bushed, I guess. Over."

There was a long pause, then Chamberlain said quietly, "Yes, I bet you are, Captain.

"I followed what I could of the battle by listening in on the radio chatter. It was pretty confusing, as one would expect. But look, can you give me a bit of a status report now? Why don't you start with the casualties we suffered?"

"Right, Commodore," replied Fitzpatrick with a bit of a slur. Then he shook his head, and after a few moments, and quite surprisingly, he found a bit more strength well up from somewhere deep inside himself. He said more clearly and forcefully, "Sixteen Rangers killed, sir. Twenty-four wounded, six seriously or critically. Sadly, Lieutenant Sweetwater said we might lose three of those injured guys. Time will tell, I guess.

"Look, sir, I'm really sorry about that! But it was a true slug-fest, or a street fight, as filthy and dirty as it can get.

"Ah, there were exactly fifty living Warriors altogether in the attack, and we had to kill them all! None of those vicious bastards even attempted surrender. They would literally keep fighting with limbs hacked off or blown away.

"I guess they must have been specially bred for this kind of nasty business, or something like that. Hell, they were all in some kind of hibernation a little over one day ago! I doubt a human soldier could be ready for a full-fledged battle that quickly after something like hibernation. Of course, the point is moot. We don't know how to put ourselves in hibernation, of course.

"Bottom line, Commodore, it took everything we had to beat them in the end. But we did beat them, thankfully. Over."

There was another long pause, then Chamberlain said, "Okay, thank you, Captain. No, we thank you all, and very much!

"You and your company did your duty, to the letter. And you went beyond that, actually. It's too early to talk to you about individual commendations, but after you get some proper rest, I want you to start thinking about that.

"Okay, now here are some new orders for you, beyond continuing to look after the wounded.

"Get everyone out of their battle gear. Tell them to make their way over to the toroidal section, and to get properly cleaned-up and properly checked-over by the medics. Not all injuries are physical, you know. Some people will be really shaken up by the ordeal. That can happen to even the toughest soldiers. And sometimes only a doctor or psychologist can tell how serious it is.

"Then order everyone to get a proper rest, and a proper meal, including the medics, eventually.

"Next step after that will be to clean up the incredible mess you no doubt have made inside the Flagship. That includes dealing with all of the freshly-killed Warriors.

"I have just given special orders to Commander Yamato. He will be working with four of your Rangers who were guarding the toroidal section while you were directly engaged with the enemy. They are currently putting six freshly-killed Warrior corpses back into hibernation chambers. I'll tell you why later.

"You might think that I overstepped your command to assign the four Rangers to Commander Yamato, but, well, I could not reach you until now.

"Perform the same routine as last time with the other Warrior corpses. Strip them naked, and itemize everything taken off their bodies. Take before-and-after digital images of each Warrior. Then pitch the corpses out into space through the shuttle docking hatch. Pitch them down-trajectory, into the Flagship's wake.

"Make sure everyone in your company knows we will be conducting proper space burial services over here for all of our dead. This is formalized action is very important for morale. People need to grieve. And funerals are for the living. It helps them on their personal journey towards full acceptance and recovery.

"But sorry, more about all of that later, when you are properly rested. Okay, Captain, that is all for now. Execute your new orders! Over."

"Yes, sir!" Fitzpatrick barked in reply. "Over."

As he started bending his stiff and cramped limbs to comply with the fresh set of orders, Fitzpatrick smiled to himself. He had just been kicked into action like he really was just a 'mad dog'. But he really appreciated the commodore's motivational and highly-complimentary speech.

He decided once again that he was glad Chamberlain was in charge.

30

Commodore Chamberlain was pleased that everyone showed up on time for the midnight, shift-handover command staff meeting.

Of course, they had not had one of these meetings for a while. He grinned inwardly that everyone had been rather preoccupied lately.

He hoped that he had given everyone enough time to get some proper rest. But there were some pressing, heady matters that just had to be discussed.

When everyone was seated around the table, in his usual way, Chamberlain said loudly and bluntly, "Commander Yamato, please provide us with your watch report."

"Yes, Commodore!" Yamato barked. "Our situation is nominal. We have no impairments with any of our systems. The same can be said for the captured Warrior Flagship. We have had no incidents of note with naval crew members or with Ranger personnel.

"Oh, and I *personally* disposed of the old coffee maker in the bridge after it crapped out on us yet again. I am pleased to say it is now in the wake of the Flagship with the Warrior corpses. I must confess I truly enjoyed the experience of getting rid of it.

"Corporal Mitterrand of Ranger Special Weapons and Equipment just surprised us by delivering a new coffee maker to the bridge. Apparently, he has been secretly constructing it from scratch, as a hobby of sorts. I must say it makes an *excellent* brew, which will no doubt improve naval crew morale. I do not think this action warrants an *additional* citation for the corporal, of course. However, I believe honourable mention from yourself would be very well received, and further improve our inter-service relationship.

"That's about it, sir." He had somehow managed to keep a straight face the whole time he was speaking about coffee makers.

"Okay, Commander, maybe we really can get back to *nominal and boring* again?" replied Chamberlain with a quick smile. Then he frowned, and said quietly, "But our well-established, comfortable, coffee-drinking routine was *definitely* broken recently, of course."

Chamberlain paused to look around the table. He was pleased to see that everyone looked well-rested, well-groomed, in good humour and very alert.

Captain Fitzpatrick had a long, stitched-up scar on the back of his right hand that obviously extended well up his arm. And he had a similar, ugly wound on his forehead. But otherwise he looked to be in reasonably good spirits. So Chamberlain asked him quietly, "How are the wounded Rangers coming along, Captain?"

"I am pleased to report that only one Ranger remains in serious condition, Commodore," replied Fitzpatrick. "But I'm talking about Private Klopp, and that proud Ranger is as strong as an ox. First Lieutenant Sweetwater believes his left leg can be saved, and that he should pull through okay."

Chamberlain then looked carefully at Sweetwater, and she just nodded, and offered a weak smile in return.

It was obvious that their first real combat experience had been highly traumatic for every member of the Ranger Company.

So Chamberlain said, "First Lieutenant Sweetwater, point forward, please provide the Command Staff with a weekly status report on the morale and condition of *everyone* on board.

"You know better than any of us about post-traumatic stress disorder. And I want to hear *fresh* ideas for keeping everyone physically and intellectually challenged with activities, preferably communal activities. Lonely people can become depressed people, especially with what this lot has been through."

"Yes, Commodore, I will be most happy to comply with that order!" Sweetwater said with passion. She now looked visibly relieved. Chamberlain concluded she had obviously been worried about this difficult matter herself.

Chamberlain paused for another long moment. Then he said, "I will now verbally share my own, highly-redacted status report with you people. Consider what you hear now as *highly classified*, and definitely for your ears only.

"Commander Yamato and four Rangers successfully injected thousands of capsules into six Warrior corpses. The capsules originated on New Earth. They contain two strains of an alien virus that we know is highly infectious and lethal to all three Master variants, even after further mutations, which we know will occur. The six virus-hosting Warrior corpses were then returned to hibernation chambers on the captured Warrior Flagship.

"Captain Fitzpatrick, I now want you to assign personally-selected Special Weapons and Equipment personnel to work with Commander Yamato to install those six hibernation chambers into Warrior scout ships. I am talking about one chamber installed per ship.

"The chambers must be able to be dropped under gravity, or slowly ejected, and then opened remotely on command from an artificial intelligence system we will install in each scout ship. So, that will no doubt require some creative engineering, and real craftsmanship. There will probably need to be a *considerable* amount of modification to the scout ships, and the hibernation chambers. But the commander will elaborate directly with you about all of that, later.

"Bottom line, Captain, make sure everyone takes their time, and gets this job done properly.

"Commander Yamato is going to be really busy. He has not exactly been slacking off lately, of course. Point forward, he and I will be *personally* working to install an over-riding artificial intelligence control system in the captured Warrior Flagship, and in each of the six Warrior scout ships. No one else will be involved with this top secret work, and I want you to *order* everyone in the naval crew and the Ranger Company not even to *speculate* about what we are doing.

"Now, I am extremely pleased to confirm that the captured Warrior Flagship, and the six attached scout ships, are *fully functional* in every way.

"And we now know the *exact* location of the planet of origin! I am talking about the place where Masters have established enough of a civilization to be able to send a Warrior seek-and-destroy Armada our way.

"And, by scrutinizing the commander's log on the captured Flagship, we now know for sure that the Master rulers intended to destroy New Earth *in its entirety*!

"So, none of us should feel *any remorse* when I tell you our *new*, very secret mission is to entirely destroy the Master colony that just tried to destroy us.

"We will be doing our part in that frankly Herculean effort by sending this now unmanned, and soon to be modified, Warrior Flagship back to its planet of origin.

"When we have sent this Warrior Flagship on its way, we will make our own way home, that is, back to Addy Moon Base.

"When we are underway, I will send a tight-beam, coded message to Addy Moon Base confirming that our mission has been *fully successful*. That is *all* I will say. And they will know exactly what that means. That's because we have executed our part of the overarching plan *perfectly*. You should all feel a great deal of pride in that accomplishment.

"Okay, that's it. I will not elaborate further.

"Some leaders back on New Earth might tell me later that I took far too much liberty with the interpretation of my letter of commission to share this top-secret information with you. If so, I will counter-argue that I simply needed your expert help. And furthermore, I will say that I strongly believed you all *earned* the trust, admiration and lasting gratitude of every member of our species. If they actually *do* take issue with *any* of our actions, my ass will be in a sling, so to speak, and not yours.

"But for the record, albeit top secret, you are now all under *direct orders* to never tell anyone what you have just heard. Breach of these orders will be considered treason, and will result in dishonourable discharge, or far worse.

"Now, are there any questions? No? Okay then, let us all work efficiently and effectively together to complete our remaining work program, so we can leave this ugly, depressing battlefield just as soon as we can, and return home to our friends and families.

"This meeting is now adjourned."

31

Prime Minister Patricia Hernandez was sitting hunched over, with her elbows resting on her massive, ornate desk. She was also resting with her chin on her fingertips, and unconsciously talking to herself.

Characteristically, she was worried about many things. Her many critics would consider most of the matters she was currently wrestling with as trivial.

But she had always struggled with prioritization. In her mind, everything *must* be dealt with, and immediately. As a result, her long term in office had taken an immense toll on her physical health. But thankfully, she was still as mentally acute as ever.

She was deeply absorbed with some rather obscure and indirect indicators about the health of the New Earth economy when the telephone on her desk rang. She was tempted to ignore the call, even though she could see by a glowing button on the hard-wired, highly-secure device that the call was from her soon-to-be-retired administrative assistant. She let the phone ring three times, then she snatched up the handset.

She snarled angrily, "Yes, what *is* it, Marge?"

This was an often repeated and blatant form of workplace harassment. If she had ever had a sincere one-on-one discussion with her subordinate, Marge would have told her this abusive, recurring behaviour was the reason she had finally decided to take up early retirement.

But Marge had always avoided conflict with her stern bully of a boss, and her intent was just to leave quietly.

So, as usual, there was a brief pause, and then Marge replied meekly, "I am very sorry to disturb you, Prime Minister, and I know this is against your scheduled meeting protocol. But General Nils Knudsen has just arrived in reception with two members of the Privy Council, ah, Chancellor Francis Maldonado and Dean Asher Weismann.

"They say they have a *significant* update to share with you, and they are looking for your immediate approval to pursue a recommended way forward. Should I send them away?"

Prime Minister Hernandez experienced a brief flash of *déjà vu*. And she briefly considered blowing off this brash, unscheduled intrusion of her privacy.

But she quickly checked herself. These three visitors were not people who could be blown off without consequence. So, instead, she sighed loudly and growled, "No, as it happens, I think I can spare a *few* minutes for them right now. Please show them in."

Then she sighed again, and added more pleasantly, "And Marge, I'm sorry I barked at you just now."

"That's okay, Prime Minister," Marge replied brightly after receiving a very rare apology from her boss. "Okay, here they come now."

The prime minister rose from her desk and formally greeted General Knudsen just inside her office door. The general's handshake was as firm as ever, and he was *still* a handsome devil, she thought. His hair was now mostly grey, but his posture and physique were as good as ever. And he still held the top post in the combined military and security force.

Knudsen's wife, Doctor Francis Maldonado, was following directly behind the general. Hernandez took a moment to carefully study her face as they shook hands. Francis now had many wrinkles around her eyes, but there was still a strong hint that she had once been very pretty. Francis had just announced that she would be retiring as Chancellor of Abubakar University. However, she was still very active in politics. Unfortunately, she leaned to the left, whereas Patricia Hernandez was solidly middle-right.

Following directly behind Francis was Doctor Asher Weismann. He was dressed in a frumpy-looking, tweed suit. He was not aging very well. After his wife passed away, he went back to wearing cheap, plastic, black-rimmed eyeglasses. But he was still the Dean of Astrophysics and Space Engineering at Abubakar University. There was a widespread rumour that he planned to remain in that position until the day he died. He was a devoted academic, and really did not give a *damn* what people thought about his personal views, or his appearance.

The prime minister motioned for everyone to take a seat in the adjacent lounge area of her office. When everyone was settled, Hernandez said abruptly, "Well, isn't this interesting? Judging by this *elite* cast of characters, and our shared turbulent history, might this meeting have something to do with *aliens*? And, you know, I am almost *certain* that I have said something like this before to you three people."

Knudsen cleared his throat, and said calmly, "Yes it does, Prime Minister. The current concern is not with our secret alien friends and allies that we have come to call the *Collaborators*. Rather, it concerns the infamous aliens of antiquity, that we have always called the *Masters*.

"Firstly, we have a highly significant update to share with you.

"Secondly, we have a forward plan that is completely aligned with our previous discussions with you, and with our overarching battle plan, which you secretly approved."

Knudsen leaned back for a moment, and quickly glanced at his wife, and his close friend, Weismann. They both looked very grim, but they nodded back at him for support.

"If you recall," Knudsen continued, while turning back to directly engage with the prime minister, "Five of our robot frigates intercepted a Warrior Armada of seven battlecruisers after they entered our Oort Cloud. Six of the Warrior battlecruisers were completely destroyed. The remaining battlecruiser was effectively disabled by a lower intensity, directed-beam gamma ray strike. As we suspected, that vessel proved to be the Armada Flagship.

"Our robot ships then chased down and destroyed three Warrior scout ships that had managed to escape the initial barrage. That took some doing. The enemy Warrior pilots proved to be tough and determined, and their little scout ships proved to be highly nimble and incredibly well-armed.

"During the search-and-destroy mission, one of our robot frigates was completely destroyed, and two others were damaged, but not to the extent that they were totally crippled.

"The four remaining frigates then took up watch-keeping duty near the disabled Warrior Flagship that was still moving through our Oort Cloud.

"In parallel, to intercept the Warrior Armada, we had deployed our only manned battlecruiser, the *Indefatigable*, with a Company of Rangers aboard. Commodore Mustafa Chamberlain was commissioned and placed in independent command of the attack force. Thankfully, as things turned out, our battlecruiser and Company of Rangers only had to deal with *one* disabled Warrior battlecruiser. Still, that proved to be a highly significant challenge. But more about that in a moment.

"That is because we are pleased to be here today, Prime Minister, to tell you that two days ago we received a light-speed, tight-beam, elaborately-coded transmission from Commodore Chamberlain.

"It took us quite a while to decode and analyse the very large file he had attached to his very short message.

"In his brief message, the commodore simply advised us that the intercept and capture mission had been *completely successful*, and that his battlecruiser and four surviving robot frigates were returning to Addy Moon Base."

The prime minister's facial expressions then went through a remarkable series of dramatic transformations. She first recoiled with surprise. Then she looked relieved, and even a bit gleeful. Then after another long moment, she returned to her typical, defensive if not outright cynical demeanour. She looked stern again, and even a bit angry. Then she mumbled through gritted teeth, "Tell me *all* about it, General."

"Prime Minister, the large file attachment that Commodore Chamberlain sent to us is his formal, complete battle report," Knudsen began. He was still calm and composed. "We will share that with you by secure email, should you wish to study it at length. And we recommend that you *do indeed* study it at length.

"What they achieved way out there in the Oort Cloud was both remarkable and heroic. We think you will agree the commodore's report is very well written, and comprehensive.

"For now, in a nutshell, please be advised that the Warrior battlecruiser was successfully boarded. That required a lot of ingenuity, as it was out of stabilizing control, and it was rotating around two axes.

"The spearhead Ranger boarding party entered the main, zero-G fuselage of the battlecruiser. No Warrior corpses were found in that section of the vessel. Of perhaps greater concern, they could not initially find a way to access the engine compartment located at the very aft of the vessel. That aspect of the initial phase of the operation proved to be highly significant.

"Thankfully, the boarding party *did* find a way to access the bridge, which they determined was located within a separate, toroidal section of the gigantic spaceship.

"Fifty Warrior corpses were found there. That makes sense, as that would place them within the more comfortable, full-gravity section of the normally spinning vessel.

"The Warriors had apparently all been killed by our Alpha robot ship's artificial gamma ray burst.

"Our computer and systems experts then tried to break into the Flagship's control and data management system. They first set about restoring the internal power and ship stability control systems. That required hacking through *seven layers* of elaborate, password-protected firewalls. But they managed it all somehow.

"Unfortunately, about a day after the power was restored in the vessel, an attack was mounted by *fifty* Warriors against our Rangers!

"They had been hibernating in a heavily-shielded chamber adjacent to the engine compartment. There must have been an independent, automated command and control system that kicked them out of hibernation just as soon as power was restored.

"A vicious, mostly hand-to-hand battle then ensued. Thankfully, our Ranger Captain, Joachim Fitzpatrick, on his own initiative, had very creatively and professionally armed and trained his company in the use of archaic but nevertheless highly lethal weapons. They confirmed the hard way that these weapons could be used to kill Warriors in body armour, while not damaging the vessel or its contents.

"In the end, eighteen Rangers were killed, and twenty-two were wounded. But *all fifty* of the post-hibernation Warriors were killed. None of them wanted to surrender. It was a fight to the death for them, which frankly led to one of the goriest and bloodiest battles that can be imagined.

"Subsequently, the Warrior Flagship was stripped of everything of immediate use to our attack and salvage force out there, or that might improve our understanding of the Masters.

"Many curious devices were found. More importantly, the Warrior Flagship Commander's log was located and uploaded to our battlecruiser. It was then fully translated and analysed. Commodore Chamberlain attached the translated variant of the log in its entirety to his recent transmission."

General Knudsen then turned to nod and smile at his close friend, Weismann.

Doctor Asher Weismann then cleared his throat and said, "Prime Minister, the ship's log has given us the *exact* coordinates of the Master colony that sent the Warrior Armada to destroy us. We now know that colony is on a rocky planet in a star system about 80.2 New Earth Light Years away from us.

"Looking back at the timelines, it seems that the Master civilization *must* have received the transmission that 'the Collaborators' told us about. You know, the one from the failed, follow-up, Master exploration visit to New Earth."

Prime Minister Hernandez just stared back blankly, so without referring to any notes, Weismann added, "If you recall, Prime Minister, that message said:

'We have confirmed the failure of our first attempt at colonization on the planet. Expect to encounter an advanced, competitive, probably hostile alien civilization when you get here. The ecosystem of this planet is toxic to us right now, and will no doubt be far worse after generations of further alien intervention and contamination. Annihilation of the entire planet is therefore recommended, if you have the technology.'

Weismann then added, "That message had been sent at light speed, and it referred, of course, to New Earth, and to our species.

"It seems that as soon as the message was received by the nearest Master colony, the leaders there ordered a Warrior Armada to attack us. It looks like that Armada had been previously engaged in another search-and-destroy mission. They had been exploring the blasted ruins of a suspected 'enemy' base on a moon orbiting a rocky planet in a star system that is only 12.3 New Earth Light Years away from us! They referred to the *enemy* as something like 'the Cowards' or perhaps 'the Retreaters'.

"They could very well have been referring to the highly-intelligent and advanced alien species that we call 'the Collaborators'."

Knudsen then intervened, and said, "Thank you, Dean Weismann. That was a good summary, sufficient for now.

"Prime Minister, when Commodore Chamberlain realized he had found this *critical* piece of information, he immediately and correctly set about making the captured Warrior Flagship ready to return to its planet of origin. Only, as planned, it would be returning with a... ah... *highly toxic* cargo, and the means to precisely deliver that cargo.

"Furthermore, the commodore and his staff officers devised a way for the Warrior Flagship to be controlled by a very elaborate over-riding artificial intelligence system. But more about that later.

"For now, just know that in line with our overarching battle plan, the one that you approved a while back, the Warrior battlecruiser is now traveling directly to the nearest and only known Master colony at about one-twentieth of light speed.

"Now, in addition, it seems the Warrior's communication protocol was highly restricted. In the event of failure, a rigidly prescribed message was to be sent. And in the event of success, a different, also rigidly prescribed and very brief message was to be sent.

"So, Commodore Chamberlain sent the prescribed 'full success' message from the bridge of the captured Flagship just before the vessel was sent on its way home. The message was directed in a tight beam at the planet with the offending Master colony, or more precisely, where that planet will be in space 80 years from when the message was sent.

"Commodore Chamberlain exercised his own initiative in deciding to send that message. But I believe his decision is fully in line with our overarching plan, so I fully support what he did.

"So, where does all of this leave us, you may want to ask?

"We suggest, Prime Minister, that we are now ready to exercise *our* part of the remaining battle plan. General Ibrahimović on Addy Moon Base has recently informed us that two highly modified robot frigates are now fully operational, loaded with... ah... *cargo*, and ready to go. The two frigates are parked in standby mode in a stable orbit around Addy.

"Are you okay with this so far, Prime Minister? I know we have presented you with a *lot* of information to absorb, and to ponder..." He trailed off with a questioning look.

"Yes, I think so," replied the prime minister with a bit of hesitation. After a moment, she said quietly, "I remember some parts of the 'overarching plan'. I *definitely* remember that it will deliver the harshest punishment we can possibly devise. Are we sure we still want to do that?"

Knudsen then looked tenderly at his wife, and asked with a bit of discomfort, "Francis, would you take that question… ah… the toughest one?"

Without hesitation, Francis said forcefully, "Yes, Prime Minister, we are absolutely *convinced* this still has to be done.

"The Master civilization that attacked us will not stop at just one attempt to destroy us. In eighty years or so, they will believe that they have succeeded. And that is exactly what we want them to think.

"They *may* be able to detect in a highly limited way our continuing artificial electromagnetic transmissions. Those are blasting out into space radially, and therefore degrading by the inverse square law. If the Masters are able to detect our transmissions from eighty light years away, they must then also untangle a hopefully indecipherable, mixed-up jumble of nonsense.

"They will eventually be able to detect their returning battlecruiser, and they will note that it is unescorted. They will also know that surviving

Warriors would have returned to hibernation for their long journey home.

"And we know by established Master protocol that *nothing* can be communicated further from a returning Flagship until the Commander of the Armada directly reports *in person* to the highest leader within the Master civilization.

"So, the Masters most likely will not suspect something is amiss until the Warrior Flagship returns to close proximity to their planet, and well after our two robot ships have covertly gone to work with their independent biological attack mission.

"All of that will not occur of course for about sixteen hundred years or so from now…" She trailed off with a gulp, and a look of horror. She had remembered again the many deaths that would ensue, albeit Master deaths.

There was a prolonged moment of silence. Everyone was very uncomfortable as they wrestled with their own thoughts.

Finally, Prime Minister Hernandez took a deep breath, and then said clearly, "You absolutely did the right thing by coming here today. Thank you all for doing that!

"Friends, we will now proceed with the rest of our secret plan. Of course we will! Only future inner-circle, government leaders will ever know about it. And I sincerely hope they will all agree that the four of us, or rather that I, as your Prime Minister, did the right thing."

"Now, General Knudsen, I can only spare about ten more minutes for our impromptu discussion. So, remind me with appropriate detail what will happen next…"

32

After sixteen-hundred and twelve New Earth years, the Collaborator-inspired, human-designed artificial intelligence system, or 'controller', was still actively managing the stripped-down, 101,408 tonne Warrior battlecruiser. The vessel had been travelling through interstellar space at about one-twentieth of light-speed since it had departed the outer reaches of the Sol-system.

The 'AI' controller decided it was time to decelerate the former Warrior Flagship at about ten metres per second squared. This manoeuvre was the long-established, Master 'standard' for a returning Warrior battlecruiser. But after eleven days, the controller greatly deviated from the Master protocol. Just prior to entering the outer reaches of the stellar system's Oort Cloud, it decided to expend most of the vessel's remaining fuel load. It quadrupled the rate of deceleration, and slowed the vessel to about 200,000 kilometres per hour.

Sixteen centuries before, the controller had been ordered, by the long departed Commodore Chamberlain, to essentially ignore the planetesimals within the Oort

Cloud. So, the controller did not worry about making any evasive manoeuvres while it penetrated the outermost regions of the distant stellar system.

Chamberlain knew that the Oort Cloud would mostly be just empty space. So, the chance of actually hitting something within it would be infinitesimally small. Chamberlain had also rigidly defined the captured battlecruiser's first and primary mission. The controller had been ordered to release the six robot-Warrior scout ships within the outermost fringe of the Oort Cloud.

The relatively small but highly manoeuvrable scout ships were each equipped with an independent AI controller. In contrast, Chamberlain had ordered each of those controllers to take *great* care to avoid collisions, and detection.

After successfully releasing the scout ships, the AI controller on the Warrior battlecruiser focused on completing its secondary mission. It fired-up the vessel's powerful ion-drive system again to accelerate at maximum thrust. Its new goal was to intercept and crash into the planet where the Masters had successfully established a colony.

The Warrior vessel quickly expended all of its remaining plasma drive fuel load. But it did manage to increase its speed to about 250,000 kilometres per hour. The ionized radiation glow from its thruster exhaust caught the attention of the Masters in charge of the planetary defence system. The Warrior vessel started receiving tight-beam, electromagnetic hails on the Master's standard orbital traffic-control frequency. The messages were repeated every few minutes or so. The space traffic controllers were requesting an explanation for the vessel's very unusual and alarming activity.

The AI controller on the Warrior battlecruiser noted the *exact* point of origin of the query messages it was receiving. It then decided it would target that location on the surface of the quickly approaching planet. The AI controller also noted with great precision the speed of rotation of the target planet, and refined its modelling of the planet's orbital trajectory. It then made minor but very precise adjustments to the battlecruiser's trajectory to impact the selected surface target on the planet.

The Masters' query messages became more frequent and more frantic as the battlecruiser continued on its now obvious collision course.

The AI controller then sent one very brief, tight-beam message directly at the target surface location. In the language of the Masters, and in a standard Master code, the message said the equivalent of:

"Mayday! Mayday! Battlecruiser Number 7 is out of control. Multiple system failures after collision with an ice ball. The Warriors in hibernation have all been killed. Only three Warriors are at bridge stations. We have no fuel remaining on board. And we are losing internal power. We are—"

The transmission suddenly ended at that point.

The Master orbital traffic controllers on the target planet then ordered multiple land-based and space-based defence systems to try to destroy the incoming and seemingly out of control battlecruiser. But even if those systems could target the vessel properly, there was really nothing they could do about it. The vessel was simply moving too fast.

What was happening was unprecedented. And no Master had ever thought it even remotely possible.

When they realized that destruction of the inbound vessel was impossible, the orbital traffic controllers relayed a message to the Warrior battlecruiser from Master high-command. The message simply said, "Blow yourselves up!" over and over again.

But the AI controller decided it would be best not to even acknowledge these last minute, frantic, self-destruct orders from the target planet.

The Collaborator-inspired, human-contrived AI system controlling the battlecruiser was not self-aware. It could not feel remorse, or fear, or even *consider* changing a decision once it had been made. Its own destruction was just part of the overarching plan. And that plan *must* be executed fully.

To determine kinetic energy, one multiplies one-half the mass of a moving object by that object's velocity *squared*.

The battlecruiser slammed into the atmosphere of the target planet at a ninety-degree angle to the planet's centroid. The resulting shock wave, heat wave and explosion transferred most of the inherent kinetic energy to the atmosphere of the planet.

The energy released was equivalent to the detonation of sixty megatons of TNT, or 2,4,6-trinitrotoluene. The explosion mostly resembled the air-burst of a thermonuclear weapon. But a large ball of still-speeding, molten debris impacted and exploded on the land surface. It created a kilometre-wide crater and a massive gas and dust plume.

The horrible aftermath of the collision was long-lasting. It proved to be a very useful distraction for the six robot scout ships. They all successfully evaded detection. They also had very little difficulty picking out their own primary landing targets on the planet.

Still, to be on the safe side, each scout ship selected and traversed its own highly-convoluted course to reach its landing target. The scout ships all made a lot of twenty-G turns. They could manoeuvre right to their structural G-force limit because they had no living cargo to protect. If an attempt had been made to stop them, nothing could have come close to intercepting them.

But as it turned out, the scout ships did not have to worry. They encountered no resistance as they made their way to the planet's surface.

It was typical for Warrior scout ships to manoeuvre in the atmosphere of a Master planet while on practice exercises. The Warriors rarely filed flight plans for these kinds of missions. The Warrior variant of the Master species had special status within the Master culture. Warriors were in fact revered, and no 'ordinary' Master would ever dare to question their actions.

The scout ships had all targeted locations with thick natural vegetation. The fundamental assumption was that where there was thick vegetation, there would also be lots of animal life.

The Masters always selected planets for colonization that had a relatively high diversity and abundance of native plant and animal species. It was thought that applying this criterion would provide them with the necessary feedstock for their genetic re-engineering programs.

And within a community of native wild animal species, there would undoubtedly be carnivores and scavengers. So, the AI controller on each scout ship had a simple goal: deposit the scout ship's cargo, the frozen Warrior corpse, in a place where the thawed-out meat of the corpse would likely be eaten by wild animals.

When animals ate a thawed-out Warrior corpse, they would also consume the thousands of tiny, virus-containing capsules imbedded in the flesh of that corpse. And those animals would then become unknowing and probably unaffected hosts for the propagation and spread of rapidly-mutating virus strains.

The Collaborators had advised their human allies that those mutated virus strains would *all* be lethal to Masters in any of their three 'standard' forms.

The scout ships had ancillary ram jets, and variable-axis turbofans. They could fly in an oxygen-rich planetary atmosphere like a fighter jet aircraft. They could also land vertically in very tight spaces. So, each scout ship had very little difficulty with landing on the surface of the planet, and then discharging its cargo load in a suitable place.

After the scout ships had each accomplished their primary mission, they all took off again. Then they each selected an isolated, secondary land location to target. This time however, they applied the criterion that their next land target must also be rocky and non-vegetated.

The scout ships all accelerated to great speed, and then slammed themselves nose-first and straight down into their selected terminal ground targets. In all cases, their destruction was almost total.

Later, a curious Master accident investigator might find some small residue bits to examine. But there would be very few forensic clues left to help identify the source of the wreckage, let alone the cause of each apparent disaster.

33

Over the span of a week, two highly-modified, interstellar, 'robot' frigates rapidly decelerated from one-twentieth of light speed to a virtual stand-still at the outer edge of the distant star system's Oort Cloud. They were each guided by an independent AI controller that did not have to be concerned about sustaining a human crew, or over-stressing such a crew through prolonged elevated high G-forces.

The arrival time of the two robot frigates was impeccable. It was now just a little over two days since another AI controller on a captured and slightly modified Warrior battlecruiser had devised and implemented that vessel's destruction, as well as its own destruction.

The massive explosion that resulted when the Warrior battlecruiser collided with the target planet greatly helped the two robot frigates penetrate the Oort Cloud undetected. And the nightmarish aftermath of the impact explosion was still occupying the Masters' full attention on the afflicted planet. The Masters were forced to deal with many highly-unusual, very concerning and immediate matters. Monitoring activity in the far reaches of their solar system simply had to be deferred until something resembling normality could be restored.

The two robot frigates immediately went to work on their assigned multi-year plan. They kept each other informed about what they were up to so they would not duplicate efforts, or interfere with each other in any way. But their New Earth human programmers had given them considerable tactical freedom to work independently within an overarching strategy.

Their fundamental, repetitive approach was simple in concept, but incredibly difficult to operationalize.

Firstly, a robot ship would search for the next potentially suitable planetesimal within the Oort Cloud. In general, a large ball of dirty ice between one and three kilometres in diameter would suit nicely.

The first step was to estimate the selected planetesimal's overall density, and the uniformity of mass distribution within it. To help refine these estimates, the robot frigate's controller would typically direct two to four heavily-armoured 'penetrating probes' to intercept and impact with the planetesimal. These probes would strike the object with high velocity so they could penetrate deeply below the surface. The impacted probes then performed a suite of passive and active subsurface measurements *in situ*, and some chemical analyses. The acquired data was then sent back to the robot frigate on a radio frequency. The number of probes deployed depended upon the degree of agreement within the acquired dataset.

Then the AI controller on the robot frigate would estimate the object's overall mass, and the location of its centre of mass. Radar and optical scans were used to map the shape of the object in great detail. Also, spherical integration and many iterations were performed using elaborate numerical methods.

With this processed information, the robot frigate's controller would then determine where to direct two to four 'cargo pods'. These pods were heavily shielded to protect their contents from infrared and other forms of radiation. Also, an 'explosive pod' was deployed in a spot well away from the cargo pods. It had a plutonium-core, and was basically an implosion-type of fission bomb, with an explosive yield equivalent to about one kiloton of TNT.

All of the pods would gently land on the surface of the object. Then they would burrow and melt themselves below the surface. They would work themselves as deep as they could go towards the centre of mass before their power reserves ran out.

The cargo in the non-explosive pods outwardly resembled the grape shot contained in the 'canisters' that were once fired from cannons to kill sailors on wooden sailing ships during Earth's turbulent, war-filled history. These canisters, however, contained thousands of capsules that in turn contained billions of the virus-like germs known to be deadly to Masters.

Each capsule was shielded with an outer coating of an insulating and ablative material, and an inner iron-compound shell that would rapidly corrode in a water-wet, oxygen-rich environment. And the billions of viruses in the centre of each capsule were mixed into a protein-rich paste that creatures like insects and wild animals might find rather tasty.

Next, the robot frigate's controller would direct two to four 'thruster pods' to the surface of the planetesimal. These pods would burrow down a bit, and then pin themselves firmly to the surface of the object by firing explosive bolts. Then the direction of thrust was remotely adjusted by the robot frigate's controller to align with the location of the planetesimal's estimated centre of mass.

Then the robot frigate's controller would fire a thruster briefly, and carefully observe the result. It would carefully note the resulting minute change in the object's trajectory, refine its estimate of the mass and centre of mass of the object, plan the next thruster burst, and then fire that thruster.

This process was repeated until the robot frigate's controller was satisfied that the planetesimal had been successfully 'nudged' on to the new, desired intercept course through space.

Then the robot frigate's controller would look for another suitable planetesimal to convert into a biological, weapon-delivery vehicle.

The robot frigate would continue its work program until it ran out of fuel, and supplies. It was highly unlikely that it would ever be observed by a Master sensing device, and by extension, destroyed by a Master-controlled weapon.

From a long way away, a robot frigate looked like any other object in the Oort Cloud. And those other, natural objects often changed course suddenly through random interactions. The cloud of dirty ice balls was known to the Masters to be a source of comets.

The ultimate goal of the New Earth attackers was to direct infected planetesimals to intersect the orbit of the target planet, ideally on the opposite side of the system's central star. There, the small nuclear device would detonate. The hope was that the planetesimal would break into smaller bits that would attract less attention and concern on the planet that had been colonized by the Masters. The additional hope was that these bits would not disperse too far, and that a lot of them, or hopefully most of them, would end up in decaying orbits around the planet.

Then, the final hope was that the ablative coating on the 'grape shot' would protect the internal biological cargo during the high-speed and very hot plunge through the atmosphere. It was also hoped that the grape shot would land somewhere wet where its iron-based shell would quickly corrode, and release the virus cargo into a natural environment.

The Collaborators had used a similar approach successfully on New Earth with their multi-eon spanning Pyramid Project.

Replenishing a supply of deadly viruses within a natural environment over a period of time was known to be an effective way to kill a lot of Masters.

By various natural mechanisms, infection would spread to unknowing and probably unharmed host animals. And some of those creatures would come in contact with domesticated animals, or even directly with Masters.

And after infection, some of those Masters might spread the disease to other Masters before dying a horrible death in one form or another. And once established within a Master population, the viruses would mutate at an astounding rate, far faster than any virologists could ever hope to combat with new, targeted vaccines.

34

The King and Queen of the Master colony were suddenly very unhappy.

Until the recent disaster, when an expected, returning Warrior battlecruiser had inexplicitly exploded over the central defence facility, the Master royal family had been living a pleasant, decadent and romantic life of idle and pampered luxury.

Their names would probably be next to impossible for a human being to mimic and pronounce properly. In the chirping, high-pitched language of the Masters, the King's chosen name approximated something like, "Farthest-Seeing of the Most Elite." And the Queen called herself something like, "Most Glamorous Mother of Future Geniuses."

Vanity was a common trait within the relatively small Royal caste. That predominant behavioural trait may not have been especially revered by the greater population of Masters, but it was definitely and purposefully overlooked.

The King and Queen were the traditional ceremonial heads of state. They held mostly figurehead positions within the burgeoning, still colonial, but once again classical, Master society.

The planet had proven to be mostly disappointing to the Masters. It was rather weak in natural resources, and it was bit too cold for their liking. However, after an unusually long era of pioneering and hard labour, and many frustrations, a sustainable foothold had *finally* been established on the planet by the Explorer and Worker caste of metre-and-a-half tall, bearded and cloned hermaphrodites.

But thankfully, the temperate regions of the planet were relatively rich in flora and fauna, and there were many places where fresh water was abundant. A mostly agrarian economy was up and working, and no Master was hungry any more. And so far, the native environment did not seem to harbour much in the way of toxins or pathogens that could affect or infect a Master.

A brutish, native, herbivore creature had provided genetic feedstock for a useful, re-engineered, beast of burden. It looked like a weird cross between an Earth zebra and an Earth elephant.

However, there had been nothing on the planet that even remotely resembled a quadruped hominid. So, re-engineered, Master-like, semi-intelligent slaves were not an available resource. That proved to be both a good and bad reality.

On the bad side, Master Workers sometimes had to perform manual labour when robotic machines were unavailable, or not completely up to a necessary task.

And on the flip-side, there were no semi-intelligent animal competitors to worry about.

There were however many dim-witted but nevertheless ferocious and hideous predatory beasts among the highly-diverse native carnivorous species.

So, as soon as they could manage it, the hermaphrodite Explorers had brought the proper genetic modifiers out of hibernating cold storage, and set to work at re-manufacturing the Warrior caste of their species.

A Warrior baby started life in a laboratory. A genetically-modified sperm cell was injected into a genetically-modified egg cell. The tiny fusion of egg and sperm was then placed in the womb of a hermaphrodite surrogate 'mother'.

Because a Warrior baby was far larger at full-term pregnancy than a hermaphroditic baby, the Warrior fetus had to be surgically removed a month or two before the full gestation period.

The Warrior baby was then raised in a series of progressively larger and more elaborate incubators until it was a year or so old.

Then the Warrior child would develop into adulthood inside a highly-specialized orphanage and training facility with its brethren of large, muscular and aggressive eunuchs.

Master societies were very harsh, and very competitive. The education of a Warrior was therefore Spartan-like. There was very little if any nurturing, or intellectual mentoring. At any stage in their development, Warrior cadets that failed to come up to high, pre-set standards were put to death in a very public ceremony. This custom reinforced a simple message to *all* members of the colony:

Failure of any kind simply would not be tolerated.

So, a Warrior cadet would never experience the love of a mother or father. And it would never fall in love, and be able to procreate. But it would always relish the company of its equally brutalized comrades, and successful cadets would all eventually become Brothers-in-Arms, and a respected part of an elite corp.

The Warrior caste had been firmly established on the planet after a few generations. The Warriors were then able to take over all of the armed-service duties within the Defence Ministry.

When that transition occurred, the colony's hermaphrodite Council Leaders then set about recreating the Ruler caste of Masters.

The Explorer and Worker caste had to use a completely different set of genetic modifiers for their Ruler caste development project. The process was almost the same as the one used to produce Warrior babies.

But to successfully produce a Ruler baby, at various stages of development, the fetus in the womb had to be injected with additional genetic modifiers.

The process was very involved, and often failed miserably.

But in the end, the Workers successfully managed to create seven unique male-female 'couples'. Each couple then formed the nucleus of a self-sustaining Royal family.

The initial group of Royal babies were raised in an exclusive, highly-sophisticated orphanage. Unless there were special health issues, subsequent generations of Royal babies were raised in traditional Royal family settings by their natural parents, or rather by professional Worker servants assigned to the Royal household.

So, members of the Royal caste could have sexual intercourse. And they liked to do that, a lot. The Master Royals of antiquity were by disposition polygamous, and it was difficult for most re-created Royals to live up to the historical monogamous expectations.

The schooling of a Royal mostly centred on the Arts. They learned to play musical instruments, and they performed the many classical compositions for each other. They also learned how to create physical art forms, and they decorated their palaces with their works. And they functioned as architectural and aesthetic critics within the greater Master society.

But a Royal was not an especially fertile or intelligent member of the Master species. In time, though, each Royal family slowly grew in numbers through natural selection, and sometimes through deliberate cross-breeding to generate and maintain healthy offspring.

Over a number of generations, it was thought that the re-created Royal caste probably approximated the original, diverse, two-sex form of the original Masters on the Mother planet.

But what the colonial Masters referred to as their 'Archaic Era' was far too distant in both time and space to remember properly, even with the help of elaborate historical databases.

The members of the hermaphrodite Worker and Explorer caste were always by far the predominant variant within the Master species. They performed most of the societal support functions. They were also the intelligentsia, and the keepers of all archival data.

In addition, the Workers were always the assigned crew members on space exploration ventures.

Also, and most importantly, the Worker and Explorer caste always remained in ultimate control. They ran the *real* government.

There were seven bureaucratic Ministries in their government, including Defence, which the Warrior caste now essentially managed according to their own command and control system. The other traditional Ministries were Resource Exploitation, Health and Nutrition, Infrastructure and Energy, Information and Knowledge, Security and Justice, and Galactic Expansion.

There was also a ruling Council of seven hermaphrodite Ministers. The Council Leader represented the Defence Ministry, and was respectfully referred to as Commander-in-Chief.

A Warrior could never be a member of the ruling Council.

Usually, a councillor had previous experience as a Deputy Minister. The Council nominated its own candidate replacements, and then they consummated each promotion to the ruling table via a secret ballot process. The Council also decided who would be their leader, by unanimous agreement, through a series of elimination, secret-ballot elections.

When their colony had been *fully* established according to historical Master norms, the Council Leader was no longer called Commander-in-Chief. Rather, the Council Leader assumed a title that roughly translated as 'Prime Minister'.

And the Council itself changed its name to something like, 'The Cabinet'.

The hermaphrodite Prime Minster was immensely powerful. One of its functions was to decide which of the seven noble families would be the *ruling* family. And the prime minister could change its mind at any time. This led to a lot of entertaining infighting, intrigue and scandals within the Royal families. But it was thought that active competition within the Royal caste would foster a healthier, more vibrant greater society. The continual conflict usually ensured that the King and Queen were reasonably competent, and enthusiastic about their mostly ceremonial roles.

The King and Queen supposedly had veto power over important matters of state. In this capacity, the pair functioned as a sort of democratic 'Senate', which could occasionally suggest, 'sober second thought'. And so, the prime minister was supposed to at least *consult* with the King and Queen before formally announcing that a decision had been made by the Cabinet.

But of course, only the Cabinet knew for sure what matters it had discussed, and decided upon.

Usually, however, the prime minister very transparently and very precisely followed to the letter the elaborate, established process of consultation with the King and Queen. Historically, the primary goal of the prime minister was to maintain peace and tranquility, and project the *semblance* of a democratic, self-critical government with built-in checks and balances.

So, it was no surprise really when the current prime minister asked for a consultation meeting with King Far Seeing and Queen Glamorous.

The King and Queen accepted the prime minister's request, of course, but to them, it was always *unfortunate* when something unplanned disturbed their comfortable, typically self-serving, daily routine.

The prime minister was escorted into the Royal Chamber by two immaculately uniformed Warrior guards. The King and Queen were seated on magnificent, intricately-molded, highly polished, solid platinum, side-by-side thrones on a metre-high dais.

They did indeed look regal! They were both relatively tall creatures when standing erect, at slightly over two metres in height. And they had perfectly symmetrical, very handsome faces. Their skin was very dark and unblemished, and their shoulder-length hair was a lustrous strawberry-blond.

The prime minister was the only member of Master society allowed to directly engage the King and Queen in conversation. However, the prime minister was required by law to avoid eye contact with a bowed head until formally addressed.

Because this was an unscheduled, *ad hoc* meeting, to express their annoyance, the King and Queen made the prime minister wait an unusually long period of time before acknowledging its presence inside the Royal Chamber.

Finally, after only a quick glance at the prime minister, the Queen chirped bluntly and crudely, "Well, what is this about?"

The prime minister paused an unusually long moment before replying, to express *its* displeasure at this obvious show of disrespect. Then it said calmly, "Your Most Royal Majesties, thank you for the opportunity to speak to you with so very little notice. But there have been some recent *developments*. And these developments are a bit confusing, and perhaps rather *alarming*.

"If you recall, about a week ago, there was a *horrible* incident when a returning Warrior battlecruiser seemingly went out of control and subsequently exploded directly over our main defence base on the other side of our planet. As a result of that catastrophe, we have lost about half of our Warrior contingent, and about half of our overall space-monitoring and defence capability.

"The explosion resembled a nuclear detonation, in that it created a shock wave, an intense heat wave, and a destructive electromagnetic pulse. It immediately killed thousands of Masters, not just Warriors, and thousands more were seriously burned or wounded. Many of those injured Masters will also die.

"The electrical power distribution system on Continent Two was severely damaged, and it will take us months to repair that damage. Also, a plume of ash and somewhat toxic gases now encircles our plant within the upper atmosphere. As a result, we expect a *slight* drop in the intensity of solar radiation at ground level, and therefore a drop in global atmospheric temperatures for a year or so. Therefore, some crops could fail, and we will probably have to manage food shortages in some places.

"We are still gathering the data we require to develop a full recovery plan. But we sincerely believe we *will* fully recover if we manage things *properly*.

"Now, if you also recall, because of the relative scarcity of resources, our colony has only ever managed to build a fleet of seven space battlecruisers. And those battlecruisers have been away on multi-generation missions during most of the history of the colony.

"Since we have never been directly threatened from space, our long-term goal, from long before the start of your reign, has been to complete our first exploration, generation spaceship.

"We were greatly looking forward to the return of the seven-cruiser Warrior Armada that has been away on a search-and-destroy mission for centuries. We understood that the mission was a complete success, according to the transmissions we received centuries ago.

"It is therefore a great mystery to us why only *one* of the seven battlecruisers apparently accomplished the successful return journey. Transponder telemetry has confirmed that the returning vessel was indeed Battlecruiser Number 7, which our historical records show was also the Flagship of the Armada.

"The only intra-star-system transmission we received from the returning battlecruiser was a *distress* signal. It indicated that the vessel had been severely damaged after a collision with what it called an 'ice ball' in the outer reaches of our stellar system. The probability of such an event occurring is extremely low, but admittedly possible.

"A few one-Warrior scout ships *may* have managed to escape the catastrophe. But if that occurred, our ground-based and satellite-based monitoring systems failed to detect them.

"Of course, we were all greatly, ah, *distracted*, by the horrific explosion of the battlecruiser.

"We have not yet heard anything from non-registered Warrior scout ships. This may confirm that they do not in fact exist.

"But to be thorough, in time, when our abilities have been fully restored, we will conduct systematic ground searches for intact or destroyed Warrior scout ships.

However, those search efforts will have to be made over the *entire* surface of the planet, and also within the region of space directly surrounding our planet. So, this systematic search exercise will probably require *years* to complete.

"Meanwhile, to allow us to recover more quickly, we have temporarily suspended the construction of our exploration, multi-generation space vessel. If we find we can resume geosynchronous orbital construction operations in a year's time, we estimate completion of the massive and highly complex vessel about eleven years from now, assuming we do not experience another unexpected and devastating *calamity*.

"To close our discussion for today, Your Majesties, do you have any questions, or perhaps some words of wisdom to guide us, or perhaps to *inspire* us, during this very difficult time?"

The King and Queen had been listening attentively with their mouths agape. Now they looked at each other in obvious confusion and fear. Finally, the King asked quietly, "How will this directly affect *us*?"

The prime minister could not help visibly recoiling with disgust at the King's blunt and stupid question. It said to itself, "What selfishness! And what the hell *good* are these *useless* creatures?"

But then the prime minister remembered the only message it really wanted to deliver to the Royal pair, and it calmly replied, "We will ensure that your personal well-being will be *mostly* unaffected, Your Majesties. But we will no doubt be asking you to make more frequent public appearances, on television of course, to help us restore morale within our society, and inspire us all to work harder."

The Queen huffed and snorted in response, and then chirped harshly with obvious distain, "*Well*, if we absolutely *must*, we must, I suppose. Now, this has been a *most* distressing conversation, Prime Minister, and *most* annoying! You can now leave our esteemed presence, so we can deal with more *important* matters!"

The prime minister decided it had experienced more than enough disrespect from these two snobbish fools.

So, it simply backed out of the Chamber, with many pauses to fully bow from the waist. It knew the well-established routine, and it gave the impression of fully respecting it, even though it found *all* royal intercourse to be tedious and demeaning.

35

The colonial Cabinet met as all Master hermaphrodite leadership councils had met, in any societal situation, for eons upon eons.

The colonial government Cabinet Chamber was circular and completely dark. The six ministers and the prime minister stood for their meetings around a circular table with a diameter of about four metres. The centre pedestal of the thick, dark-black, dull-finished, solid aluminum table was positioned in the exact centre of the room.

The prime minister stood on a quarter-metre-high dais, so its head was slightly higher than the other six ministers, or 'Speakers', as they traditionally called themselves in their meetings. A low-intensity, spherical, yellow-white lamp was positioned over the exact centre of the table, about half-a-metre higher than the head of the prime minister.

Everyone wore identical, form-fitting, flat-black coveralls so that only their pale, bearded faces could be seen. And everyone trimmed their head of short black hair, and their full black beard, exactly the same way.

Their positioning around the table was fixed, and sometimes that was the only way to remember who was saying what.

When they met for their meetings, the Cabinet members, including the prime minister, worked very hard to avoid eye contact with each other. They expected each other to keep their heads perfectly still, and their eyes fixed on the centre of the table. In fact, there was a small, red, flush-mounted, light-emitting-diode in the exact centre of the table to help them maintain their demonstration of proper etiquette.

In some of their meetings, the Cabinet would work towards making an important decision that the prime minister could then take forward for public referendum. Usually, however, a Cabinet meeting was simply for information sharing.

Normally the prime minister would start with some sort of welcoming statement, and a summary of Warrior Defence Force activities. Then each minister would speak in turn according to their position around the table, starting with the minister standing directly to the left of the prime minister. Positioning around the table was according to seniority. No government Ministry was ever favoured over another.

The six Speakers were free to say whatever they wanted when they had the floor. But they were all politically astute and ambitious Masters, and they all had their own agendas. To prevent bickering and grandstanding, the prime minister was the only Master allowed to interject at any time.

On this occasion, the prime minister started the Cabinet meeting in a very unusual way. It chirped harshly, "Speakers, the direct and indirect death toll from the mostly air-burst explosion over our primary defence base has probably peaked at three hundred and twenty-seven thousand, five hundred and twelve. The negative impact on our economy has been highly significant, but not totally crippling. Master life goes on mostly as before in most places. The climate has cooled a bit, but thankfully, not enough to lead to prolonged food shortages. We now expect to recover fully in seven years or so.

"We cannot dwell upon the bad things that have happened to us. But we *will* continue to fully investigate this calamity, to determine if there are ways we can better protect ourselves from a recurrence.

"As we discussed in our last meeting, we *all* have a role to play in refining and executing our modified space defence plan. We will not re-visit that program today, as we have just embarked upon it.

"However, Speaker Two, we have been hearing rumours that some sort of *epidemic* has started. *Illuminate* us all as to what is actually happening!"

Speaker Two was the Minister of Health and Nutrition. It was always highly prepared, and so it immediately and forcefully replied, "Cabinet members! We could be facing the emergence of yet another *crisis*, as if the one we just experienced was not bad enough!"

"Come, come, Speaker Two, it *surely* cannot be as bad as all that!" interjected the prime minister immediately with a series of sharp, admonishing chirps. "Calm yourself, and just relay the facts as you know them!"

Speaker Two deliberately paused for a moment, and then said slowly and carefully, "There are now *six* predominantly rural regions spread over three continents that are reporting outbreaks of diseases. The diseases have different and highly variable symptoms. But the diseases always seem to progress to death. And they are clearly highly *infectious*.

"We have performed numerous autopsies, of course. Analyses of tissue samples show the infections were most likely caused by microbes that we have *never* encountered before. They are extremely tiny, really just a protein shell that contains something resembling our core genetic material.

"No, that is not quite right. The stuff inside the protein shell is the *antithesis* of our genetic material! These barely living creatures use our cells for their sustenance and propagation, and they also seem to have the ability and propensity to *unravel*, so to speak, our controlling, six-component double-helix genetic molecule.

"And the propagation rate of this suite of probably related diseases is truly *alarming*! And the suspect microbes also seem to mutate at an alarmingly high rate.

"Therefore, we must *immediately* enforce quarantines to slow down the spread of these infections within our species, or better yet, completely *contain* the infections until they die-off on their own, or until we can eradicate them completely by some currently unknown means."

The prime minister showed its discomfort by blinking rapidly a few times, but it somehow managed to maintain its rigid stare directly at the centre of the table.

But some of the Speakers just could not help flashing their eyes around to take quick peeks at both Speaker Two and the prime minister.

After a long pause, the prime minister asked, "Speaker Two, as a result of your emotional outburst, I have three rather *obvious* questions for you.

"Firstly, when did these disease outbreaks begin?"

"Prime Minister, first reports of these probably related diseases began about eighty-two days ago."

"Okay, then secondly, have the Warrior and Royal castes been affected as well?"

"Prime Minister, not yet, possibly because those revered variants of our species do not visit rural or agricultural areas that are often adjacent to wilderness areas. But there is nothing to suggest that the Warriors or the Royals have some sort of differentiating natural immunity."

"Okay, thirdly then, can your Ministry devise and manufacture vaccines to either cure infected subjects, or to prevent infection from occurring in the first place?"

"Prime Minister, we believe so, but that very difficult and highly technical work has only just begun. And of course, evolving mutations could possibly frustrate our efforts, no matter if the vaccine research and development program proceeds with our typical efficiency, dedication and intelligence."

The prime minister paused for another long moment, then it ordered loudly, "Then a*ccelerate* the vaccine production effort, Speaker Two. We must try to out-race the speed that mutations occur."

The prime minister then took a quick glance at both the Minister of Infrastructure and Energy, and the Minister of Resource Exploitation.

Then it ordered, "Speakers One and Three, give the Ministry of Health and Nutrition whatever it needs for this priority activity.

"And Speaker Six, resources of *all* kinds are now scarce, obviously. Assist this priority effort by continuing to suspend work on our exploration generation space vessel. Ah, and issue a public statement, that we are, ah, investigating an exciting *new* technology for improving the vessel's design and functionality. But stress that we need to suspend the construction program for only a *very brief* period of time.

"And Speaker Five, how soon can your Ministry put in place *total* quarantines around the six infected regions? And can we do that without overly alarming the *unaffected* population?"

Speaker Five was the Minister of Security and Justice. It paused for an unusually long period of time before answering. Then it said, "Prime Minister, rumours are already rampant that there is an epidemic of some sort underway. I think the best we can do now is issue calming public statements, you know, to assure Masters that we are *right on top* of this epidemic. Furthermore, we should say that we are extremely *confident* solutions will soon be found, please stay calm everyone, do not interfere with our efforts, help us when we ask you for help, or for your patience, *et cetera*.

"That may not be enough of course. Enforcing curfews, and cordoning off very large areas will require *far* more resources than we normally have at our disposal.

"Unless, of course, we could enlist the services of some otherwise idle *Warriors*..." It trailed off, knowing it was taking a big political risk by crossing a jurisdictional demarcation line into the prime minister's exclusive domain.

But it need not have worried about that possibility. The prime minister immediately chirped in harsh tones, "Consider that *done*, Speaker Five. *Of course,* we can put our Warriors to work to help with this critically important effort. After all, we may be working for *our very survival* as a species.

"The Warriors, of course, will not like being under your authority. So, ah, try to allow them as much *independent* command and control as possible. And tell them this *request* for their help with domestic security matters came directly from *me*.

"Use those words *exactly*, Speaker Five. Stress that this is a *personal request* from me, even though *we* know if they balk, in any way, it will immediately become a *direct order*."

The prime minister then glanced briefly at Speaker Four. For the whole meeting, Speaker Four had impressively managed to maintain a fixed stare at the red dot in the centre of the table. The prime minister knew its character and wondered if it was holding something back. So, it abruptly barked, "Speaker Four, Speaker Two has just told us that *nothing* like this epidemic has ever occurred before. Is that a true statement?"

The Minister of Information and Knowledge hesitated briefly before answering. The prime minister risked taking another quick glance in its direction and noted that Speaker Four now looked *very* uncomfortable. Beads of sweat were popping up on its forehead!

Then the prime minister could not help turning its entire head to stare directly at Speaker Four. Then it barked again, "Speaker Four, answer the damn question! Right now!"

"Prime Minister, it is true that no epidemic like this has ever occurred on *this* planet," Speaker Four began tentatively. Its agitation was now disturbingly obvious to all of the other Cabinet members. After a short pause, it added quietly, "However, there are records that suggest this sort of thing may have occurred on *other* Master-dominated planets.

"Some of those other, related calamities led to some theorization that our primordial galactic enemies, ah, the 'Cowards' as we call them, somehow created the diseases, and *aimed* them at us, so to speak.

"It seems we were the *only* animal species affected in all of these recorded instances, which may give credence to the remarkably consistent origin theories that arose on other affected planets."

Then the Cabinet members all silently struggled for a while to assimilate and rationalize this rather shocking new information. They all had different paradigms, even though they outwardly looked to be identical creatures. This meant that they all took slightly different introspective routes towards personal understanding and acceptance.

After a very long pause, the prime minister said quietly, "All right, Speaker Four. Thank you. Keep exploring these theories for us."

The prime minister paused again to think for another moment, then it added, "Our colony has never directly encountered the Cowards, of course. But our colonial ancestors *did* send our only Warrior Armada to investigate some ruins on a distant moon that they thought might once have been a base used by the Cowards.

"That same seven-battlecruiser Armada was then sent on to attack and destroy *another and different* suspected dangerous race of alien competitors. But for some reason, only *one* colonial battlecruiser has returned to us from an apparently successful combined expedition. And that battlecruiser *somehow* ended up destroying itself and thousands of Masters by colliding with our planet!

"I think we can all agree that the recent rash of calamities are probably too remarkable and too mysterious to be *unrelated*?

"So, Speaker Six, point forward and until I order otherwise, work very closely with Speaker Four. Assist the minister in any way that you can! Work *together* to answer the most pressing question.

"Here is that question. Is there a potential link between the return of the Flagship battlecruiser and the emergence of these diseases? And if so, what is that link?

"Bring the answer, or perhaps answers, to our next Cabinet meeting, that we will have in, ah, five days' time."

The prime minister then paused to take a long, slow, deep breath. Then it loudly chirped, "Right, Speakers, that is enough for today. Thank you for your preparation, and your close attention.

"Our meeting is now adjourned."

36

The Warrior Commander knew it was a losing battle.

'Battle' was hardly the right word for this disgusting scene. It was really a brutal, small-scale, civil scrimmage, made worse by an invisible fifth column that killed from inside the bodies of the group of quarantined Masters.

The 'soldiers' of the fifth column were microbial foes that could not be seen, only felt. And when an unfortunate Master encountered the microbial enemy directly, the end would only be a few weeks away. And death by microbial infection was truly a horrible way to go.

The vaccines that had been issued to the general Master population seemed to be have been effective for a hundred days or so. But the situation was now degrading rapidly. And for some reason, infection seemed to spread quicker within the Warrior population than the hermaphrodite Worker population.

As for what was happening to the members of the Royal caste, well, who the hell knew? There were so *few* of them, and the spoiled bastards had always quarantined themselves, going back long before the first outbreak of infectious diseases.

But the commander had a job to do, no matter how risky that was on a personal level. Or, for that matter, how *disgraceful* it was on a professional level.

It walked over to the high, open window in the guard post again. It used binoculars to closely scan the nearby barbwire perimeter. There were still no signs of life on the other side of the wire. It had been this way for two days now. That was not necessarily a good thing.

There was nothing moving on the near side of the wire either. Warrior guards were either maintaining proper discipline by staying well hidden, or they were really sick, and maybe even giving up. The commander suspected it was now a mixture of the two possibilities.

And indeed, things were getting far worse.

Then the commander looked at its adjutant again, not with sympathy this time, but rather with disgust. The beastly, dirty, dishevelled creature had slumped down in a corner of the outpost, and fallen asleep!

"Number Two, wake up, you lazy bastard!" growled the commander in deep chirps.

The adjutant stirred a bit, and then leaped to its feet. It wobbled a bit, and croaked in raspy tweets, "Yes, Commander! Sorry, Commander, sir! I... I don't know *how* that could have happened. I am truly sorry,

Commander, Sir..." It trailed off with a look of both confusion and shame.

The commander glared angrily at its adjutant for a few long moments. Then it sighed, and shrugged, and said quietly, "I *know* how it happened, Number Two, and so do you. We both have not slept for over two days now. Our food is worse than lousy. Biting bugs are crawling all over us because we cannot clean ourselves properly. And our comrades are finally becoming *fed up* with this undignified guard duty, and they are getting sick, and some are dying.

"Now, I obviously need to vent a bit, Number Two. Your job is to carefully listen to me, and to offer alternatives for my consideration.

"Firstly, our morale is the *shits*!

"Our barbwire fence and our blasters have successfully kept the farm Workers inside the wire. That is just great. But we do not know how many of them are still alive in there. And that is *totally* unacceptable!

"But there cannot be many left, because we do not see them anymore. Now, I *could* send in a sortie of Warriors wearing germ suits and masks to investigate, but what is the damn point of that?

"It is *obvious* that the barbwire cannot contain the spread of the disease, or diseases. *Our* people have been getting sick for ten days now. And we cannot wear germ suits all the time. That is just not practical.

"And we cannot retreat either! Our orders are very clear on that point, and they have been reinforced to me *three times* over the last two days. Command treats us all like cowards. But we are not cowards. We must hold our station and guard the perimeter.

"Now, what are your suggestions for me, Number Two?"

The adjutant was a good officer, but it had obviously been highly stressed for a long period of time, and it was visibly fatigued by that ordeal. But after a long moment of thought, it seemed to relax a bit, and it said, "Right, Commander. Fully understood, sir.

"The fact is, sir, we clearly are all *doomed*, and there can no longer be any doubt about that.

"So, I suggest we wait, ah, one more day. If we still only see animal life on the other side of the wire, then I suggest we should *all* cross through the wire, without wearing germ suits. Because there *must* be food over there, and clean water. If we are all going to die eventually, then we should die with *dignity*, with a full belly, lots of intoxicants, and a few final laughs with our comrades.

"That is my suggestion to you for what it is worth, sir. It is made with the utmost respect for you, and for our company of heroic Warriors."

The commander initially looked angry at the response from its adjutant. But then it shrugged again, and smiled weakly. Then it said with a laugh, "Yes, that is actually a good, noble suggestion, Number Two. It honours and respects the finest traditions of our caste.

"So, I say… why the hell not!

"We are Warriors, damn it! So, we will all *die* like Warriors, and pretend we have won this *stupid* battle against an invisible, cowardly enemy."

37

The prime minister entered the extensively renovated Royal Antechamber with two attending Warrior guards. The room had been significantly reduced in size to about six metres wide, six metres long and three metres high. The two guards were wearing full-body, biological protection suits. They were also carrying rather large, bulky bundles on their backs.

Security cameras silently observed as the guards methodically unpacked their bundles. Then the cameras captured the work of the two guards as they patiently and gently helped the prime minister into its own, form-fitting, full-body biological protection suit.

When a sealed helmet had been firmly locked and sealed in place over the prime minister's head, the two Warriors sprayed the prime minister's 'germ suit' from head to toe with disinfectant. Then they carefully and thoroughly vacuumed all of the liquid off the prime minister's suit, and the deflected spray that had accumulated on their own suits, and on the white ceramic floors, walls and ceiling of the Antechamber.

Then the attending guards carefully re-packed their bundles and left the room. They closed the door they used, and re-sealed it from the outside.

The prime minister decided to sit down on the only bench in the room. Then the air flow dramatically increased. The prime minister remembered that over a half-hour period, the air in the room would be completely displaced at least twenty times with filtered, irradiated and chemically disinfected air.

Finally, the air flow subsided, and the door to a small, attached airlock automatically opened. The prime minister entered the airlock and closed the door behind itself. It then closed its eyes as fierce ultraviolet lights were turned on. It held on to handles on the walls while a very strong blast of circulating air bounced it around the tiny chamber. This battering went on for about five minutes or so.

Finally, the fierce air blast subsided, and the surrounding UV lamps were turned off. The prime minister opened its eyes and watched as the door to the Royal Chamber automatically opened.

The prime minister was now sweating profusely inside its germ suit. The suit itself made movement very difficult, and it greatly restricted peripheral vision.

The prime minister stepped very carefully through the open door. Two attending Warrior guards in full germ suits then stepped forward and assisted the prime minister as it lurched towards the King and Queen, who were sitting sedately on their thrones at the far end of the large hall.

When the prime minister finally reached the foot of the dais upon which the King and Queen were seated, it flipped on the microphone inside its helmet, and waited to be addressed.

After all of the indignities it had just been subjected to, incredibly and inconsiderately, the King and Queen made the prime minister wait while they continued a quiet and private chat with each other. This absurd scene went on for ten minutes or so. The prime minister noted with disgust that the Royal banter was trivial, and that the regal pair laughed with glee at stupid, silly, private jokes.

Finally, the Queen looked up at the ceiling and said, "You were *summoned*, Prime Minister, because we are *slightly* curious as to what has actually been going on out there in our world for say, the last one hundred days or so.

"We sometimes watch the domestic news reports of course, but they are so *boring*, and we *know* your government spins the worthless information presented to suit your own, selfish, political agenda.

"So, *illuminate* us now, with the *truth*! Begin!"

The prime minister deliberately waited a full minute before replying. When he could see the King and Queen were suitably angered by the obvious show of impertinence, it said calmly, "With the deepest respect, I take issue with your harsh criticism, my Queen. I *always* deliver the truth to you, and to the King. That is a matter of record. I know that everything said in this Chamber is recorded for posterity. And I have full access to *all* of those records."

The prime minister's voice was being projected over a loud speaker in the Chamber. The confining helmet over its head made its chirps sound muffled, and there was a slight time lag. The lag was annoying, but the prime minister decided it could be managed well enough with a little discipline on its part.

The King suddenly looked angered, but before he could reply, the prime minister added, "But you have ordered me, just now, Your Majesties, to tell you the *truth*, so of course, I will comply.

"The *truth* is, that after about three years of sometimes frustrating, and always intense struggle, we may *finally* be getting on top of the horrible epidemic that has been killing us in great numbers.

"The latest suite of vaccines are proving to be effective. And by escalating our rather *ruthless* quarantine program, disease outbreaks are quickly and effectively being confined so infected groups can die out on their own. Every corpse is being completely cremated, of course.

"But we have lost a staggering *three-quarters* of our Worker population through disease! That means our current *global* population is only about eleven-million Masters.

"For some reason, the Warriors have been especially hard-hit. They now number only about *twelve-thousand* in total.

"The Royal families, of course, have been effectively isolated from the epidemic, as you well know. But that is because they are venerated and privileged, and no expense has been denied them to install and maintain elaborate protection systems, like the ones we have installed for you in the Royal Antechamber.

"Our economy, and our defence capability, have obviously been devastated. We are just now starting to re-build, and to re-populate. It will take *generations* to fully recover, of course.

"We are *decades* away from resuming work on our first exploration, generation space vessel.

"And we no longer have the means to properly defend ourselves from attack from space. We *may* be able to start building a battlecruiser in five years or so. If so, it will not be ready for deployment for at least *ten years* after construction starts.

"We strongly suspect, but so far have been unable to prove, that the infections that have been afflicting us were *artificially produced*, by a foe, somewhere off of this planet. They seem to be remarkably tailored to affect us, but not other animals, like the native animals on this planet. Furthermore, those stupid beasts seem to be unwitting hosts for the spread of the infecting microbes.

"Worse still, these no doubt *alien* microbes mutate very quickly. This makes their ultimate and complete eradication very unlikely.

"The historical timeline suggests the appearance of these microbes *must* be linked somehow to the return of the Warrior Flagship battlecruiser, but we do not yet know how exactly.

"The Flagship completely disintegrated when it blew up in our atmosphere. No microbe could have survived that catastrophic, intense-heat event.

"However, we believe we have found the wreckage of one or possibly two single-Warrior scout aircraft, or more correctly 'spacecraft', in isolated locations. There are no colonial records of the loss of these scout craft, so they *may* have originated from the returning battlecruiser.

"But if so, we do not know how they managed to remain undetected when they entered our atmosphere, and then possibly flew around for a while in controlled airspace. Of course, we may have been rather *distracted* at the time.

"But there is nothing in the wreckage of these scout craft that indicate they could have been carrying biological weapons of some sort. And no Warrior bodily remains have been found with any of the wreckage, or near any of the wreckage, which in itself is puzzling. That line of investigation is continuing, but likely will lead us nowhere.

"Now, Your Majesties, this suit is *extremely* uncomfortable. Will that be enough of the *truth* for today?"

The King and Queen then covered their mouths with their right hands, and whispered to each other for a few more minutes. Then, while fixedly staring at the King, the Queen dismissed the prime minister with a callous flip of her left hand.

Then the two Warriors guards helped the prime minister back across the entire expanse of the Royal Chamber and into the air lock.

The prime minister did not even attempt to bow in the traditional manner during its long, tedious exit from the Royal Chamber. It knew it could blame the bulky germ suit for restricting its movements.

And it was frankly completely fed up with Royal protocol.

38

Speaker Two, who was also the highly stressed and greatly over-worked Minister of Health and Nutrition, called for an *ad hoc* Cabinet meeting right after the prime minister and Speaker One had passed away. Speakers Three, Four and Five were far too sick to attend, and in fact, were near death.

But Speaker Six, the bored, largely ignored and under-worked Minister of Galactic Expansion, showed up right on time for the meeting.

Speaker Two started the meeting with the usual formality. It stared at the tiny red dot in the middle of the table in the darkened Cabinet Chamber, and said quietly, "Thank you for coming on such short notice, Speaker Six, and for respecting the starting time that I requested.

"By default, I am today's Chair Master. I will not claim to be the prime minister. But we can talk about that later. That point might be moot anyway, considering our *horrible* and quickly deteriorating state of affairs.

"We are no longer even *trying* to keep up with rapid disease mutations through the research, development and manufacture of new vaccines.

"Three years ago, we naively thought we had achieved some sort of a steady-state stasis with our biological defence program. But then, the highly variable suite of infections seem to have become even *more* aggressive. We concluded that *wildly* new types of mutations were somehow appearing in our natural environment.

"Then two independent studies suggested that the original two strains of pathogens had somehow suddenly reappeared in our ecosystem!

"These two strains were, or rather are, especially *nasty*, using crude terminology. They mutate rapidly and unpredictably, and their mutated forms travel down entirely new and unpredictable pathways.

"One of our top scientists postulated that the two strains were, or perhaps are, being continuously replenished by comet or meteor debris. This scientist even claimed to have found some physical evidence to support this possibly unnatural phenomenon. The scientist alleged it had found, in widely dispersed wilderness areas, some small, spherical, metallic nodules with a protein-rich, probably *microbial-infused* centre.

"A few other scientists began to agree with this alarming new and unproven theory. But then they *all* died from a form of the infectious disease with millions of other Masters.

"But even if this greatly disturbing theory can be proven to be correct, there is frankly *nothing* we can do about it now!

"It *does* lead one to wonder, however, if we have been deliberately attacked with biological weapons, say by our arch-enemies of antiquity. I am referring, of course, to the alien race that we call the Cowards.

"But *again*, and frustratingly, we are no longer in a position to defend ourselves from such an attack, or to seek retribution.

"In summary, Speaker Six. I believe we are well past the point of recovery. My blunt assessment is that our colony has *failed completely*.

"Now, do you agree with this assessment?"

Speaker Two then turned to look directly at Speaker Six, and Speaker Six turned to look directly back at Speaker Two.

Speaker Six was obviously shaken by the information it had just received. It was trembling, and it looked highly stressed. It grabbed the edge of the circular table to steady itself. Then it said in wavering chirps, "Yes, and I am greatly sorry to say, that I *fully agree* with your assessment, Speaker Two.

"We are clearly all *doomed*!"

Speaker Two simply nodded in response. Then after a long moment of struggle with inner turmoil, it suddenly appeared to relax a bit, perhaps in resignation. It said quietly, "Right, that's *it* then, Speaker Six. This means, of course, that the remaining members of the Cabinet, specifically you and I, have but *one* task remaining.

"We must send out a high-powered, radial, electromagnetic broadcast, in all standard frequencies, and along all exploration mission vectors, to tell other Masters, wherever they are, of our humiliating failure to successfully colonize this planet.

"Now, before we terminate our final Cabinet meeting, please help me formulate the message we will send…"

39

The King and Queen of the Master colony had summoned the prime minister to the Royal Chamber, but for the first time in the history of their colony, the prime minister had failed to respond.

In fact, suddenly *no one* was responding to a Royal summons.

There were no longer any servants to call upon to bring them their rich food and drink, or to dress them in their fine clean clothes, or to bring them fresh, plush towels, or even to clean the many exotically-furnished rooms in the vast Royal Palace.

There was no running water in the palace. The toilets were full of their disgusting bodily waste, and the toilets would no longer flush.

And there was no electrical power, and no one to replace all of the emergency candles that had burned down to stubs. And it was almost as cold inside the palace as they imagined it must be outside in the open air.

Of course, they had never actually been outside of the palace during their entire lifetimes. But they had been told that the external environment could be harsh at times, and highly variable.

The King looked at his wife with compassion, and grave concern. Her eyes were closed, and she was shivering uncontrollably. She was emaciated, so her health problems might stem from starvation, and not from one of the horrible infectious wasting diseases that they had heard was killing commoners in great numbers.

Still, did it really matter at this point?

The King then realized he was feeling very hungry and very weak too.

After a long, agonizing, pensive moment, he finally accepted that their decline in health would accelerate until it ended with their rather horrible deaths.

So, he gently shook his wife awake, and softly chirped, "Open your mouth, my dear. I have a morsel of *exquisite* food for you, fresh from our chef!"

The Queen slowly opened her mouth in a semi-conscious state. The King placed the little pill on her tongue, and said tenderly, "Now, swallow that down quickly, my dear, so it can do you some good!"

The King watched as the Queen obeyed his suggestion. Then her eyes closed again, and she became very still. Her mouth opened slightly, and she made a little gurgling sound. And then her breathing completely stopped.

Then the King placed a similar pill in his own mouth, and quickly swallowed it down. He was unconscious in only a few moments, and his heart stopped shortly after that.

40

Eons ago, they had originated on an Earth-like planet.

Their system of counting time had always centred upon the archaic year, or the full cycle of orbital transit of their home planet around their home star.

They knew that distant star still existed. But they could never forget that their home planet had been completely destroyed by their arch rivals in the galaxy, the evil and selfish Masters.

Their clan had creatively fashioned a moon to suit their needs. It had a rocky, warmish core, with a thick outer layer of frozen, solid, low-molecular weight organic and inorganic compounds that included water. They lived far below the ice-rock interface.

But they still had many means to monitor activity in regions of special interest to them within the galaxy.

The two Elders surfaced together, and then swam over to a secluded part of the subterranean pool of warm, mineralized water.

They were quadruped amphibians, and they were naked. With a bit of imagination, they sort of resembled Earth's sea iguanas, minus a tail. In fact, the members of their clan called themselves something like 'The Sea Divers' or 'The Pool Divers'.

Over hundreds of thousands of years of evolution, their feet and hands had enlarged and flattened, and webs had grown between what once had been bony digits. Their skin was shiny and translucent, and was tinted with a swirling mixture of the many possible shades of blue and green. They had both lungs and gills, and they had a pair of forward-looking, rather large, membrane-covered, green-flecked eyes that could no longer blink.

They could speak under water when they wanted to, but it required more effort to speak properly, and to hear properly. And of course, sound travelled further under water, and the two Elders did not want anyone else to overhear this particular conversation.

Their language was both melodic and rhythmic. If a human being could hear them speaking, that person might think they were singing or chanting to each other. Of course, their words or lyrics would be unintelligible to any human being.

In any situation, the First Elder always had the honour of speaking first. When the pair were comfortably floating with their faces close together, the female First Elder whispered, or quietly chanted, something like, "Greetings, Second Elder. I understand you have something important to share with me. This is not really an opportune time, but I also understand that you think it is *very* important. So, please proceed."

"First Elder, thank you for this opportunity to speak with you on such short notice," said the other Elder very quietly, who was also female. "We have just intercepted an electromagnetic transmission. It heartens me greatly. We will keep it secret, of course, but I thought *you* at least should immediately know about it, too.

"It was broadcast radially. It was sent in the language of the Masters, using an ancient code that we easily recognized. Let me quote the translation for you now:

"*Colony two-four-eight has completely failed. Our condition was nominal until infecting microbes appeared in our ecosystem. The microbes may have originated from comet or meteor debris, but that is uncertain. Or, these microbes may have been carried back in a returning Warrior battlecruiser that visited the ruins of a suspected nearby Coward base. So, the Cowards may have done this to us, intentionally. But that is probably a moot point. Be advised that this planet is now completely toxic to Masters. Our vaccines only worked temporarily because the invading microbes mutated significantly and very rapidly. The native animals on this planet are hosts for the disease, or rather diseases. But the offending microbes do not appear to affect those simple creatures with their vastly different genetic make-up. So, we believe this place is now a threat to the survival of our species. Annihilation of the entire planet is therefore recommended, if you have the technology."*

"Now, what do you think of that message, First Elder?"

The First Elder silently pondered the startling new information for the equivalent of about five long minutes. Then she quietly said, or sort of sang, "Second Elder, Master Colony Two-Four-Eight is, or more likely was, about eighty light years away from us. I think this message means that our covert *allies* have successfully used our technology, and closely followed our guidance, to completely destroy a relatively nearby Master colony.

"The *allies* I am referring to are the intelligent creatures that called themselves *human beings* during our only meeting with them. That meeting occurred a long time ago, on a distant moon in this solar system. But if you recall, these human beings settled on the third planet in our adopted solar system, and eventually on its moon as well, the same one where our meeting occurred. Their adopted planet is watery and rocky, and they only live on land."

The Second Elder smiled pleasantly in the manner of their species. Then she sang, "Yes, First Elder, that is what the other Elders think, too. Except, two of our *brothers* think we should now send a brief 'thank you' message to our allies. However, all of the *other* Elders have spoken out strongly against that idea. What do *you* think we should do next?"

Without hesitation, the First Elder replied, "Second Elder, I will not agree to the sending of *any* message to *anyone* in response to this intercepted, widely-broadcasted plea to destroy a planet. We must remain, as always, *completely silent*!

"You see, we told our *allies* they would never hear from us again. And we asked them not to search for us, and they have complied with that request. Furthermore, we asked them to never visit the icy moon around the gas-giant, fifth planet in our adopted solar system, and they have complied with that request as well.

"So, our allies have *proven* to be as intelligent, trustworthy and brave as we hoped they would be. And they have learned to be much more careful about announcing their location, and by extension, *our* location.

"Since we first met them, they have reduced the density of their intra-planetary wireless communication broadcasts by at least *four orders of magnitude*.

"And with the many gifts we gave them, and our indirect mentoring, our allies are now almost as technologically advanced as we are. They can defend themselves properly, and by extension, unknowingly defend us as well from another Master attack.

"And they no doubt have also intercepted this message from the devastated Master colony, and they can determine what it means as well as we can.

"So, I say we must continue to leave our allies alone, in peace. And therefore we will *all* remain as we are just now, in blissful ignorance of each other. Their reward will be the same as our reward. We will both be free from Master invasion, hopefully for a very long while."

"As always, your words are both wise and welcome, First Elder," replied the Second Elder formally. "And as always, I completely agree with you. Your voice, when mingled with other supporting Elders, will no doubt sway the two dissenters on the Elder Council, to see it our way.

"So, we will send *no* message at all, and we will therefore not risk interception by old enemies, especially by other Master colonies."

The First Elder simply nodded respectfully in response.

Then the two Elders sank beneath the surface of the comforting, warm water in the quiet, subterranean pool, and swam their separate ways.